I0601800

Isabella Macdonald Alden

Mrs. Solomon Smith Looking On

Isabella Macdonald Alden

Mrs. Solomon Smith Looking On

ISBN/EAN: 9783337317188

Printed in Europe, USA, Canada, Australia, Japan

Cover: Foto ©Andreas Hilbeck / pixelio.de

More available books at **www.hansebooks.com**

Mrs. SOLOMON SMITH

LOOKING ON

LONDON

GEORGE ROUTLEDGE AND SONS

Broadway, Ludgate Hill

Glasgow, Manchester, and New York

1889

CONTENTS.

CHAP.   PAGE

- I.   A good Listener   7
- II.   She attends a Sunday-school Convention   17
- III.   She has Trials and Compensations   . 28
- IV.   What Solomon learned   .   .   . 39
- V.   "Some Things is queer"   .   .   . 46
- VI.   "I think and Mrs. Smith does"   .   . 61
- VII.   "Whom have We here?"   .   . 73
- VIII.   "I'm glad Solomon ain't along"   .   . 85
- IX.   "Poor Lida and the Rest"   .   . 97
- X.   "Perhaps She's right"   .   . 110
- XI.   "I think there was an Unbeliever"   . 122
- XII.   "I suppose He knows what He meant" . 133
- XIII.   "I do dislike Scenes"   .   . 144
- XIV.   "I have to stay outside and wait"   . 156
- XV.   We feared, We hoped, We trembled   . 167
- XVI.   "Auntie always sees Things"   . 179
- XVII.   "You are right, I am a Relation"   . 191
- XVIII.   Meditations that meant Something   . 203
- XIX.   Lumps of Clay   .   .   . 216
- XX.   You've helped along in this Work   . 227

XXI. "Principles is inconvenient Things" . 239

XXII. "And behold, They were engaged" . 251

XXIII. "Sho! that Argument upsets Itself" . 262

XXIV. "They up and called Him a Fanatic" . 273

XXV. "Them Smiths ain't the common Kind" . 284

XXVI. "There wasn't Anything else to do" . 295

XXVII. "Deliverance" 306

MRS. SOLOMON SMITH LOOKING ON.

CHAPTER I.

A GOOD LISTENER.

She was just the nicest old lady. We were always glad to see her coming down the walk. "So original," we said, "so good-natured," "so large hearted," and "so quaint." In fact, we had a long list of sentences beginning with "so" to describe Mrs. Solomon Smith. In winter she always had her knitting. She had it this afternoon. And Laura took her crochet, and Mary her braiding, while I gave the block of coal in the grate a vigorous poke, and sent the red glow flaming up before I settled myself to enjoy her.

"That's for all the world like some folks!" she remarked, meditatively, resting her knitting-needle on her lip and staring into the glow on the hearth. "You have to give them an awful poke, every now and then, before they set themselves to amounting to anything." Then she returned to the subject about which Mary had questioned.

"Yes, I went to the Olin Park Sunday-school. I didn't mean to stay over Sunday when I went to town, but the folks were real cordial, and I'll own

that I've had a hankering after Sunday-schools ever
since Solomon was made superintendent.   The Olin
Park Church is famous, you know ; and so last Sunday morning I just went there."

"It's a great big room—a dozen rooms, for that
matter—and glass doors shutting you up all alone
with your class. I'd like that first-rate if I was
a teacher.   And thay have carpeted floors, and
cushioned seats, and an organ, and maps, and mottoes,
and a bell, and everything. There ain't anything
that you can get with money to add to that school.
I like that, too ; if the work is worth doing, it's worth
having the tools, and the best kind you can get.   It
didn't seem to me a mite too fine for the use they
want to put it to."

"But, Mrs. Smith," interrupted Laura, who likes
nothing better than to get into an argument with
Mrs. Smith, or, for that matter, with anybody who is
quick-witted, "what do you think about spending so
much money for carpets and cushions, and all such
things, when the Missionary Boards need money, and
when so many good things are waiting to be done,
and can't move on for the want of money ?"

"Well, I dunno, child," said Mrs. Smith. "There's
a chance to make two sides to it, I s'pose ; and a
good deal might be said both sides, I dare say. Maybe it ain't just the thing. I don't feel over and
above sure about it in my own mind ; and yet I'll
own that I hate to see folks coming from their handsome houses in their handsome dresses and setting
down on old worn-out cushions, with their feet on

bare, dusty floors, as if anything was good enough
for the Lord. It don't seem quite right. If they
don't have no better than that at home, most of 'em,
why that's another thing. Some folks say that there
oughtn't to be nice fixed-up churches, on account of
poor people not feeling to home. But it always did
seem to me as though that depended on the way
they was treated after they got there. I ain't never
had such a carpet in my hull house as this one in
your setting-room, and never expect to have; but as
long as you act real glad to see me, and treat me jest
as well as though my house was all Brussels carpets
from garret to cellar, I'll own that I kind of like to
step my feet on the pretty vines and flowers, and
have a good look at them. Like enough folks feel
so in handsome churches. As for the money being
needed, well, it's a question I don't understand, and
it stretches out so many ways I don't know how it's
ever going to be understood. Red cushions in a
church ain't necessary, maybe; but, for the matter of
that, neither is red worsteds. And though one don't
cost as much as the other, if the idea is wrong, why
it's wrong, whether it's penny's waste or a dollar's;
and the hull thing snarls itself up, you see, and who's
going to find the end of it ?"

Laura bent her head lower over her red worsteds
and coughed, while Mary laughed outright. Then
Laura, blushing and smiling:

"You needn't laugh, Mary, red worsteds don't cost
any more than serpentine braid."

"But about the Olin Park Sunday-school ?" said I.

"Oh, yes. Well. I liked all the pretty things; but I'd agree with Laura, here, about some of the dressing. It was too fine for the place. You see, it seems to me such a different thing from having fine churches. If my pew in church is carpeted in green Brussels and my seat covered with green velvet, or something, and stuffed with down, I can offer a piece of it to the ugliest-dressed woman that comes in, and hand her a book, and look pleasant at her, and make her feel that she has got as much of the softness and prettiness as I have, and has as good a right to it, because it all belongs to the Lord. But you see, if I wear a blue silk dress trimmed with white lace, I can't go and spread a breadth of it over her, nor make her feel as if it was as much hers as mine, nohow I fix it. Don't that make a difference? Them girls stood side by side, some of 'em in blue silks, with knife pleatin's, and box pleatin's, and paniers, and puffs, and with bright ribbons flyin', as gay as peacocks; and then one in rusty alpaca, darned here and there, and frayed at the wrists, and made like nothing is nowadays; and they felt uncomfortable—you could see in their eyes—and it didn't look right.

"No, child, I dunno's I'd have a uniform. I don't like Sisters of Charity ways of doing it, nor I don't like the Quakers' exactly; and if I was the matron of an orphan asylum, the thing that I *wouldn't* do would be to have all the dresses and aprons alike. You see, it doesn't look home-like. But the way I'd manage it would be to have all the people have common sense, and then pick out their dresses for church with an eye to the best good of everybody, and it would be all right."

This brought a merry laugh from Laura.

"That is an excellent way of managing it! But how would you arrange it so that all the people would have common sense? Don't you think it is one of the scarcest things in the country?"

"Maybe so, child," with the gravest and most earnest old face imaginable; "but it's easy got, after all. If people would only put themselves under the lead of the Lord Jesus Christ, they would have common sense as well as everything else. Maybe, though, I did those young things injustice. But it seemed to me they was so busy fixing the ribbons, and shaking out the paniers, and admiring the set of their kids, that they hadn't room for much else. They didn't act like thinking beings; that was the trouble. I ain't one that expects folks sixteen years old to act as though they was sixty; but I did hate to hear them sing, 'Jesus, keep me near the cross,' and giggle right at the end of the lines. The cross seems such a solemn thing to me, I can't make out how the very thoughtlessest of them can take the word on their lips with a laugh. It can't be because they are young and frisky. It is some mistake in their bringing up. If one of 'em had lost a dear friend, and somebody was speaking of it in solemn language, they wouldn't have any trouble in keeping from laughing. I expect I'm an old fogey, but it kind of seemed to me, as I sat there, that some of

the hoity-toity singing helped along the giddy feelings. ' We are soldiers for Jesus,' and ' We'll battle
for the right'—that's what they sung, loud and
strong, four hundred voices ; and they didn't look
nor act like soldiers. I'm dreadful afraid some of
them didn't know the meaning of the words. ' Sound
the battle cry,' one of 'em sang, right in my ears—
a loud, shrill voice she had—and then she whispered :
' Charlie Parks has got his hair parted in the middle !
Did you ever see the like ? · He'll be wearing an
overskirt next.' And then she came into line with
the singers : ' Gird your armour on for the Lord.'
Now, how could them two thoughts find place in
her brain at once ? It don't stand to reason, you
see. And there she stood, pretending to be singing
praise to him, speaking his name ; and if her heart
wasn't praising, wasn't she takin' his name in vain ?
The whole thing just made me shiver.

"I couldn't help watching that class of girls the
whole blessed time. The visitors' seat ran right
along behind theirs, and I never did see such restless
beings since I was born. They couldn't keep still
in prayer time either. They nudged each other,
and passed slips of paper down the seat, and
whispered a little ; and this same girl who sang so
loud giggled every now and then. Now, Mary, you
look exactly as though you would like to say—if I
wasn't so much older than you—that I couldn't have
been praying myself, or I wouldn't have had time to
see all this. That's just as true as you live. I was
sort of distracted with the flutter and noise, and I

couldn't keep my thoughts anywhere. There, again, is the question of who is to blame for them girls growing up in that way? You see, the grown-up folks didn't keep as still as they might. The four young fellows who tended to books and papers and such things, kept tiptoeing around, up this aisle and down that, and the leader of the singing turned over the leaves of his book, and, if you'll believe it, the superintendent himself seemed to be trying to find his place in his Bible while the minister was praying.

"Well, they began the lesson; I listened hard, then, for Solomon and I had been studying that lesson by spells all the fore part of the week, and I wanted to see what new ideas I could get. And you never see the beat of that teaching in all your life! 'This is a funny lesson for us,' one of them said. 'I knew all about the birth of Christ when I was a baby.' And then they went to discussing. They talked about that Star, wondering whether it was a new star, or a new look to an old star, and how it looked, and how long it shone the first time it appeared; and then they didn't know a mite more about it, you know, when they got through than they did at first; and then they tried to find out just exactly what part of the East the Wise Men came from, and how long a journey they took; and then they talked about Herod, and all the wicked things he had said and done; how he murdered his wife, you know, and his children, and how old he was, and how long he had been sick, and what year he died, and everything about him. And then they

went back to the Wise Men again, and they talked
about the gold they brought, and wondered how
much there was, and in what shape it was; and
described frankincense and myrrh, and told how one
was used for putting around dead folks, and the other
for burning incense; and then, if you'll believe it,
the bell rang. I didn't tell you about the bell, did I?
It kept ringing every few minutes. There seemed
to be something that somebody ought to be warned
by that bell to tend to most of the time. It would
have distressed me if I had been a teacher. Well,
it rang this time, and that lesson was done. You
see they had been interrupted lots of times; the
Secretary had come along, and the Librarian, and the
Treasurer, and the boy with the new Lesson Papers,
and I don't know what not. But I guess they
wasn't disturbed; it didn't break the thread of their
thought, you see, for they didn't have none to break.
And that was all them girls got, that day, out of that
lesson!"

"What did you and Mr. Smith get out of it?"
Mary asked her, looking roguish.

"Bless you, child! it is just alive with thoughts.
Them things they talked about was good enough,
some of them; but the teacher didn't get to anything. I thought, more than a dozen times, 'Now
she is coming at the thought.' But she didn't; she
slipped right around it, just as easy!

"How do you suppose, now, she could have got
rid of saying something to them young things about
the trouble that the Wise Men took to find Jesus;

what a long, hard journey it was, and how much they had to go through ; and how it is such a simple thing to do, that it seems strange that everybody don't do it ? And there they was, so sharp with their answers, and knowing so much about history, and quoting Scriptures, and all that. Why didn't she remind them how much Herod's chief priests and scribes knew about history, and prophecy, and all that, and what good did their knowledge do 'em ? And when I see them a fluttering there, and nudging each other, and having so little heart in it, I couldn't help wondering whether any of 'em professed to be a worshipper of Jesus—had their names on the Church book, you know ; and was it real, or was it kind of like Herod's—not so ugly looking, but not much more honest.

"Then that bright Star coming out and guiding them men. Dear me ! how could she help reminding her girls that he himself is the bright Morning Star, and stands all waiting for the chance to guide them home. And then the gifts ; how they brought their best to him. She didn't say a word about our gifts ; how our hearts are better to him than all the gold and silver, or the cattle on a thousand hills ; nor a word about the altars where our frankincense ought to be burned every morning and evening ; nor nothing at all, only just the bare facts about Herod, and the gold, and the gums.

"Will they be any likelier to find Jesus by the help of that teaching ? ' Where is he ?' the Wise Men asked, and my heart ached to lean over there

and ask them girls if there wasn't one among 'em
that would like to know where he was, and go and
worship him? To think that she had a chance to
talk about finding him, and giving him our hearts,
and giving him our prayers, and being lighted by the
Star of Bethlehem all the journey through; and she
threw away her chance! It made me sick."

"I would like to go to Sunday-school and be in
your class, Mrs. Smith." Laura said this, and every
touch of humour had gone out of her voice, and her
eyes shone with tears.

"My class, child? Bless your dear heart! I'm
nothing but an ignorant old woman; I don't know
enough to teach a class. But if I did try to teach
one, and had a lesson all about finding Jesus, and
giving the best things to him, I wouldn't leave both
them ideas clean out of sight. But there! it's easier
to grumble than it is to teach, I dare say."

CHAPTER II.

"GOOD-MORNING, Mrs. Smith," said both girls at once. "We were so glad last night," continued Laura, "to hear of your return. Here, take this arm-chair."

An event had happened at the little house in the Hollow. Mrs. Solomon Smith had been away from it for an entire week.

We who knew her so intimately were sure that wherever she went, she would go with her eyes open ; so that her return was, to her friends, an anticipated pleasure; hardly less than anything she might have enjoyed herself while away. We knew she would permit us to see with her eyes, and to hear with her ears ; adding the sharp suggestions of her own mind besides. So we were glad to welcome her, and willing also to give her time to breathe a bit, and to ask all the questions concerning home and friends that her loving heart might suggest. Then smoothing down her apron with her wrinkled hands, untying her cap-strings and settling back for a long talk, she began, "Well, I've been, and I've got back ; and take it all in all, I ain't had such a spell come over me never as I know of. How did I happen to go? Bless

C

you, child, I couldn't help it. The papers were so
full of it, you know. Couldn't take one up for six
weeks beforehand that something about that Convention, and the wonderful things they were going
to do and say, would stare you in the face. 'What
is a Sunday-school Convention, anyhow?' says I to
Solomon, and I thought he ought to know, 'cause he
had been superintendent for more than a year, but *he*
didn't know. Says I to him, 'Well, now, if I pre-
tended to be a Sunday-school man I'd go the whole
thing; I'd find out about those things, and if they
are worth going to I'd have the good of 'em.'

"'Can't afford it,' says Solomon.

"'Oh, no,' said I, 'of course not; I knew you'd say
that; it comes so handy; but, then, you know, you
went to the Cheesemakers' Convention last year, and
to the Agricultural Show, and to the Dairymen's
Meeting, and to the Cattle Show, and I dunno what
not.'

"'Yes,' said he, 'of course I did; that's my
business; it stands me in hand to know all that's
going on about farming, and keep up with all the
new things.'

"'Exactly,' says I. 'And you can afford money
to tend to all such things; but Sunday-school teaching and superintending is kind of a pastime; you
only do it because you've got a spare hour on Sunday
that you can't use for hoeing or mending fence, and
put it in there because you don't know what to do
with yourself; but it wouldn't be the thing to go
and spend money jest to help along such an amusement. Is that it?'

" Solomon looked at me kind of sharp like, and was right still for about two minutes. Then says he:

" ' Come, now, if you think it is so important, suppose you go to the meeting ; I'd like to have you first-rate.'

" ' I don't belong to Sunday-school,' says I.

" ' That don't make no difference,' said he. ' You can tell me all about the meeting, and I shall know more about it than if I was there myself, and I'd like to hear about it. I ain't got time to go myself; you know we are uncommon busy this season.'

" Well, at first I didn't mean to go, no more than nothing ; but I went on talking jest for the sake of it, and says I :

" ' I thought you couldn't afford the money.'

" I only said that for the sake of saying it, cause Solomon, he ain't a mite close with his money, only being a man, you know, he got so used to saying ' I can't afford it,' that the words jest spring to his mouth before he knows it. He looked a little foolish, and says he :

" ' Well, I can't afford to waste money, but if you think it is so important, and would help, you know, why, that's another thing.'

" Says I : ' I think it's important for you, cause it's right in a line with your work ; if it's to help that kind of work along, of course it would help you ; but I dont s'pose it would help me make any better butter or cheese, or look after the chickens and turkeys, or get any earlier garden sauce, than I have now, and you know that's my work.'

" ' Well, now,' says he, ' you know I always did understand things better for your telling of 'em, and if I had the time to go, and there couldn't but one of us go, why, for the improvement of it, I'd ruther it would be you, 'cause you could tell it off to me of evenings all winter, and I could take it in better.'

" Well, I always was a master hand, Solomon thought, at telling things, and I knew he paid attention to what I said better than to most folks ; but for all that, I hadn't the faintest notion of going to a Sunday-school Convention ; nor didn't give it a sober thought till we got a letter from Hannah, my sister, you know, and she told me about her Jessie being tuckered out and needing a rest, and they wished she could have a change and go somewhere for a few days before school commenced again ; 'twouldn't hardly pay for her to come down to the country to see us for so short a time, and the journey was expensive, too ; but they did wish she could get away somewhere ; and then I looked up at Solomon, all of a sudden, and he nodded his head, and says he :

" ' That Sunday-school Convention is the very thing.'

" And Solomon, being a man, you know, is dreadful set in his way when he gets a notion ; and he was so took up with that one that he give me no peace till I up and started, he a counting out the money for me and for Jessie, as if he ruther enjoyed it. I knew I'd have to pay Jessie's way if I took her, 'cause her pa ain't a mite forehanded—never was. He lives in a town, and has a large family, and there's always shoes and hats and gloves and things wanting, and it takes a sight more to live than it does on a farm, and he ain't nothing to depend on but a store where they keep dry goods. That always did seem to me a dreadful uncertain way of living! Suppose folks should take a notion to go without new clothes for a spell? You can't eat the things lying there in the cases waiting to be sold. But now on a farm it's different; folks has got to have wheat, and corn, and potatoes, and even if they shouldn't want 'em, why then you can eat 'em yourself. So I always felt kind of sorry for Hannah's folks.

• Well, I went for Jessie, and her and me got started. She thought it was the funniest notion I ever took yet! Just as funny for her as for me, for she never went to Sunday-school since she was a little girl, she said; she ain't a mite over seventeen this minute, and there she talked about when she was a little girl. But land! She wears trains, and all them things, and looks as old as any of them. I'll own up that I felt real queer as we began to get near the town where the meeting was.

"'Well, well,' I said to Jessie. 'I've always heard it said that there ain't no fool like an old fool, and I believe it. The idea of my going to a Convention at my time of life! It would be bad enough if I was woman's rights!'

"'Auntie,' said Jessie, 'let's give it up, and go back home.'

"'Jessie,' says I, 'did you ever know your uncle Solomon's wife to give up a thing after she once got

started ? I ain't one of them kind. I shall see
what a Sunday-school Convention is before I'm three
days older ; you may depend on that.'

"Well, we showed our papers, and got our street
and number, and did it all up regular, and went to
the nicest kind of a house, where they treated us like
queens; and the next morning we went to the Convention. Land ! it wasn't an overpowering place at
all ; just a big room, with three or four dozen folks
in it, sitting as far apart as they could get, and singing, each one of 'em, a different kind of a tune—by
the sound. It was very faint singing anyhow ; Solomon could have beaten them all hollow.

"'My patience !' says I to the man at the door, ' I
thought this was a dreadful big meeting. Why, you
ain't got as many here as we get out to our country
singing schools.' He smiled as pleasant as could be,
and says he :

"'The people haven't got in yet; we are having
devotional exercises.'

"'Oh,' says I, 'the people don't come till after
they are over, and there's something important to be
done, eh ? Well, now, that's curious, I should think,
for a Sunday-school meeting ; the devotional part
ought to be kind of important.'

"' It's early yet,' says he.

"'Do you think so ?' says I. 'Why, the men folks
where we are stopping went to the store two hours
ago ; and the women went to market and got back
before we started. Why, it's after nine o'clock !'

"But Jessie, she was blushing like a peony—the

land knows what at. She's great on blushing, Jessie is ; kept at it half the time we were gone. · And she kept twitching at my sleeve, and a coaxing me in ; so I went along. Of all the doleful meetings I ever was in, that one named 'Devotional Exercises' was the worst. I didn't think there was a mite of devotion about it. Now, that's the truth. Why, Solomon and I have sat down in our kitchen, with the old Psalm book, and a tallow candle, and grandfather's big Bible, and had enough sight better meeting than that was, many a time. I can't think what ailed the people. The man who prayed acted as though if he should ever get through and sit down, he was afraid that the meeting would come to an end ; and so he went on and on, seeming to think that it was his duty to keep the thing going. And he prayed about things he didn't care nothing about, I believe. His voice sounded like it, but we oughtn't to judge. Anyhow, my heart felt pretty heavy, and I looked at Jessie, and I was afraid if they had many 'devotional exercises,' she wouldn't get chirked up a bit. After a spell, though, that man did get through, and somebody found out, by accident, that the time for devotional exercises was up. You can't think how glad they all acted ! They was as lively as bees right away. A brisk little man hopped up and went on that platform, and says he : ' The Convention will please come to order.' And where he had kept himself, and that brisk, ringing voice of his through all them devotional exercises, I don't know. Why, his voice sounded just like a breeze from the

sea. It kind of waked everybody up. But, bless
you! the Convention didn't come to order; it couldn't.
If they had sent a telegraph all over the town,
saying, 'The devotional exercises are over, you can
come on,' they couldn't have crowded and squeaked
and rustled in faster than they did. Such a hubbub
you never did see. They came talking and laughing,
too; kept up their talking—pretty loud voices at
that—till they got fairly inside the door, and a little
bit down the aisles. And there was that man on
the platform trying to do the talking himself. I
whispered to Jessie. Says I: 'Them folks appear
to be so tickled to think they didn't get here to them
devotional exercises that they can't stop laughing
and talking.' Then Jessie, she giggled, and I was
ashamed of her.

"Dear me! I wish I could tell you all about that
meeting. I could talk all summer about it; and
Solomon says I've got to. He is particular to hear
of every little thing. Some of the things was grand.
That's the trouble. There ain't much comfort in
telling about it after all. You get right into the
middle of it, and it comes over you how the man
looked, and how he walked across the stage, and
threw his arms, and how his voice sounded, and you
seem to feel that that was a good deal of it, after all;
and there's no use in trying to tell it. Lots of things
I didn't understand.

"'The next thing on the programme,' said the
leader, 'is an exercise in chronology, by Dr. Date.'

"'What's that?' I said to Jessie, and she didn't

seem to hear me, and I gave her a nudge. 'What's that big word he says?' I asked her, and do you believe that child knew? and there's been sights of money spent on her education. She shook her head at me, and I thought she meant that I wasn't to whisper; and I didn't mean to be put off by that *child*, so I said it again a little louder. Her cheeks were just like peonies, and she bent forward, and says she softly:

"'Auntie, I don't know.'

"Then I felt real sorry that I had asked her, she seemed so kind of beat. There was a nice-looking young gentleman sat just the other side of me, and says he, very pleasantly, not laughing at me a bit:

"'It is to show us about dates in the Bible; just when things happened. See, the professor is putting it on the blackboard for us.'

"Sure enough, there he was dashing off a long line of figures and letters to stand for words. He made real pretty figures, and he worked most amazing fast. I watched him a spell, and then says I to my young man:

"'I don't quite see what is the use of filling up one's head with all that mess of figures; it would take me half a lifetime to learn 'em, and then I should blunder; I always was dreadful at figures, and if I knew 'em all like a book, I don't see how it would make me any fitter to teach the children the way to heaven; they don't need them figures to go by.'

" He smiled again ; not a saucy smile, you know, but a nice, pleasant one; and he leaned over to me, and says he :

" 'There is a fellow out West who has written a book to show that the Bible can't be true, because he thinks he has proved that the world is more than six thousand years old.'

" I looked back at the blackboard, and the very first words that that Dr. Date had written there were these three, in great, big, handsome letters : ' *In the beginning.*'

" ' Why,' says I, ' s'posing it is ? It might be a million years old, for all that the Bible says about it; that only says in the beginning. How did he find out when that was ?'

" 'Exactly so,' says he, and he laughed outright. ' But you see the poor fellow has never studied Bible chronology, and he forgot anybody else had. He makes a great many statements that a careful look at Bible figures proves to be false ; and one of the reasons why we study Bible chronology is to be able to correct the mistakes of just such ignorant fellows as he, so that our children won't be led astray by them.'

" Well, after that I paid attention to them dates and names ; and, if you'll believe it, it was quite interesting and not so terribly hard to remember. He strung some of the words together making poetry like, and a good many of 'em began with the same letters ; and—well, I don't know how he did it. Jessie said she believed I was bewitched, but I got quite excited learning of them figures, and I said most of 'em off to Solomon last night. I couldn't help kind of liking it ; and I thought if I was young I'd go into it with all my might and know all about it."

CHAPTER III.

SHE HAS TRIALS AND COMPENSATIONS.

"THERE was some funny acting folks as ever I see at that Convention. They had a conference about mistakes in teaching. The man who commenced it told off a lot of mistakes, and then he called on others to give some ; and, if you'll believe it, they seemed to be all used up on mistakes. Not one of them opened his lips. The man coaxed, and coaxed, and they just looked at each other, and some of them gaped and looked at their watches, and were as dumb as oysters. I had forty notions to speak out. Says I to Jessie: 'For the land's sake! what ails 'em? I should think they could talk about mistakes; why, I know two or three myself, and I'm a notion to give them.' Says Jessie: 'Auntie, don't you do it; I shall sink through the floor.' 'Well, then,' says I, 'I won't; though if you sink as easy as that I wonder you are not at it half the time.' But I felt sorry for that man up on the platform, a leading people who wouldn't be led. I always did think balky horses were the most provoking critters that were ever put on a farm. He took out his handkerchief and wiped his face, and it looked red enough to blaze.

"At last the leader of the whole thing, or the conductor, they called him, came to the poor man's help. Says he : ' We have but three minutes left for the discussion of this subject.' Well, why on earth he didn't say that before, if he had any idea of the good it would do, I can't imagine. Their tongues were all loosed by it. They all wanted to talk at once, and they all wanted to say a great deal. They kept hopping up all over the room, and trying to get in their word, and the leader had to call them to order. Said I to Jessie : ' That's for all the world the way your uncle Solomon acts when he gets in the house a little before dinner is ready. He looks at the clock, and he watches me, and he gapes, and he acts as though there was nothing in the world he was so near ready for as his dinner, till I get it all on the table, and say, Come, Solomon ! and then he's off. He finds out that the gate isn't shut, and that the stove in the front room needs a stick of wood, and his hands need washing, and there's no end to the things that he seems to think he must do while the dinner sets there and spoils. Some-times I say to him, Solomon, what a pity it is that you couldn't have found some of those things to do while you sat there waiting. And so I say of these men ; if they could only have found their tongues before it was time to keep still. I believe men are all alike.'

"I didn't think I was talking so loud, till the pleasant-spoken gentleman began to laugh so hard he shook the seat, and then I saw that Jessie was blushing again. Well, now, wasn't it queer that they should act like that and that man a-coaxing them for dear life, and they having plenty to say all the time ?

"Then you never see the beat of that Convention for arguing. They just liked it. There was two or three of 'em who sat all ready bristled, waiting for a chance to say, 'I don't agree with Brother Jones,' and then their eyes would glisten, and they would talk, and talk, and argue about whether it was so or wasn't so, till I couldn't help thinking some of 'em forgot which side they begun on, and jest went on talking because they was kind of wound up, you know, like a clock, and couldn't stop till they ran down. I never did like eight-day clocks; and I'm dreadful glad they've gone out of fashion. Some of the things that they argued about was just as plain as that two and two make four ; and some of them argued as though it didn't make no difference to them whether two and two make four or forty, and they went right along with just as much vim when the thing wasn't of a mite of consequence as they did when it was important. I really think they did it because they liked to, just as boys wrestle, you know ; and I must say they kept their tempers first-rate.

"'My sakes!' says I to Jessie, 'if these were women talking like this, in about three minutes more they would pull each other's hair and scratch each other's eyes. I don't believe it would be a good idea for women to have conventions.'

"These men, some of them, looked pretty fierce,

and talked so, but, if you will believe me, the whole
thing ended in a laugh at last. I didn't get hold of
the joke, and I'm sorry for that, for Solomon does
enjoy a good joke. But I laughed with the rest; it
seemed so kind of pleasant to see them get good-
natured, and give it all up and turn to something
else, as nice as if they all thought alike ; and for the
matter of that, who knows but they did ? Men are
such queer creatures.

"There was one man who was in powerful earnest.
I shan't ever forget him. He lectured to the teachers
about helping their scholars to come to Christ, and
I tell you he did make solemn work of it!—grand
work, too. I felt like I would give almost anything
to know enough to teach, or to be young again and
learn it all. And I looked around on that young
thing that I'd took there, and I prayed to the Lord
to let me do some of my work through her. I can't
help wishing you could all have heard that lecture.
The tears just run down my cheeks ; I couldn't
keep them back, I felt so solemn like, and yet so
glad and happy ; for he told about heaven, and
about the glory, and the lasting for ever, and all that,
in a way that made us feel as though we couldn't
think of running any risk of missing it.

"That was in the evening, and I sat by my
pleasant-faced young man again, and when we were
coming out I couldn't help holding out my hand
to him. I felt exactly as if I knew him, and says I:

"'Mine eyes shall see the King in his beauty.
I'm sure of it, young man, and I do hope you are.'

And I'm beat if there wasn't tears in his eyes too. He catched hold of my hand and shook it hard, and says he:

"'I am indeed, thank the Lord.' And then what did he do but turn to Jessie, and says he, 'You, too, I trust.' And Jessie's voice was all of a tremble, and her cheeks like roses, and she said, 'Oh, I hope so.' 'Don't leave it that way,' says I. 'Make a sure thing of it, child.'

"I couldn't help it. It did seem dangerous, as well as kind of sad, not to feel certain as you were alive about it, and I knew I did. But I'll never forget that lecture: it was worth all the money we spent just to hear it, and I know it will do me good for ever. 'What is that man's name?' says I, and I gave Jessie my programme. 'You mark your pencil all around it,' says I, 'for I want to thank him when I see him in heaven for this night's work,' and I mean to.

" But I tell you, it takes all sorts of folks to make a world. Some of the people didn't like that speech. He was 'dry,' they said. I heard one woman say that two or three times; she sat right before me, and she kept wetting up her throat with candy all the evening, and giving some to the man that sat next her, and then they would whisper and giggle. She was nothing but a girl, and I told Jessie if she had been mine I should have felt like whipping her and sending her to bed; and I do think mothers ought to keep their girls by them till they learn them how to act. It does put me out of all patience to see

folks whispering and laughing at the meeting; if the
lecture or preaching, or whatever it was, was as dry
as chips—and I won't deny but that some of those
men were dry enough; and those that had the most
letters at the end of their name seemed to be the
dryest—but I'd pretend I understood, just for the
looks of the thing, and give other folks a chance to
hear.   It was curious, though, about them titles;
they stand for learning, and the more they have of
them the more learned they are.   D. D.'s, you know,
and LL. D.'s and Ph. D.'s, and the land knows what;
I didn't understand the letters, nor the men either,
some of them, and says I to Jessie:

"'I suppose they've got to prove that they deserve
all them letters, and so they don't dare to come down
and use words that we ever heard before; more's the
pity.'

"But for all that, if there's any one thing more
than another that I do despise, it is whispering and
laughing, and bringing folks' meals to the meeting-
house?   Why, some of those people munched candy
and nuts and chewed gum the whole living time.
There was two girls, and sometimes a boy, that seemed
possessed to sit somewhere near me—I suppose because they aggravated me so—

"Did you ever see them Orientals?   The same
man showed 'em.   No, they ain't pictures, they are
real live folks; he took 'em right there out of the
Convention.   But, land, you'd never have known
them in the world!   They were dressed up just like
the folks used to dress in Bible times, and they talked

like them and acted like them. You knew it was
just as they talked and acted then, because they fit
right into the Bible as complete as though they had
been living when it was written. The women carrying water-pots on their heads, you know, and glean-
ing in the fields, and gathering sticks for the fire, and
wearing veils ; and the bridegroom coming at midnight, and they a-going out to meet him with lamps,
and all that. All complete just as the Bible tells it.
And, if you'll believe it, the folks out in them coun-
tries are at that same kind of life yet ; veils and all.
Such looking beings as they are ! And such actions !
I tell you what it is, we ought to do more for the
heathen. I joined the Missionary Society first thing
I did after I got home ; and I mean to work for it,
too, with all my might. I never thought much about
it before, but I couldn't get them women out of my
mind, nor the men either, for that matter. I believe
they looked the most outlandish of the two. I know
it was all natural, cause it fitted into the Bible, and
made you understand what some of the verses meant.
I tell you them folks need converting. We must set
right to work and do our best for them.

"But, oh, I wish you could have seen the Holy
Land ! Soft, pretty paintings of the sky, and the
water, and the grass in the country where the Lord
Jesus Christ was, you know. I declare it made me
feel so queer, when the man was pointing out the
well where he sat, and the road to Bethany, and the
palm-trees, and all ; I most couldn't keep the tears
back.

" There was a picture of Jerusalem, lying still and pleasant there in the sunshine, and the great hills all around it, and as we sat gazing at it, the man who was showing them said suddenly, in his strong, solemn voice :

" ' As the mountains are round about Jerusalem, so the Lord is round about his people.'

" I never felt so safe before. There they was, you know, the great mountains, looking stronger than time itself; and there was the promise; and it seemed the silliest thing not to trust him. You needn't go to thinking it is because I am old and foolish that it had such a power over me. There was Jessie, with her young face all shining, and the tears just ready to drop, and says she :

" ' Oh, auntie, I'd like to go there.'

" ' You shall, child,' says I, ' to his own country. He has gone to prepare a place for you, you know, and he will come back and get you ; all you've got to do is to see to it that you are ready when he comes.'

" I tell you the whole thing seemed realer to me than it ever did before. After that, how do you suppose we felt to hear two women say, just as we was going out :

" ' Why in the world do they want to spend so much time over those pictures of Palestine ? They are nothing but outlines anyway, and I don't think they are interesting at all ; the description of them is always so dry.'

" There was quite a good many people there who

were troubled with dryness. They wanted something funny the whole blessed time, but they didn't
like to own it, and so when things wasn't funny they
just lumped them and called 'em 'dry.' The Bible
readings was dry, and the lectures on Bible History
was dry, and the lessons on Bible Geography was dry,
and the Normal Classes was the most dreadful dry
of anything; and I'll venture to say that if them
kind of folks had been willing to own it, they thought
the Bible itself was as dry as dust. Oh, well, of
course folks of that kind creep in; they like to get
to places and see the sights and hear the funny things,
and what harm does it do? Maybe now and then
they get an idea; who knows?

"The folks wasn't all of that kind, I can tell you;
only here and there one thrown in. And them Convention people know enough to understand that
there is no kind of use in trying to please everybody
all the time. There's no trade on earth so easy to
learn as grumbling, you know. I shouldn't wonder
if more folks got to be head workmen in that line
than any other. Why, if I had really set out for it,
I could have found something to grumble at the most
of the time. There was one man that most made me
feel like flying out of the window. He was real
smart, and I wanted to hear all he said, but when he
got into about the middle of his sentence he was sure
to drop his voice away down into his boots, so that I
couldn't make anything out of it. I did get so provoked !

"'For the land's sake,' says I, 'I do wish he would

take breath enough once to carry him through a whole sentence so I could hear the end of it.'

"But he didn't, he went on that way to the very last. I told Solomon that I could give him the first half of a good many good things, and, if he had brains enough to finish them out, they might help him. But that seems to me like downright cheating. The last part of them sentences all belonged to me, and he had no right to go and mouth them up, and finally swallow 'em without giving me a chance. They said he was the finest orator at the Convention.

"'Well,' says I, when we was at our boarding-house, eating dinner, 'the first half of him is a good deal of an orator, but the last half is a dead failure, I think.'

"Still, I said, and I say it yet, if I couldn't have heard the first word that he said, I wouldn't have got up and squeaked and rustled out as so many of them did. When I got commenced I'd have stuck it out if it most choked me. I do hate to see folks nipping out of church during a meeting. They kept doing it there all the time; it did seem queer to me that a few of them couldn't have made up their minds to go together, and have it done with; but no, right in the middle of somebody's speech, up would bob a woman and rustle herself out, and that would seem to give another one the notion that she would like to do the same; but mind you, she would wait until the other had got down the aisle, and opened the door and shut it, and had time to get to the foot of the stairs, and then she would start, and she would

suggest the idea to another one, and so they kept it
a-going by spells, all day.   Says I to Jessie:

"'Now, if I faint dead away, and don't appear to
be coming to, after five minutes or so, why I suppose
you can have me carried out; but for anything less
than that, I won't go out of this house till after the
benediction is pronounced!'

"And I didn't; though some of the speeches was
most mortal long!"

CHAPTER IV.

WHAT SOLOMON LEARNED.

"I HAD one queer time," said Mrs. Smith, after a careful pause, during which she set the heel in the grey stocking. "It worried Jessie dreadfully; but it didn't me a mite. We heard ourselves talked about. I have always heard it said that listeners never hear any good of themselves, and so far as my knowledge goes, it's true.

"There was two women walking along up the street real slow, spreading out so that you couldn't get by them. They were talking about some Convention folks. And don't you believe one of them went on and described me to the very life, dress, bunnit, and all? They was to be pitied, I think; for they had the worst of it. My dress was clean if it hadn't an overskirt; and my bunnit was last year's shape to be sure, but it was paid for, in good, honest money, and so long as I don't mind wearing it, I didn't think they had any call to worry.

"Well, they went on talking, and they said that was the way with these Conventions. A lot of people came to see the country, and to do shopping along the way, and didn't know nothing about Sunday-schools, nor care nothing about them, and didn't have brains enough to understand what was said, and wanted to get boarded for next to nothing, so they just made the meeting an excuse; and for their part they thought it was an imposition.

"Now it happened that I had seen both them women before. They set right behind me all the forenoon, and bothered me most amazing, keeping up a whispering about how they preserved plums, and canned tomatoes, all the time that man was telling us about the Holy Land. They were the ones who thought the lecture was so 'dry.' I made up my mind it was my Christian duty to help them women a little, so I spoke right up, though Jessie, she twitched at my sleeve:

"'See here,' says I, 'it's no more than right that I should let you know that I'm just behind you with the very dress on that you've been describing, only you didn't get it quite right; the side-breadths ain't cut goring at all; I always make mine straight, and it didn't cost but twenty cents a yard, instead of twenty-five, as you thought. But now I want to tell you: I do know a little bit about Sunday-schools. My husband, Solomon Smith, is the superintendent of the one at the Hollow. He couldn't come himself—at least, he thought he couldn't—so he sent me, and I've been a listening every single minute—when I could get a chance for the whispering—and I shall tell Solomon all about it as soon as I get home. I didn't come to do no shopping. Every living thing I've bought since I left home is a tin horse to send to my daughter's baby, and it

stands to reason that I wouldn't have come a hundred
and thirty-two miles just to buy that. As for getting
my board cheap, I have got it cheap—good board,
too—and I'm thankful for it. I know the folks I'm
stopping with ain't grudged me a mite of anything.
They've about promised me that they will stop next
fall on their way out West, and spend a few days
with me, and if they do I shan't grudge them a sight
of the country and they may go a shopping to the
store at the Corners if they want to. I'm glad I
come. I listened to every word of that lecture, when
you was doing up your plums, and canning your
tomatoes over again at the Hall this morning. I
didn't think it was a bit *dry*. And I mean to help
Solomon along in his Sunday-school work by that,
and some other things as soon as I get home.'

"Warn't they beat, though! They went to work
trying to apologise. 'Didn't mean *me*,' they said,
though how their consciences would let them say
that, after describing of me to my face and eyes, *I*
don't know. Jessie, she cried a little about it, and
Solomon says he thinks I was ruther hard on
them. Solomon is sort o' chicken-hearted, you know,
where people's feelings is concerned. But I really
shouldn't wonder if it done them good. I didn't
bear them no malice, not a speck, and I told them
so.

"What do you think Solomon said to me the other
night, after I had been talking about that meeting to
him for an hour on the stretch? 'Maria,' says he,
'it's all just as interesting as it can be. But it's

getting near to Sunday, and what I want to know is: What am I to do next Sunday that will make our school better? As near as I can make out, you ain't told me anything yet that will help the school along.'

"Now do you know for about a minute I was *beat.* Then says I: 'Why, Solomon, yes I have. Haven't I told you a dozen things that you want to stop doing? For one thing, you are never to go and have devotional exercises on purpose to fill up—making a prayer about things that you ain't thought of before in a month, and won't think of again in another month. It's disgraceful. Long prayers ain't devotional, anyhow; I always thought they wasn't, and now I know they ain't; and you are apt to make just a trifle too long prayers, Solomon, now that's the truth.'"

At this point Laura broke the spell which had held us by laughing immoderately.

"I can't help it," she said, when I shook my head, "I've kept it bottled up all the afternoon; but this is too funny."

"Bless your heart, child!" said dear Mrs. Smith; "laugh away; I like to hear folks laugh in the right places."

Then Mary called us to order, and started Mrs. Smith again, by asking what Solomon said.

"Why, he thought about it a spell, and then he said, in that thoughtful way of his, 'Well, I dunno but you're right.' So while I was about it, I made up my mind I'd mention a matter that has bothered me some, and says I : ' There's another thing, Solomon, you can stop when you get through.' Some of the Convention folks would say, ' But my time is up and I must close,' then they would move along, without any more idea of closing than a clock has of not ticking. Stealing other folks' time, and easing up their consciences, and kind of encouraging folks by owning of it every few minutes. ' Now, Solomon,' says I, ' I have thought that you now and then used up some of the time that rightly belonged to the teachers, and, if I was you, I wouldn't do it. Then you can stop picking out a tune every little while that no living being but you and Job Simmons can sing. And then you can give up that habit you have of squeaking them heavy boots of yours up and down the aisles, attending to some business while Mr. Brown is summing up the lesson ; I never knew how kind of aggravating that was till the men and women, especially the women, squeaked through that Hall times when I wanted to hear. Not but that I wouldn't most as soon hear your boots squeak as to hear Mr. Brown sum up the lesson. But that's neither here nor there ; it don't look like the right thing.

" ' Why, Solomon,' says I, ' I could keep on all night. There's hundreds and hundreds of interesting things in the Bible and about the Bible that you never dreamed of, and you ought to know them. History and dates and all them things. It proves that you can't be mistaken ; it makes you feel as sure of there being such a place as Bethany as that

there is such a place as the Hollow and the Four
Corners. And "Peter" and "John" and all them as
real as Job Simmons and John Stackhouse; and
heaven itself seems realer than the solid earth.
There's no use in saying that such things don't save
souls; neither do sermons. But they make things
look plainer and seem truer; leastways they ought
to. There ought to be a lot of Bible studying done
by anybody that undertakes to superintend a Sunday-school; and a great deal of praying, too.
Nothing ever seemed more certain than that.
Solomon,' says I, 'if you could have been at that
closing meeting, and heard them pray for the Sunday-school superintendents and teachers and scholars,
that they might all work just as the Lord Jesus
Christ would have them work, you would have gone
to Sunday-school next Sunday holding your head
steadier than you ever did before in your life;
because you would know that it was being held up
for you with that kind of praying, and you'd have
been a better superintendent than you ever was
before, because, after joining in them prayers, you
would know now that you had promised before the
Lord to do your best, and you would have gone to
work to get ready for it. I tell you it's solemn
business! That's one of the things I learned, anyhow.'

"'The long and short of it is,' said Solomon, after
thinking of it over, 'you've learned at the Convention
that a Sunday-school man must study the Bible a
great deal, and pray a great deal, and think about

his work a great deal, and do the very topmost that
he can, every time.'

"'Yes,' says I, 'that's about it.'

"'Well,' says he, getting up and going over for
the big Bible, 'I think that is about enough to learn
in a week, especially as it'll last a lifetime.'

"'I've learned another thing,' says I, 'and that
is that you're to go to the next Sunday-school meeting
that comes along, if I have to wear my old grey dress
year in and year out, and have to sell my speckled
calf in the bargain. It's all very nice as far as it
goes to tell you about it, but it won't do; you ought
to be there to feel it.' 'What about Jessie?' Well,
now, do you know that's the cream of the whole
thing! I can't think of her without the tears coming. That child's woke up. She heard the voice
of the Lord himself speaking to her, right there in
them meetings.

"Says she to me: 'Auntie, I do thank you for
bringing me here; and I'm going home to work; I
can do it.' And I knew she could.

"The other night I had a letter from my sister
Hannah—her mother, you know—and in it she says:
'What did you do to bewitch our Jessie? The child
has gone to work as if all the children in town were
dependent on her. She has even taken a class in
Sunday-school; dreadful little scamps, who never
behaved in their lives till last Sunday; but some
way, nobody knows how, she contrived to bewitch
them.'

"It was just before family worship that we was

reading the letter, and Solomon he wiped his glasses
a good deal while I was reading of it; Solomon sets
great store by Jessie.   I wish you could have heard
him pray for her!   My!   I knew then, jest as well
as could be, that them boys of hers would behave
the next day.   I'm waiting to hear that they did.

 " Yes, I've joined a class at the Hollow.   Never
too old to learn, you know.   We had a real good
time yesterday; and Solomon didn't pray but four
minutes by the clock, and he never squeaked them
dreadful boots of his around once ; and the singing
was nice old tunes.   I never did see such a master
hand as Solomon is for taking a hint."

CHAPTER V.

"SOME THINGS IS QUEER."

"Solomon can't go," said Mrs. Smith, musing in her knitting, and looking meditatively into the fire.

"And he is dreadful set on my going. Jonas is the only kin he has left; they ain't been much like brothers, so far as visiting goes; it must be nearly twenty years since they've laid eyes on each other, and as for writing letters, Solomon is no hand to write; but he has a very warm heart towards Jonas and all his family, and he thinks a wedding is something uncommon, that ought to bring the family together, and the long and short of it is, he wants me to go."

"Of course you ought to go," my Mary said, speaking in the first pause; "I shouldn't think you would miss it for anything; a city wedding is a grand affair. I hope you will go if it is for nothing but to tell me about it when you get home. I suppose it will be ever so splendid; they are rich people, aren't they?"

"As to that, I don't believe they've any too much to spend on flummeries, child," Mrs. Smith said, looking with such loving eyes on Mary, that, while the child blushed and laughed over the searching

glance that went up and down the "flummeries" on
her dress, she was in no wise displeased. Mary never
was annoyed by Mrs. Smith's plain speaking.

"I don't know much about them ; never was there
in my life. Jonas, I knew, when he was a young
man, and Sarah, his wife, walked over from Dean-
ville to see me once ; she was dressed plain enough
then, and was a meek and quiet body. They've
lived in the city for more than twenty years, but I
guess they've had hard rowing. Solomon has a note
of his brother's that there ain't been no interest paid on
for more than five years now ; and Solomon thinks he
wouldn't have done so, if he had been forehanded.
If I go I shall take the child a nice little present, to
show them that we feel all right about the interest,
as of course we do ; for when a man can't pay, why
he *can't*."

A singular combination of circumstances had made
us, or rather was about to make us, what Laura
called "almost related" to dear old Mrs. Smith. I
had a gay young nephew in a distant city, a mother-
less, fatherless boy, whom, in his quite early life, I
had mothered as well as he would let me. He had
been, however, for ten years so independent of us
that he rarely visited us, and more rarely wrote.
Last week he had surprised us by a cordial
invitation to his wedding, and the lady whom he
was to marry was Solomon Smith's niece, Lida, or
"Elizabeth," as Mrs. Smith called her — Jonas
Smith's only daughter. Irving, my boy, had been
very eager in his urgings that we—uncle, aunt, and

cousins—should come to see him made into a " grave old man," but his uncle could not get away from business, neither did Solomon Smith believe that he could. So, after many talks and numberless plans, it was finally settled that Mary should stay at home to care for her father, while Mrs. Smith and Laura and I represented the two families at the wedding. In view of the fact that our boy Irving had no home, our invitation to stop with the Smiths was most cordial, and made it very much " nicer" for our old friend.

So imagine us one winter morning, duly packed, lunched, and with the usual number of bundles, seated in the eight-o'clock express, ready for whatever experiences the next three or four days might have to furnish.

Laura began the journey by looking volumes of indignation at those who dared to smile over Mrs. Smith's appearance , but really I did not blame them: the dear old lady certainly had the faculty for getting herself up in a unique fashion. Her trim black dress was completely hidden by a long heavy cloak of dark-green cloth, an old-fashioned cloth, such as I fancy our grandmothers might have worn —I think it was called camlet, and nothing like it, so far as I know, can be found in the stores of to-day. The shape in which it was fashioned was as quaint as the material. The bonnet which accompanied it was of velvet, and in its better days the pile on it had been heavy; even now the velvet was of a rich, glossy black—not a thread of cotton about it; but

the shape of the bonnet suggested at least ten winters
of duty, I don't know but many more. The sweet
old face looking out from the old-fashioned frill that
gathered full about the old-fashioned bonnet, was
beautiful to us, but those who did not know her
were apt to smile. Laura, with her flashing eyes and
cheeks aglow over what she felt was disloyalty to a
noble soul, had no idea what a pretty contrast she
was. She had finished her dark-green travelling suit
but the day before, and it became her wonderfully ;
she had taken counsel of the dear old lady's taste
somewhat, I fancy, for there were no " furbelows" of
any sort about it.   She turned a seat and made herself comfortable, sitting backwards, establishing Mrs.
Smith beside me, for protection from " gigglers and
simpletons generally," she whispered, as she leaned
over to arrange my valise as a footstool.

   But before the day was done, many who had
smiled learned to respect the figure in the dark-
green cloak and large bonnet.   It was a curious
study to watch her, so quiet and unobtrusive was
she, yet so alert; nothing escaped her keen grey
eyes.

   To begin with, of course there was a baby on the
car, and of course it demanded more than its share
of attention.   Now a sweet-faced, cooing baby
arrayed in fine white-broidered garments, with bright
eyes, and dimpled chin, and mouth that breaks into
radiant smiles whenever one looks that way, is an
exquisite bit of enjoyment for anybody.   I have seen
Laura go into raptures over such an one, and borrow

it of a doting mother, and kiss it and coo to it by the
hour together; but this baby was not over-clean,
bearing about on its coarse dress the marks of a long
journey. At his best, he was not pretty, for he was
wide-mouthed and tow-headed, and had dull, unre-
sponsive eyes; besides, he was tired and sleepy, and
yet would not sleep; hungry, too, and the bill of fare
spread out before him in the shape of watery-looking
milk in a cinder-covered bottle, and a molasses cooky,
seemed to disgust him; on the whole he was undeniably cross. He threw away the cooky, and tried to
send the bottle after it; he pulled at his tired, discouraged mother's nose, and at her hair, which was
in such disorder that it did not need this touch to
add to the dreariness of her appearance; by turns
he whined piteously or yelled outright. The mother
lifted him from one tired arm to the other, and
coaxed and petted as well as she knew how, and
scolded a little, especially at the four-year-old tow
head who clung to her shawl, and was in every way
dirtier, homelier, and more objectionable-looking than
the baby. This group sat nearly opposite us, the
father absorbed, most of the time, in a newspaper.
Laura watched them furtively, annoyed by their
close proximity, annoyed by the molasses cooky on
the floor, surrounded with puddles of tobacco juice
which the father from time to time poured around it;
annoyed, apparently, that so forlorn a specimen of
baby should turn all the poetry connected with childhood into disagreeable prose. Mrs. Smith watched
them too, but with an entirely different face. In-

tense sympathy with both mother and baby were so
strongly written on it that I was not in the least surprised, presently, to have her give a brisk little
spring forward and come back with the angry baby.
His irritation was, however, held in check by astonishment; I am sure he was not used to motherly old
arms.

"Poor little fellow!" murmured his new friend;
"how tired he looks! Cinders in his eyes and cooky
in his mouth and nose; no wonder he cries. Laura,
if you would just wet my handkerchief for me, I
could make him more comfortable in a minute, and
rest his poor mother a bit."

Very gravely Laura arose, very slowly she drew
off the dark kid glove that matched her suit, and
prepared to go to the water-tank and wet the capacious clean handkerchief, which was intended to
cleanse baby's face. The deed was done, however,
in process of time, and baby, far from resenting,
seemed soothed and pleased with the entire performance. He actually smiled, and though his mouth
was undeniably large, that lovely mystery which
dwells in a baby's smile came instantly to glorify
this one. Then he nestled in the comfortable arms,
and laid his little tow head against the motherly
bosom, and was softly crooned to sleep. The look on
the mother's face, meantime, must have paid Mrs.
Smith; I know it softened the look of annoyance
in Laura's eyes. The mother came presently with
grateful, homely words; she was "dead tired," had
been travelling three days and two nights: all the

clothes she had brought with her for the children were soiled, and they were both as cross as two sticks, and she was clean discouraged. She would take baby and lay him on the seat beside her, maybe he would take quite a nap.

"Poor thing!" Mrs. Smith said, looking compassionately at the mother, and cuddling the baby; she would lay him down herself, and sit beside him. "I won't let him roll off," she said, with delightful assurance of strength in her voice; "I've done the same thing for my children and grandchildren; here's an empty seat right behind us, I'll make a nice bed for him, and I'll coax the other little fellow to me, and keep him comfortable; there's a big apple in my satchell he'll like: then you just lop down and take a nap; it will do you good."

"Johnny won't come," said the mother, looking volumes of thanks that she did not know how to express. "He's awful bashful." But Johnny did come. He was magnetised. He had his face washed, too, and his dirty little hands, with another corner of the capacious handkerchief that Laura obediently wetted for the purpose; then he leaned against the old green cloak, and listened to a quaint sweet story, beginning about a kitty and a naughty puppy, and changing, I hardly understand myself by what transition, only I know it seemed sweet and natural, to the story of a nice little unselfish boy, who let his mother take a nap, and was a help and comfort to her all through a long journey. Then the story branched again: "Once there was a little boy, a

beautiful baby boy, who started with his father and
mother in the night and took a long, dangerous
journey—not on the cars, oh no, indeed! but sometimes on foot, and sometimes in his mother's arms,
on a donkey's back, and all the way that little boy
did not once do a naughty thing." And I sat and
listened, and heard the old, old story of the flight
into Egypt grow into marvellously vivid power and
beauty, and the four-year-old Johnny, who by this
time was curled into a corner of the seat with a bit
of the green cloak wrapped about him, listened as
one spell-bound. Evidently the old story was a new
one to him. He had many questions to ask; wise
little questions that hinted at thoughts hid away
beneath that shock of yellow hair; thoughts which
might some day grow into deep ones. Who knows
to what extent our dear old lady was shaping and
moulding them that day?

Presently the father roused from his tobacco and
his paper sufficiently to remember that he had some
responsibility in life, and looked about him for his
family.

The distinct, steady breathing—if I should by
courtesy call it breathing—of his tired wife, told all
her neighbours that she was making the most of her
much-needed rest. The father seemed greatly
astonished at the condition of affairs, and came presently and leaned against the back of our seat and
talked with Mrs. Smith.

"My youngster there will tire you all out."

"Not a mite," spoken in a hearty way that might

have been a joy to any father's heart. "Nice little
boys don't tire me; and he is a nice little boy; he
has been as good as gold, and let his mother and
little brother sleep. He has had a nice story, too.
Haven't you Johnny?"

Johnny nodded.

"He's a first-rate listener, Johnny is," continued
Mrs. Smith, and as the boy slipped away from her
and gave himself up to staring at Laura, who had
her watch out, she added : "He did more than listen.
You ought to have heard his wise little questions.
I think they were real wonderful in such a little
fellow."

"Johnny is a cute enough chap," said the gratified
father, and the fatherly look that came into his eyes
began to reconcile me somewhat to his appearance.

Up to this time I had not liked him at all.

"He is as bright as a button," was Mrs. Smith's
emphatic statement. "Two nice boys you've got;
the baby is uncommon strong with his hands and
feet. In just a little while you'll have them trotting
about after you, copying every single thing you do.
Boys is almost certain to copy their fathers; that's
one reason I was sorry that mine were all girls. I
wanted them to copy Solomon; he's my husband :
and Solomon hasn't a habit about him hardly, that a
boy wouldn't be the better for copying. I think
fathers ought to look out for that; specially if they've
got bright boys."

The father in question looked down at his boots
and said nothing. I was glad he could not see

Laura's curling lip. She evidently was thinking of ways in which he might be copied that would not improve his boys. Mrs. Smith was silent only a moment, then she returned to the charge.

"I was thinking of that when I sat looking at your baby's fat little face and clean, sweet mouth, after he had gone to sleep; what a dreadful pity it would be to have it all stained up with tobacco. They'll go to chewing before long, I suppose; time flies fast, and boys begin uncommon early now days; but doesn't it seem most too bad to think of it?"

He might have been an uninterested third person, to judge by the innocent tones of Mrs. Smith's voice. It was certainly a bold experiment. I watched him curiously to see how he would take it. His dark, reddish skin grew a shade redder, and his eyes flashed a little; but the wrinkled old face was so kind, and the large old hand patted his sleeping baby so tenderly, that, apparently without knowing it, his face softened. He moved uneasily, as one unwilling to leave the subject, yet unwilling to talk about it.

"I don't know as I care about my young ones taking to chewing," he said at last; "not while they are boys, anyhow. I calculate to bring 'em up about right; and smoking and chewing is no kind of business for a boy."

"Well, I dunno. Don't it seem a kind of a pity that a boy couldn't be allowed to copy his father? It seems so natural like, they begin it before they get

their first boots, and they're always at it; trying to
walk like father, and eat like father, and talk like
father; that is, if they have good fathers. It seems
almost as if it was what the Heavenly Father intended—one of the ways to teach them. Don't you
think so?"

He shifted uneasily from one foot to the other.
This was evidently a new idea, and suggested other
serious thoughts to him.

"There's no particular harm in chewing that I
know of," said he at last in a dogged sort of tone.

"Well," said Mrs. Smith, tucking the plaid shawl
carefully about the baby, "I always thought that
depended on what you chewed. Tobacco, now, brings
a good deal of harm along with it. Besides spoiling
of the breath, and making things untidy all
around"—and whether she meant it or not, her eyes
wandered to the baby's cooky still swimming in the
river of tobacco—"it's injurious to health, and expensive; I know all about it, you see. I had a
cousin, once, who smoked and chewed up a whole
farm, well stocked."

"A farm!" repeated the father, his voice expressing astonishment and incredulity; "not a very large
one, I guess."

"Well, as to that, it was pretty considerable of a
farm for them times. Forty acres or so, all in good
order, and cows and horses, and farming utensils, all
complete, and he just made away with the whole
thing."

"Smoking and chewing?"

"Well, that was the beginning. You see, his father took to smoking soon after he was married; then he went to chewing, and the boy when he was a little fellow liked the smell of tobacco, seemed to kind of hanker after it; inherited the taste from his own father, you see. He wasn't to blame, poor fellow; he wasn't fourteen when he could smoke a cigar with the best of them, and it worked just as it often does; by-and-by tobacco didn't satisfy him; nothing that he could smoke or chew was strong enough for the craving he felt. It was born in him, poor boy. He'd tried beer, and then brandy; and after a while he couldn't seem to live at all, without having a bottle in one pocket and a chunk of tobacco in the other. Of course, he chewed up and swallowed down the whole of that farm; didn't leave enough of it to buy him a coffin, or bury him; so the town buried him. The father's money was all gone, of course; but he is living yet, the father is, and manages to get enough money to keep him puffing and spitting. He's a queer father, now, ain't he? when he looked on and saw all that, and just chewed and puffed away. He never drank a drop in his life, so far as I know: the tobacco satisfies him; but when the next generation took the disease, they took it stronger, just as they're apt to, and tobacco didn't do. Some things is queer."

Thus concluded Mrs. Smith, rubbing her chin meditatively with her disengaged hand, while with the other she patted the baby. I studied her quiet face, and tried to decide whether she really knew that she had been reading the father the sharpest kind of a lecture on parental responsibility and inherited tendencies.

"Wall," the father said at last, after turning quite to one side to eject a quid of tobacco, "wall," he continued, "I've known boys who didn't smoke or chew, though their fathers did."

"That's true," said Mrs. Smith pleasantly; "oh yes, that's true. If there warn't a sign of a chance for the children it would be awful; but then the chances are against 'em, dreadfully against 'em, and the curious part of it is, if they have nice, good fathers who do about right in other things, the chances against 'em are a great deal worse, because you see they can't help kind o' wanting to follow father and be like him, and they can't see no harm in what he does. It seems a dreadful pity for a father to keep doing what he wouldn't have his boy do for a good deal. That's an uncommon fine shaped head of your Johnny's. He is great on mimicking, isn't he? You ought to have heard him tell me how the engine went. He had it complete."

This sudden transition from tobacco to Johnny surprised me, but the father answered with a gratified nod:

"He mimics everything and everybody like a monkey."

Then immediately that dark-red streak rolled up into his face again. He plainly saw that he had caught himself in the meshes of his own admission.

He went back to his sleeping wife, and if I am a judge of faces, he revolved two thoughts:

"What if the old lady is right, and the little monkey should go to mimicking me?" and "I don't want the little scamp to smoke or chew. I don't see the harm in it for me, but it is different with him. I'd just as soon he wouldn't."

CHAPTER VI.

"*I THINK OF THINGS TO DO, AND MRS. SMITH DOES THEM.*"

" I COULDN'T do such things, mamma," Laura had said
to me, earnestly, as she watched Mrs. Smith cuddling
the baby. "Nice sweet children I can fondle, but
these are so disagreeable-looking; and the father
and mother are disagreeable. Besides, what is the
use? She will wash their faces, but how long will
they stay clean, and when will they be washed again,
and what does it matter, anyway?"

As she had poured these questions out on me,
seemingly irritated over her own thoughts, they
amused me so much that I could only laugh in
answer, and wonder who was arguing with Laura,
to convince her that she ought to be as benevolent
as Mrs. Smith. But while the conversation between
the father and his new friend was in progress, I
noticed that Laura had drawn the boy Johnny to
her side, had shown him the machinery of her
watch, and the queer little picture set in the charm,
had allowed him to finger the chain, and then to
count the bright buttons on her sack, and finally
seated him beside her, and was in full tide of earnest
talk.

"He really is an interesting little fellow," she explained to me with a slight blush and laugh, as she saw me watching her.

The baby took a long nap, and awoke in peace, was straightened out and kissed, and made comfortable by Mrs. Smith before the mother roused from what had evidently been her first rest since the journey began. I had noticed with interest that, after the father took his seat again, he had carefully drawn his wife's head from an uncomfortable position, and rested it on his shoulder; after which he sat in perfect quiet, neither spitting nor reading until the nap was concluded. The tired woman awoke with a start, as if she had stolen time from duty, and her cheeks grew hot over the condition of things. I either saw, or fancied I saw, a shy sort of smile quiver for an instant on her face, as she observed where her head was resting. If I am not mistaken, such care for her comfort was new, and was born of the example set by our old lady. She came with haste and thanks over to her smiling baby.

"He is as good as gold," said Mrs. Smith, and she made room for the mother to sit beside her, asking a question that detained her.

There was some earnest talking after that; baby accepted of his cleansed and newly-filled bottle with a smile of satisfaction, and absorbed himself with its contents, while the two women talked. Of course I did not hear the words, but the change on the younger woman's face was so rapid and so marked

that there was a sort of a fascination in watching it.
She ceased speaking presently, dropping into the
rôle of a listener, and occasionally lifted an ungloved
hand, seamed with many days of hard work, and
wiped away a tear. Suddenly there was a commotion. Sooner than they had expected, the station at
which they were to stop was called out, and it took
us all, working rapidly, to robe the baby and Johnny,
and see that no bundles or baskets were left behind.
There was little time for farewells, though both
mother and father managed to grasp Mrs. Smith's
hand, and I am sure I heard the mother murmur
low : " God bless you ; I'll not forget." As for Laura,
she kissed Johnny heartily, and bought an apple and
a bag of nuts for his comfort.

" Poor thing ! " said Mrs. Smith, as the cars having
filled up, Laura established her once more in the seat
beside me.

" Poor mother ! there she is, trying to bring up
them two babies without any of His help."

" The pronoun was so reverently spoken that I
acknowledge my stupidity and absent-mindedness in
asking :

" Who ? her husband ?"

" No," spoken meditatively ; " I didn't mean her
husband ; though the Lord does use that name to
make us feel how tender he is of us. I dunno as I
ever thought of it that way before ; queer I didn't,
too, when I have Solomon. ' Thy Maker is thy
husband'; them are his very words ; and then, when
he is calling on his people to turn away from their

follies and do right, he says, 'For I am married unto
you.' Shouldn't you think that the young men and
women would take right good care how they made
the wedding promises, when they saw from that how
much they ought to mean? 'Thy Maker is thy
husband!' ain't that wonderful, now! I suppose
Solomon has thought about that verse a good deal,
but it never came to me just like this before. No,
child, I was thinking of her trying to get along
without the Lord's help. Think of trying to bring
up children in this wicked world without asking the
Lord about it all! Boys at that! Satan seems to
have a special spite at boys; I've often wondered
whether it wasn't because they was apt to be out
and out *something.* Girls, now, can slip along somehow, and be six of one and half a dozen of the other,
and not much of anything; but boys are either
downright good or downright bad. That's true,
Laura, you needn't go to shaking your pretty head
at it; Satan don't much care which side you are on,
so long as he can keep you just about milk warm.
That's the kind that sort o' sickens folks; bilin' hot
water won't do it, and ice cold water won't do it; I
tell you it's the half-way between things that do the
mischief."

"And are girls always half-way between, auntie?"

"Oh, not all of them, bless the Lord! But then
they're more apt than boys not to know what they
think, nor which way they may happen to turn; so
you can never be sure of them. That's the reason
they do so much mischief; a downright wicked man

you can look out for; you know just about where
he will stand on all questions, and you can plan
accordingly: but a slippery sort of half-way one you
may coax into a corner where you would like to
have him stay awhile; and when you go to look for
him he ain't there; he has slipped out at some
knot-hole and gone! They was uncommon interesting folks somehow, that family, wasn't they? When
I felt that little baby's heart beating away, close to
mine, I couldn't help asking the Lord to keep him
safe; there's such a lot of evil to keep him from!
How that mother can stand it without running to
him every few minutes I don't see. And there he is
willing to be as interested in it all as even her husband could be! 'Thy Maker is thy husband.' I
wish I had thought of that verse to tell her; if you
had said it right out when you was thinking of it,
you might have done a sight of good."

I winced under this unintentional rebuke. Mrs.
Smith's mind ran so much on Bible words that the
connection was complete to her, but I had not
thought of the verse.

"Still," I said, "it might not have done any good
if I had; the woman did not impress me as one who
had very refined ideas of the marriage relation. I
doubt if the figure would have helped her."

Mrs. Smith shook her head emphatically.

"Yes, she had; real true ideas; when she talked
of her trials, she took great pains—went out of her
way, in fact—to show me that her husband warn't
no ways to blame; was as good a man as ever lived,

F

and provided all he could for the family. She's true enough to them promises; the trouble is she hasn't thought much of anything about the Lord all these years. Sent two babies to live in the other city, too; I asked her if she didn't feel grateful like to him for taking care of them for her and keeping of 'em safe for her. - I told her I didn't see how she ever stood beside their graves and had 'em covered up, unless she was leaning on him all the while, and hearing his voice a whispering, 'I've got them in my arms this minute, and I'll carry them in my bosom.' How do folks get through the dark places without the Lord? I don't understand it. If the sun shone, year in and year out, and there warn't any such thing as trouble, seems to me it would be hard enough; but when the clouds are thicker than the sunshine, it beats me."

At this point there came one of those nuisances of modern travel, a peanut and candy and apple and orange and book boy, making his way through the car, pitching packages of prize candy right and left.

"I thought there was a law against gambling," complained Laura, in a somewhat fretful tone; news agents on the cars always trouble her.

"There's no gambling about these, ma'am," explained the bright-faced young man respectfully; "there's a prize in every single package."

Whereat Laura laughed; but Mrs. Smith said:

"A prize in every one, eh? Nobody need go without unless they choose. Why, what a good illustration that is!"

"A great many folks choose to go without, don't they ?"

"Ay, that they do; and complain of you for offering them a chance," he said significantly.

"So they do about the other prize," she said gravely. "I've heard 'em, many a time. They think folks are meddling with what don't concern them, and they wish they'd mind their own business; and all in life you are after is to get them to take a prize that's ready and waiting for them."

The flush on the young man's face led me to think that he understood the illustration; but he moved on without making any answer, and Mrs. Smith fingered the paper of candy curiously, read the statements concerning it carefully, then got out her old-fashioned leather purse that had belonged to Solomon since he was a young man, and counted out ten cents ready for the agent's return.

"I've decided to buy a prize," she said, looking up at him with a smiling face; "though my prize that I'm talking about is without money and without price. Not that it didn't cost enough, but a rich friend paid for it."

It is impossible to give you an idea of the sweet earnestness on her face as she said these words. The young man seemed by no means displeased, yet he had no answer other than to say :

"You'll find the candy fresh and good. I deal in honest articles."

Then Mrs. Smith fumbled for her key, and unlocked with some trouble the old-fashioned satchel

F 2

at her feet, and got out and studied over carefully
certain little paper-covered books, selecting one
presently whose title was *The Great Prize*, and under-
neath was printed in black letters, with a hand
pointing to it, *So Run That Ye May Obtain.*

In the course of the next hour the busy young
agent whisked through the car again, and was halted
by a winning beckon from Mrs. Smith's hand.

"I tried your prize," she said briskly, "and it's
real good, too; nice, fresh candy, the kind I like.
Now I want you to look into the prize I was telling
you about; if you'll read this little book, it will give
you the whole story. Will you do it?"

"Turn about is fair play," he said, laughing, albeit
the colour deepened in his cheeks; "how much is to
pay?"

"Not a cent. Didn't I tell you the prize was
free? You will be sure to read it? Remember,
you promised an old woman."

"I'll read it," he said, and went his way.

"I hope I'll meet that young man in the Father's
house," was Mrs. Smith's simple comment. "I wish
I had asked him his name; but then, I'll remember
the face."

In due course of time we spread out our lunch
and dined. Mary had pleased herself in preparing
a sumptuous one, which Laura arranged on the seat
in as dainty a fashion as her limits would allow,
bewailing meantime the fact that there was no palace
car with its portable tables on this train. Mrs.
Smith had also a capacious basket, from which she

produced generous slices of bread and butter sand-
wiched with baked beans. I think we never told
Mary how delicious those sandwiches were, nor how
we neglected the cream biscuit and cold chicken to
enjoy them. A ruddy-faced German family, seated
a few seats forward of us, had claimed our attention
more than once. They were neat, and clean, and
quiet-looking. Two of the children had petitioned
with hungry eyes for fruits and candies from the
passing baskets; their appeals, however, being
always denied by wise shakes of the head from
father or mother.

" I believe those children are hungry," Laura said,
as we were spreading our meal. " See how wistfully
they watch us."

Mrs. Smith said nothing. I had not thought that
she heard; but she suddenly laid down her own
sandwich, dived into the bottom of her basket for
three others, large, thick, substantial, and went toward the German group. Eager words followed in
a jargon that the old lady did not in the least
understand, noddings of heads, smiles, German
thanks, and she came back richer with the gratitude
of warm hearts.

While she was absent Laura made this brief comment:

" I think of things to do, and Mrs. Smith does
them. I was just wishing I had the courage to
give those people some of our lunch."

" The courage! Did the act call for any special
grace in that direction ?"

"Oh, I don't know. Suppose they had been indignant—thought I was offering them charity—and refused it?"

" Wouldn't that have been dreadful!" I said. "I don't think you could have survived such an affliction."

Laura laughed. The child is a little inclined to moral cowardice in these minor directions.

Mrs. Smith trotted back presently with some bright-looking cards, illuminated texts in the German language.

"There are so many little Germans live in that lane back of our house," she explained to me half-apologetically, as I watched her selecting them with care ; "I keep a lot of these on hand. The children like them, and seeing they are the Lord's own words, there's no reason why he can't use them for his glory if he thinks best."

"Laura," said I, as she trotted away with them, " Mrs. Smith gives more than lunches. They are only to prepare the way for that which she believes the Lord will use."

" Yes'm," Laura said, looking at me with laughing eyes in which there shone tears ; "I couldn't do that part, but I might have helped to prepare the way. I wonder if some of this cake would have any influence in that direction?" Then, after a moment of silence : "Mamma, there is another thing that keeps me back quite as much as the danger of being misunderstood and harshly repulsed ; I'm afraid of ridicule. See how that elegantly dressed lady, sitting just behind those Germans, is watching her, and whispering to the gentleman at her side. They are enjoying themselves at her expense. When they get home to-night they will tell how she looked and acted, and repeat all the queer things she said, and make their audience shout with laughter. Now, I'm afraid of ridicule : it shrivels me all up, and it makes me indignant to think that she is the subject of their fun."

"You draw on your imagination for facts," I said. "Remember you are by no means certain that they are ridiculing her."

But Laura gave her head a positive shake.

"Yes, I am ; as sure of it as though I heard what they were saying. They look like people of that class."

Mrs. Smith came back to us presently ; but her ministrations were not over. The elegantly dressed lady and gentleman had by no means escaped her sharp eyes. She had designs on them.

"While I was up there," she began, addressing herself to Laura, "I heard that lady in the silk cloak say she was so thirsty that it made her head ache ; and that she would give anything for a bunch of grapes ; he tried to get her some, but grapes ain't plenty this time of year, you know. I was thinking, dear, that if you would take her a few of that great big bunch you've got left, it might do a sight of good. Poor thing ! she looks tired out."

Poor Laura flushed to the temples. Her moral cowardice, or whatever it is that holds her back, came to the front at once.

"I couldn't do it," she said in a distressed tone; "they would consider it an impertinence. She might have the grapes and welcome, if she would come after them; but I can't get up courage to offer them."

"I don't believe she will come," said Mrs. Smith dryly. "Maybe you could get up courage to give 'em to me, then, and I'll run the risk of her thinking me impertinent."

Of course Laura was lavish at once with her grapes, and Mrs. Smith hurried away, not without stopping, however, to hunt over her package of little books.

"I like to slip in one of his messages for the thirsty soul whenever the Lord gives me a chance," she said, by way of explanation.

"Mamma, I *wish* she wouldn't," Laura said, twisting nervously on her seat; "the idea of offering a tract to such a stylishly dressed lady as that! Seems to me it is just another instance of 'casting pearls before swine'."

CHAPTER VII

"WHOM HAVE WE HERE."

" THEY seem to receive her advances in a good spirit,"
I said, as Laura and I watched to see what the
elegantly dressed lady would say.

" Oh, of course," Laura answered, "they are too
well-bred to be other than courteous to her face."

There were some, however, who proved to be less
" well-bred." There had entered the car at one of
the stations a lady whose description, in brief, might
have been, that she was over-dressed; at least that
was the main impression which she left on one's
mind. No, I mistake; she was also loud-voiced,
conversing with her travelling companion in so distinct a tone that we on the opposite side of the car
had often the benefit.

Presently she began to bewail the fact that she
had left behind her silver drinking-cup, and was
" wretchedly thirsty," yet she would rather "die of
thirst" than drink from that "horrid cup fastened
with a chain." Face and feature expressed intense
disgust. Mrs. Smith looked her sympathy, looked
significantly at Laura's silver cup that lay exposed
to view; but Laura, her cheeks aglow, refused to
take the hint. At last—the grumblings continuing

—the dear old lady plunged into her satchel once more, and drew therefrom a little old-fashioned tumbler of rare glass—a choice souvenir of the past century. I fancied that it might be designed as part of the young bride's outfit. It had lain unused, carefully wrapped in a fine linen towel. She wiped off the possible dust with great care, and went with benevolent face to her neighbour oppposite.

The cars were again stationary, and we heard her pleasant voice in explanation:

"Will you borrow my little glass to drink from? I haven't used it at all, and you're welcome to it."

It is almost a pity that I cannot photograph the expression on the stranger's face. In its extreme hatefulness it might have served as a warning to that class of travellers. For what seemed a full minute she continued her ill-bred stare, then said, with all the haughtiness of an insulted princess:

"No, indeed! thank you."

After the retreating old lady she shot these words:

"The idea! the perfect idea!"

Laura's face was aflame. But when I ventured presently to steal a glance at Mrs. Smith, her eyes were as quiet as ever, and her mouth wore its placid smile. She was turning the leaves of one of her little books, and seemed to find peaceful words along its pages. Laura studied her curiously. Presently she leaned forward for a talk.

"Auntie, how do you feel when you meet such people, and they treat you that way?"

"Feel as though the poor things had had very bad

bringing up, child," with a twinkle in her eyes and
a little twitching at the corners of her mouth.

"I know, of course; but don't you feel the least
bit in the world provoked; as though there were no
use trying to be kind to some people, and you wouldn't
any more ?"

I was not prepared for the sudden gravity that
overspread the worn face, and the dimness, like that
of tears coming into her eyes. For a moment she
was silent, then she said with quiet voice :

"I don't mean to be irreverent, Laura, nor impertinent to him. I think he understands all about
it. But I can't help when such things happen, now
and then, like being a trifle glad in my heart—not
for their sin, you know, but because I remember
just how the people treated him, and how he said
'the servant is not above his lord,' and it makes me
feel kind of sure that I'm his servant. Do **you**
understand, dear ?"

"No," said Laura, bluntly, "I don't understand
anything about it. I know I should feel like telling
that woman over there that she had shown herself
to be lacking in the first principles of common
politeness, and I'm not sure but it would do her
good. Whether it would or not, I couldn't help
it. I could never tamely submit to such insulting
ways."

"And yet, He was led as a lamb to the slaughter,
and as a sheep before his shearers is dumb, so he
opened not his mouth."

It was a sermon; that one text and the manner

in which it was repeated. It seemed to flash before us a sense of the tremendous difference between the poor little trials, which we are fond of calling "crosses," and the prolonged, far-reaching, thorny cross which He bore for us. Laura had no answer to make. She sat back with a curious mixture of annoyance and admiration visible on her face.

I often thought of it during those days, how much my daughter Laura would have admired, yea, and it seemed to me, loved Jesus of Nazareth, could she and he have been on earth together. Yet she was not one of his disciples. I do not know; it may be that she would have been tried by his mingling too much with the common people. I am not sure that she could have borne the ridicule that was heaped upon him, nor endured the publicity of the scene when even his friends said, "He is beside himself."

I knew my daughter's face so well that I could study her thoughts as I looked. It was evident that while she admired her old friend, she still believed her to be mistaken. I could almost hear her thoughts: "It will not do. Mamma may talk, and Mrs. Smith may act, but the world will sneer; as long as we have to do with the stuff that the majority of the world is made of, we must keep ourselves to ourselves or else be ridiculed or insulted."

There was a little rustle down the aisle, and the elegant lady who had been the recipient of the grapes, paused at our seat. She was elegant in the extreme. Everything about her betokened wealth

and refinement. A quiet dress enough, by no means
so noticeable as our neighbour's across the aisle;
yet the long silk circle, with its rich fur linings,
represented in itself more money than possibly
would have furnished the other's entire wardrobe.

"I beg pardon," she said in a clear, musical voice,
"but I wanted to speak with you. Will you tell
me, please, where you found that delightful little
book you gave me? It expresses exactly what I
have wished put into language for a friend of mine,
and have not been able to find."

The desired information was given with a beaming
face.

"You like it, then?" said Mrs. Smith in great
delight.

"Indeed, I do! How beautiful it is! And so
simply and plainly told! Nothing could more
clearly explain our Heavenly Father's loving dealing
with us. I thank you for bringing the book to me.
It was a very sweet thought."

"You are one of his daughters, then?"

I think I have mentioned before what a peculiar
way Mrs. Smith had of speaking those personal
pronouns. A sort of lingering tenderness, mingled
with something very like awe--an indescribable way,
indeed, but it left its impress.

"I have that great honour," the lady said, with a
happy look shining over her face; "and I am very
glad to meet you, one of his saints, so much farther
along on your pilgrimage than I. You will reach
home sooner, perhaps; if you do, give the Elder

Brother my greeting, and tell him I am following
on."

"The Lord bless and keep you," was Mrs. Smith's
tenderly spoken answer.

Then the two clasped hands, as though they were
relatives, and, indeed, now that I think of it, they
were : "He that doeth the will of my Father, the
same is my brother, and sister, and mother."

I glanced at Laura to see what she thought of
this development from the one whom she had
planned was to give an entertainment to her home
friends, by turning Mrs. Smith into ridicule ; but
she kept her eyes persistently turned away, and
refused to give me the benefit of her thoughts.

It was curious to watch human nature in our car
after that. A party sitting two or three seats ahead
of us sent a plate of very rich cake, with their com-
pliments, to "grandma." Our German friends hunted
among their treasures and produced a book, three
inches square, in German, not a word of which Mrs.
Smith could read, but on being told of the contents
her face was radiant. The newsagent, on one of
his rushes through the train, paused long enough at
our seat to drop a particularly fine-looking orange
into her lap, with the words: "There, grandma,
that's a sweet fellow." The ambition to show attention to our friend spread through the entire car, men,
women, and children making special efforts for her
comfort. The lady who had scorned a drink of water
from the pretty, old-fashioned tumbler, watched
these developments in perplexed astonishment for

some time; then, seeming to conclude that she had
made a mistake, and this was some royal personage
in disguise, she resolved on making amends, in a
direct line with her selfishness, of course, which is
the way in which this class of persons always make
amends :

"On the whole," she said, leaning across the aisle,
and speaking with careless condescension, "I don't
care if I do borrow your queer little glass for a few
minutes. I am excessively thirsty."

"It is packed up now," said grandma, regarding
her in utmost good humour. "I wrapped it all up in
the towel, and put it in the inside pocket of the
satchel ; but here is a bright tin cup I bought for
the baby ; that you can take, and welcome."

So my lady, at whom Laura could not help laughing a little, accepted the bright tin cup with what
grace she could, and went for her drink of water—
quieter, certainly, if not wiser. There was not a
particle of triumph in Mrs. Smith's calm old face ;
she had simply done what seemed to her entirely
reasonable and proper.

There was a good deal of confusion attendant upon
our change of cars. Everybody acted just as everybody always does act on such occasions ; as if
breathless haste were the necessity of the moment,
and it really made no difference how many baskets
and bundles and persons you upset in your transit,
so that you reached the other train first. Each one
seems to have an absorbing ambition to be first.
Laura, who is apt to be nervous when her father is

not of the party, looked about her somewhat wildly
on emerging from the train, and repeated, " Where
is our car? where is our car?" very much as if she
were owner of an entire line. Nobody, answered, or
indeed, heeded her question, and the babel of voices
grew every moment more confusing.

" Here is the man to ask," said Mrs. Smith's cheery
voice, and she elbowed her way to the side of a
policeman.

" Your train hasn't came in yet, grandma," was
his prompt answer. " Stand right where you are
until this one starts, then yours will run in on that
track, the first train in, after this one is out of the
way, on the track nearest you. I'll see that you get
on all right."

Another tribute to the kind old face. Burly fellow
though he was, his voice took a gentle, protective
tone as he talked to her; I fancy he may have
thought of his old mother. Mrs. Smith, alert though
she was to give attention to his directions, seemed
also to be thinking of something else. Her eyes had
that earnest, far-away look in them, that I had often
observed when she became interested in a new
thought. Presently she gave expression to it :

" Here you are day after day always a pointing
out the way for people ! It must be kind of nice to
be everlastingly helping folks out of muddles, and
starting of 'em off in the right direction."

The policeman laughed ; this evidently struck him
as a new idea. He had not the appearance of a
person who ever wasted any sentiment on his work.

But Mrs. Smith had not yet finished; before he could make answer, if such had been his intention, she said:

" I wonder if you could point out the way to heaven, and see folks started on the right train to get there ? Have you learned that road yet ?"

He looked at her for a moment in blank astonishment, then shook his head:

" I'm afraid that road ain't on my beat, ma'am."

The words were spoken respectfully, and with a tinge of what might have been regret in his voice.

" Look to it," she said with energy. " Look to it right away. Death is on your beat, you may be sure of that, and it ain't safe to wait till he comes after you, before thinking of the right road. I wonder if you wouldn't read my little book ?"

Whereupon, without fumbling, she produced from somewhere, as if it had been carefully thought of, and laid aside for this particular man, a little paper-covered volume, entitled *The Right Road.* I learned afterwards that it was a book, or tract, designed especially for railroad men, policemen, and other public servants ; and that Mrs. Smith kept a package on hand, ready to use as opportunity offered ; but at the time the appropriateness of the title amazed me.

It was just as the winter day was settling into early twilight that the train rolled in at the city depot, which was our stopping-place, and we joined the hurrying, crowding throngs once more. In just as much haste they were as though the train were to

G

thunder on the next minute, instead of having
reached its terminus, as most of the passengers, at
least, must have known was the case. Irving was
to meet us at the depot, and looking eagerly for him
though we were, we had almost missed him because
we failed to remember how much, at a certain period
of life, five years count. How the boy had changed!
In fact, he was not a boy at all; it seemed absurd
to apply the old name to him. A bearded man, tall,
slightly built, it is true, yet with an air of manliness
about his very overcoat. It was of the latest pattern
and finest quality. That, at least, was natural;
Irving had always been elegant; his uncle used to
say of him, "Whether Irving has a roof to cover him
or not, or any money to pay his board bill, he will
be sure to have the latest fashion in boots, and the
best fitting kids." I remember what a sore feeling
it used to give my heart, because I realised the truth
of the criticism: and Irving had been so nearly my
own that I shrank from recognising about him that
which was not perfect.

He looked very handsome to me as I caught sight
of him, moving patiently up and down the crowded
platform, peering into strange faces, in search of one
familiar.

"Ha! auntie at last," he exclaimed, as I motioned
him toward us. "I thought I was to be disappointed.
How did you happen to be the last ones out? What
a distracting, pushing, irritating crowd this is! They
have too many elbows. And this is—Laura, I
declare!" This last after a slight hesitation. "I

should not have known you if you had not been with
auntie. You are wonderfully changed. She looks
a little like Mary, and yet she doesn't. Who is it
that she resembles? I believe it is uncle. What a
cruel thing it was in uncle to desert me at such a
trying time as this? Checks, please, auntie, or
Laura, whichever is manager-in-chief."

How fast Irving could talk! There was a good
deal of the old dash about him, accompanied with a
certain man-of-the-world ease and freedom. Evidently he admired his cousin; while he hurried off
these and kindred eager nothings, he cast approving
glances on the trim, graceful figure, and his face took
a satisfied expression which I remembered well on a
beardless face. Laura suited his æsthetic taste. He
was so eager, and so voluble, and in such haste about
checks and trunks, and so determined to secure the
best carriage for us, that up to this moment Mrs.
Smith had been overlooked. In his haste he jostled
against her, just as I was saying:

" Irving, my boy, you have not welcomed one of
our party."

" Ha!" he said—that indescribable little interjec-
tion; Irving used it often—" whom have we here?
Your attendant, auntie?"

His face was genuinely puzzled; either he had
heard nothing about the old aunt, or had forgotten
her, he thought Mrs. Smith was a servant, yet
evidently he considered the situation a strange one,
for two American ladies, of moderate income and
quiet tastes, to be accompanied by a servant, when

on so brief a trip as ours! Especially by one so old as Mrs. Smith.

" Irving," said Laura, cheeks and eyes aflame, " is it possible you do not recognise our old neighbour, Mrs. Solomon Smith ? "

CHAPTER VIII

"Ha!" he said again, wheeling quickly, and bestowing a searching, peculiar glance on Mrs. Solomon Smith. He had not known her very well; it was not strange, perhaps, that he had forgotten her existence. Yet he did not lose his self-possession in the least. "Mrs. Smith, how do you do?" he said, lifting his hat with grace. "If I ought to remember you, I beg pardon for my delinquency. Laura, I remember those eyes; you look more natural now. Do you know how they used to flash at me, auntie, when I was guilty of any special wickedness, in her estimation? Well, Jake, is your carriage ready?" This last to a grey-coated driver who appeared before us at that moment, touching his cap. "Then we will go. Mrs. Smith, can I do anything for you before we depart?"

Whereupon the good lady seemed to consider it time to come herself to the rescue.

"He doesn't remember me, Laura," addressing herself to Laura's angry eyes rather than to Irving. "Of course not! How should he? He was just a slip of a boy when I saw him last. Why, bless your heart! Elizabeth herself doesn't know me, though

I am her old aunt. I haven't seen her since she
wore long-sleeved aprons made of pink gingham."

"Elizabeth!" repeated Irving, still in utmost
bewilderment: evidently the name was unfamiliar
to him.

"Yes, Elizabeth Smith, my niece; Lida, they call
her mostly, I guess; though it seems a pity, when
she has a good Christian name."

"Lida!"

It is impossible to convey to you an idea of the
tones in which these brief words were exploded
from our elegant young man's lips. But he understood at last who Mrs. Solomon Smith was.

"I beg pardon," he said, in the easy tone common
to him. "I had not heard of your expected arrival,
and was therefore in fog. Your relatives will be
delighted, no doubt. Allow me." And he helped
himself to her bundles and boxes with the speed and
grace of a gentleman. Still, the colour on his face
was heightened, and there was a slight cloud over
the former sunniness. "Here, Jake," he said to
that official, "take these. Now, auntie, we are
ready at last, I believe," and he gallantly offered me
his arm; but Laura interposed:

"I will take care of mamma," she said, coldly,
evidently not having forgiven his greeting to her
friend; "the steps are icy; please give your arm to
Mrs. Smith."

He did it, promptly and courteously but the frown
on his face deepened.

The Smith mansion was a blaze of light. As our

carriage stopped before the steps, the door was
thrown widely open, revealing a large and richly
furnished hall, with every jet in the handsome
chandelier sending forth a glow of welcome. A
lady and gentleman stood in waiting, and a trifle in
the back-ground was a pretty girl in faultless home
attire. This was evidently Lida. Our greeting was
warm, even profuse in its cordiality; yet the same
astonishment that Irving had shown at the cars, met
Mrs. Solomon Smith. We actually had to introduce
her to her relatives.

"Why, Jonas, you certainly know me," she said at
last, a touch of asperity in her voice; "fifteen or
twenty years isn't such an awful while, to people of
our age, that all trace of what there was of us has
disappeared. I should know you in Joppa."

"Is it possible that it is Solomon's wife?" the
dignified and somewhat portly Mr. Smith managed
at last to say; and there was added to his astonishment a touch of embarrassment.

"That's exactly who I am. Solomon couldn't
come, so he sent me. And this is Elizabeth, is it?
Dear child! you outgrew your pink gingham aprons
long ago, but you'll never outgrow your eyes. I
remember them; they was about the prettiest baby
eyes I ever looked at; as blue as a piece of the
sky, and the outsides of them looking as though they
were made of the finest kind of china."

They were pretty eyes yet, and they sparkled over
this delicate bit of praise, their small owner submit-
ting to the hearty, old-fashioned kiss which her aunt

gave her with passable grace, though she had much
smoothing out of drapery to do when the old arms
were withdrawn.

Altogether, it was a somewhat embarrassing time
to all parties. The Smiths covered their surprise
and annoyance with what grace they could, and
seemed anxious to overwhelm Laura and me with
attentions, to atone for the momentary bewilderment.
It transpired that it was genuine bewilderment.
The country brother, Solomon, and Solomon's wife,
had been duly invited to the approaching wedding,
" Jonas" having insisted on so much respect being
paid, either out of regard for the brother, or in
memory of the note on which " interest had not been
paid for five years." But it had not seemed to occur
to any member of the family that the country relatives
could by any possibility accept the invitation. Mrs.
Smith's carefully written letter, apprising them of
her coming, was brought in with the evening mail,
about two hours after our arrival. Our note to
Irving had been more prompt—not having travelled
first in the wrong direction, as Mrs. Smith's evidently
had—but we had neglected, naturally enough, to
mention our travelling companion ; and to make the
bewilderment more complete, none of the party knew,
until we told them, that we came from the same
village. As for Irving, despite Laura's indignation, he was not to blame. The Smiths had not
moved to the little place near us until more than a
year after he was gone ; and if he ever knew that the
old lady from the farm, where we got butter and

eggs, was named Smith, all knowledge of it, and of her, had certainly departed from him.

We were shown to our room, Laura's and mine, a front one on the second floor, arranged with every detail of modern elegance that could be imagined—warmed by furnace, lighted by gas, Brussels carpet on the floor, rich and expensive curtains at the windows; mirrors, long, and wide, and clear, reflecting our figures whichever way we turned; delicately embroidered, lace-finished pillow-shams on the exquisitely made bed, and every bright and tasteful toilet appliance that we could, by any stretch of luxurious tastes, contrive to want; in short, the guest chamber *par excellence* of the house. Of course we were to receive special honour at their hands, for were we not the aunt and cousin of the prospective bridegroom? We recognised the naturalness of all this, yet I think Laura and I had the same unspoken anxiety as to how it fared with the dear, tired old lady who had borne so cheerily the fatigues of the all-day journey.

"I wish I knew which was her room, mamma; I would like to go and straighten her cap for her, and brush her dress, and coax her to leave her knitting upstairs for this one evening. I am afraid the pretty bride that is to be would faint if she should appear in the parlour with one of those grey socks she is always knitting. Oh, mamma, I hope they are not all shams, Irving and all!"

The seven o'clock dinner was gotten through with at last, though it was an ordeal more or less trying to every one of us. Mrs. Smith, in her round-waisted and short-waisted dress and her very old-fashioned cap, looked unlike anything that the city ladies had probably ever seen at their own table before. Moreover, she ate with her knife, and did not use her napkin, and poured her tea into a saucer, and swooped up the last drop of soup from her plate with a distinct sound for each swallow—common enough mistakes in an old lady; entirely pardonable if the people surrounding her had loved her, or if she had been a stranger to them ; but to have to acknowledge her as a relative was, I suppose, more of a trial to them than we were able to appreciate.

We were discussing the situation in our room the next morning. Laura was in a bubble of indignation.

"Mamma, her hand was as cold as ice when I touched it on our way downstairs. If they have put an old lady like her in a cold room, I think it is a shame !"

I tried to comfort her with the reminder that she was merely surmising again; that perhaps Mrs. Smith was quite comfortable. I tried also to excuse our hostess, by recalling the number of guests to be entertained and the improbability that they had many such sumptuous apartments as our own. It was all to no purpose. Laura refused to be charitable.

"I don't care if there are a hundred guests mamma. They ought not to have invited more people than they could treat decently. She is the only old lady among them, and should have had

special consideration. Sending her up two flights of
stairs! I am sure they do that, for she was quite
out of breath when I met her, and her teeth were
chattering with the cold. I am certain she dressed
in a room without a fire. I don't suppose she has
done such a thing before, at this season, in forty
years. I meant to go up with her, and see how she
was situated, but she slipped away while that silly
little Lida was talking to me. How Irving *can*—!"

The sentence was left unfinished, as though words
had failed her. Somebody fumbled at our door-
knob in an uncertain manner, turned it hesitatingly,
then apparently repented, then gained courage, and
at last pushed the door open an inch or two and
peeped in. It was Mrs. Solomon Smith.

"For the land's sake!" she said, pushing wide the
door, as she caught sight of familiar faces. "I've
found you at last. I thought I never should. I
believe I've peeked into twenty rooms since I
started. A body could get lost in this house as well
as in the street. Where's that black hole that you
stand over to get warm? My feet are all but froze
off."

"Auntie," exclaimed Laura, "haven't you any
'hole in the floor' in your room, nor a stove, nor
any means of warming you?"

"Not a sign of a hole, child. I guess all the
holes that was made to order gave out before they
got as high as my room, and they had to take them
that come by chance. Ain't you fine, though! This
is a pretty room. I guess it is the prettiest one in

the house, and I peeked into some nice ones. I
declare, I'm beat a little, at the way they live.
Must cost something to pay the rent for this place,
and get all the fixings put into it. I'm glad they're
so much better off than Solomon reckoned; but I
don't understand it for all that; I declare I don't."

Meantime Laura had drawn the easiest chair in
the room to the register's side, and gently seated
her old lady in it.

"You look completely tired out," she said, still
speaking indignantly; "I don't believe you feel as
well as you did last night."

"Well, the fact is, child, I didn't get more than
a dozen winks of sleep. I had the sociablest kind
of bed you ever see in your life; I couldn't even
turn my elbow, but it would squeak out something
or other at me. I kind o' got witched with the
thing after awhile; it seemed to me it squeaked
every time I breathed; so I just opened my eyes
wide, and gave myself up to the business of lying
awake, and keeping that thing still. I felt worse
about it, because them too hard-working creatures that
tugged up and down stairs with satchels and towels,
and then waited on the table, and tended door, and
flew two ways at once all the evening, was right
next to me, and it did seem a pity that that squeaky
thing should keep them awake. I'm going to borrow
the oil-can to-day, and put an end to its tongue; I
peeked into a room that had a sewing-machine in
it, so I s'pose they've got an oil-can."

Laura looked volumes at me before she spoke:

"Auntie Smith, did they send you up to the *fourth* floor to sleep ?"

"I don't know how many floors there are, my dear, but I guess I'm about as high up as they get, unless they swing a bed out on the roof. I don't think it would be a bad place of a summer night; but I guess nobody sleeps there now."

"Auntie Smith, I think it is a perfect outrage! I just don't mean to' endure it. The idea of sending an old lady, their own aunt at that, upstairs to sleep with the servants !"

"Bless your heart, child ! I don't mind being along with the servants; they're clean-looking girls, and they are not in the same room, anyhow ; it seemed kind of comfortable to have them there ; I believe I'd a felt skeery like without them. My door wouldn't lock—that is to say, there wasn't any key there to try whether it would or not; and though I've slept along with Solomon year in and year out, and never thought of locking the door, I'm just that foolish that the minute I get away from him I go to hunting around for locks and keys, as if all the evil-disposed folks in the world was bound to get hold of me."

"I think it is a perfect shame !" repeated Laura. "I wonder what your husband would say to it all, Mrs. Smith ?"

I had been wondering the same thing. I had a vision just at the moment of the slow-spoken, oftentimes silent, Solomon Smith; an old man whom people called commonplace, who yet had shielded and cared for this plain old woman during all the years of their married life, as tenderly as he could possibly have done it on her wedding day.

She laughed a little at Laura's question, and a tender light came into her eyes as she answered:

"I dunno what he would say, exactly; but there's some things here he would think kind of queer. I tell you what it is, for the first time in all the forty years we've lived together, I'm glad that Solomon ain't along! Now that's just as true as you live. Solomon is kind of slow about some things, especially things that he ought to be slow about; and he is gentle and long-suffering, if ever a body was; but when he is riled it means something, and the folks that rile him are apt to know it. I'm most amazing glad he didn't come."

"I'm not," muttered Laura; "a 'riled' person would be a decided relief to my nerves at this present time."

Mrs. Smith paid no attention to her; already she had passed from these minor matters to a thought of more importance.

"Mrs. Leonard"—turning suddenly to me, with an anxious look on her wrinkled face—"Irving was a good boy when he lived with you, but as near as I can remember, he wa'n't a Christian. Do you believe he can have got to be a man without paying any attention to that?"

"I am afraid he has," I said, and I felt my voice trembling; it was a sore subject with me. I had tried to do my duty, yet I seemed to have failed, both with my own and with Irving. "I have never seen anything in his letters, nor heard anything about him that would lead me to suppose him a Christian."

"And he is going to set up a family—take a young thing like my niece Elizabeth, and play at living without having that matter fixed."

The dismay in Mrs. Smith's voice might have been ludicrous to some, to me it gave a sense of solemnity. Laura, too, looked grave.

"Do you think it is wicked for people to marry unless they are Christians?"

She asked the question with perfect gravity, and without a suspicion of a sneer on her face. Mrs. Smith turned towards her, and regarded her steadily for a moment, while she seemed to be revolving the question.

"Do I think it is wicked, child?" she repeated slowly. "Why, when was it anything but wicked to live along in this world neglecting the Lord Jesus, and his call to come and follow him? Getting married and settling down in life, without asking him anything about it, just piles up the wickedness; of course it doesn't begin there, but it makes another long step the wrong way, and piles up the responsibility, too. Besides, it always did seem to me a kind of mockery. He had the 'twain become one flesh' in the first place just for a kind of continual picture to us of the love that there ought to be between him and us; and if we snatch at the picture, and are satisfied with it, and let the real thing go, it seems to me we are kind of tossing up our heads at him, and saying, ' Aha! Aha!' just as them wretches did around the cross. But there, that's just an old woman's notion. I'm afraid there's two of 'em. I ain't heard the child say a word, but I seem to kind of feel it in my bones that *she* ain't a Christian either. I guess Jonas ain't much of a one nowadays; he used to be a church-member, but it don't look like it now. I tell you, Laura, you flash them bright eyes of yours like stars, over my going up three pairs of stairs, and sleeping next to the servants, and breaking the ice in my pitcher in the morning, and all that, but the whole of it ain't nothing to going to bed without having a word read in the Bible, and kneeling down together at family worship. I could most have cried last night to think of Solomon kneeling down all alone, and me doing the same. A great big household like this breaking up and going to bed without family prayer! Laura, don't you never marry a man who can't get down on his knees and pray for you, as your father has done all his life; mark my words, you'll be most awful home-sick if you do."

CHAPTER IX.

"POOR LIDA AND THE REST."

THE next three days were trying ones. The Smiths were undoubtedly much annoyed by their relative.

Very well-meaning people they were, and, in the main, warm-hearted. Had it been an ordinary occasion, and the house free from other guests, I think they would have bestowed every courteous attention on Mrs. Solomon. But as it was, her unexpected advent at a time when many stylish guests, dear, particular, fashionable friends of Miss Lida, gay young men, college intimates of the son Harris—whom, by the way, I find I have not mentioned at all; possibly because at that time I thought there was little or nothing about him to mention—and a dignified aristocratic aunt or two on Mrs. Smith's side, were all at hand to demand special attention, I really don't consider it strange that the country aunt was sent to the fourth floor to sleep. Not that they intended any indignity thereby; they knew the room was clean, the bed ordinarily comfortable, and that the necessary conveniences were at hand; they knew, also, that people in the country were not accustomed to gas or furnaces, nor many of the luxurious appliances of modern city life. They

II

believed, no doubt, that they were giving Mrs. Solomon every whit as good accommodations as she had at home. How could they know that the grave and commonplace Solomon regarded her as the apple of his eye, studied day and night her comfort, would not, for all the worth of his little farm, let a breath of adverse wind touch her if he could help it? How could they know that before the sunrise of each winter morning he was moving around the room, stepping as if shod in velvet, not to disturb her last nap, while he raked out the coals and set the bits of wood in the old stove to burning, so that the atmosphere when she awoke would be that of summer? Comparatively few wives, after forty years of travelling together, receive such care it may be. Mrs. Jonas Smith, in her elegant home, had no such experience; perhaps she may be pardoned for not understanding what the loss of it was to her more favoured sister-in-law.

Some of the guests were rude enough to amuse themselves at the old lady's expense, even before her face, trusting to a supposed obtuseness, which did not exist, that her feelings would not be hurt thereby; others of the guests were foolishly annoyed by her country ways and homespun language. I occupied that most embarrassing position—a sort of confident of all parties.

"Poor Lida," Mrs. Jonas Smith would say to me, half laughing, half sighing, "it is really a great trial to her to have her aunt Maria here; she is as good a soul as ever lived, of course—we all recognise that

—but she is queer, both in looks and actions, there
is no denying it; and Lida is young and sensitive;
she declares she can never have her in the parlours
during the ceremony, and her father assures her that
she must, as of course she must—there is nothing
else to do; and then poor Lida cries; I hate to have
her last days of girlhood made miserable. What a
pity the dear old soul chose this time for a visit!
We could have made her so comfortable when we
were quite alone, and her little peculiarities would
have passed unnoticed. My dear Mrs. Leonard, you
are so very kind to care for the old lady as you do,
and keep her comfortable in your own room so much;
I assure you we appreciate it. Lida was speaking,
only this morning, of your and your daughter's
thoughtfulness."

She had talked on, like a smooth-flowing stream,
up to this point, giving no chance for a counter-
current; but now common honesty demanded that
I should interpose, to assure her that there was no
unselfish thoughtfulness about our action; that we
respected and loved Mrs. Solomon Smith; that she
was an honoured guest at our home, and that we
delighted in her quaint ways and keen-sighted
observations. I might as well have let the stream
flow on.

"Indeed!" Mrs. Jonas said, and "I want to
know!" and "Oh, to be sure; she is as good as gold;
my husband always said that; he has great respect
for his brother's character, too"; then she purled on
about our "thoughtfulness," and their "apprecia-

tion," and "Lida's trial," and the general mortification it was, until I gave myself up to rejoicing over the fact that Laura was not there to grow hopelessly angry at her. One little hint I ventured:

"I am afraid she is careless about her fire, and will take cold; I notice her hands are very cold mornings, and she seems quite in a shiver."

Mrs. Smith gave me in return what I suppose might be called an evasive answer. She bemoaned the fact that the house was so unexpectedly full; it was impossible to make everyone as comfortable as she would like; Harris had brought home with him two more friends than he had written about, and that called for an extra room, of course; then one of Lida's dearest friends had a cousin visiting her, and could not come without her. "That's made still another unexpected one," she explained. "And do you know, poor Lida had to give up her own pretty little room, and occupy a lounge in my dressing-room? I feel so sorry that the dear child should be turned out just at this time."

All this meant, of course, that she had no spot for Mrs. Solomon Smith save the attic room, which there was no means of warming. I really suppose this was true, and that she had done the best she knew how; but it was only out of respect for Mrs. Solomon Smith's own feelings that Laura did not give up her place in our luxurious room, and herself mount to the fourth floor; indeed, it was not until the old lady had pleaded earnestly that she secured a promise from my daughter to do no such thing.

" I shall feel hurt if you do," Mrs. Solomon had
said. "A great deal more hurt than I am about
getting my clothes on in the cold a few mornings ;
it won't last long."

Irving, too, seemed to consider me the proper
person to express his mind before.

" Isn't she a queer sort of party, auntie ? How
came you to pick her up ? "

" Are you speaking of the aunt of your prospective
wife ? " I asked him, and his handsome face flushed
a little ; then he laughed.

" Well, now, auntie, one isn't to blame for having
queer relatives, I suppose. I don't care, of course,
but it is rather hard on poor Lida and the rest. I've
no doubt she is the salt of the earth, as my dear
cousin Laura hints out of angry mouth and flashing
eyes, whenever I cross her path ; but if she would
wear a little less startling cap and spectacles, and
look a little less like a guy generally, I think I
should recognise her worth fully as soon."

I was nearly as vexed with him as Laura could
have been, and spoke very coldly about the appreciation that depended on the style of dress being hardly
worth striving for ; and then I went away without
having a word of that talk which I had longed to
have with Irving, and which I fancied he might have
planned for, in seeking me. Laura, too, poured out
the vials of her indignation before me ; she continued to be exasperated with the entire family,
guests included ; she hardly saw me alone that she
bad not some new grievance, a special slight of some

sort that her dear old lady had endured at their hands.

"It humiliates me, mamma!" she would exclaim, tossing right and left the bright-coloured wools with which she was working. "The idea that because they have a little more money than she, and dress a little better, and all that sort of thing, they should presume to look down on a woman of her worth! It is such a shoddy state of society to make money the all-important factor in friendships, even!"

"How do you know that they have much more money than she? Solomon Smith is considered a pretty well-to-do farmer, you know; and you remember she herself told us that these city friends were ' not a mite fore-handed.' "

Laura's sensitive lip curled.

"That makes me all the more vexed, mamma, whenever I think of it. The idea of their cheating Solomon Smith out of his lawful interest on hard-earned money, and then trimming even their pillow-shams with such lace as that! I tell you, mamma, there are a great many kinds of shams! Money is at the root of it all. Suppose, for a moment, that dear old auntie Smith had fifty thousand dollars to leave to that simpering little bride downstairs, do you suppose she would sleep in the attic? Not a bit of it; and they would just dote on her 'eccentri-cities'—that is the name they would call them, then; I hate it all; I am sorry I came."

I was sorry that circumstances had seemed to call for so long a stay; it had been a special petition of

Irving's that we should spend a few days with them before the wedding; Monday had been the unusual day chosen for the ceremony, because Irving's official vacation commenced on that day, and as he held an office under the Government, he was obliged to be rigid in his dates; the young people coveted the entire time to themselves, hence a Monday wedding.

If Mrs. Smith had been a meek and quiet little woman, with eyes less keen, it would have been much less embarrassing; as it was, she saw everything, heard everything, and was painfully given to speaking her mind. She was overwhelmed with astonishment at the idea of a rehearsal of the marriage ceremony, which was to take place in the back parlour on Saturday evening.

"A rehearsal!" she repeated, in a mystified tone; "what might that be?"

Two of the elegant guests giggled together, one of the aristocratic aunts frowned, and Laura explained.

"But what do they want to do it for? They surely know how to stand up in a room together, and promise to love each other, without saying it over beforehand, like children do their school pieces! I should think they would want to do the repeating of it just to each other, and let the outsiders have their turn once for all."

The little bride blushed at this, and Laura further explained that they wanted to go through with the ceremony once, with the attendants, lest some one might make a mistake, and that would be embarrassing in public. But the dear old lady shook her grey head emphatically over this.

"Too late to correct mistakes. If there has been one made, it's my opinion it will have to be corrected before it comes time to make the promises. When Solomon and I was married, we was sure enough of what we was about; wa'n't in the least afraid of making any mistakes. I was only too glad to speak out 'I do!' loud and clear, so all the folks in the church could hear me; and I've never seen the minute in all the forty years that I was sorry I said it. I hope, Elizabeth, that forty years from now you can say as much."

But Elizabeth was pouting. Something in her aunt's words had jarred on her sensitive nerves, and I have reason to know that she threw the Smith family into a turmoil, and made her mother miserable, by declaring, late that evening, that she didn't care; she wouldn't have that horrid old thing at her wedding, so, now; she wouldn't be married at all if she had got to be there, and they would see what a horrid fuss that would make.

The rehearsal, however, took place, the younger portion of the household attending, and pronouncing it all "perfectly lovely," while Mrs. Smith sat upstairs with me, and expressed her views:

"I don't like it. I can't help thinking it is all satin, and flowers, and frosting, and make-believe. I don't mean that she don't love him, poor young thing, it is plain to be seen that she does; and he watches her with them great eyes of his wherever

she turns, but there don't seem to be anything
solemn and earnest about it. The idea of *rehearsing*
such solemn promises as them are! I wonder if
they have the prayer and all said over, for fear some
of the words won't be in the right place? I don't
like it."

"But, Mrs. Smith," I hastened to explain, "they
don't rehearse the ceremony exactly: the idea is
simply to see if their positions are understood, and
are pleasantly arranged, and if all understand about
the moves to be made."

"Well," she said, after having paused in her
knitting to fix earnest grey eyes on me while I talked
—eyes which, some way, embarrassed me so much
I could hardly finish the sentence, "I'm an ignorant
old fogey, I dare say. It may be all right, but I
don't see how they can do it. I wouldn't have liked
folks a-peeking around to see whether Solomon and
I stood just in the right place, and winked just when
we should, and all that. Bless your heart! what do
you suppose we cared whether we stood right or
wrong, so long as we heard the minister say, 'I
pronounce you husband and wife,' and joined with
him to ask the Lord's blessing? I dare say it is
the thing to do nowadays, times change, but I don't
believe I could have done it."

My room was directly over the parlours, and the
hall doors were open; so from time to time we were
entertained by outbursts of merriment from below.
A marriage rehearsal certainly seemed to be a very
amusing thing. I went over, in memory, the solemn

and tender words of the marriage ceremony, with its terribly suggestive sentence, " until death us do part," and I wondered whether Irving and Lida, when they repeated the formula on Monday evening, would be able to hold their minds away from the frolic in which they had been repeated on Saturday evening.

Modern fashionable society is a curious thing, full of new devices ; perhaps one of the most innocent is the rehearsing of solemn vows in a kind of panto-mime, before the hour for the real thing. As Mrs. Smith says, " It may be all right," yet I confess myself in sympathy with her last century views. I found myself wondering curiously whether they would have rehearsed the funeral service if one of the bridal party lay dead in the house.

Sunday morning dawned upon us ; as bright and beautiful a winter morning as could well be imagined.

" I was really in hopes it would rain," murmured Mrs. Jonas to me confidentially, as we went to the breakfast-room in company. " I don't know what to do with aunt Maria to-day. Poor Lida's nerves are in such a twitter that she declares herself not equal to the thought of aunt's bonnet in our pew ; and I suppose of course she will go to church ; that class of people always do, you know."

Query : Just what class of people did Mrs. Jonas mean ?

At the breakfast-table the matter of church-going came up. It transpired that a small number of the guests were going out ; indeed, the hour was so late that those who, like ourselves, had not prudently made their church toilets already, could not have done so if they would. Mrs. Jonas Smith declared herself too much worn with excitement and nervousness to think of doing anything but resting.

"I was so glad this morning to remember that it was a day of rest," she said, looking around upon us with a benevolent smile. "I don't know what I should do if it were not for the regularly occurring Sabbaths to make a break in the week's excitements and responsibilities."

"Yes," her sister-in-law said, with sweet seriousness; "Sunday is a blessed day of rest, and to think that the Lord gives a wonderful promise to them that keep it! 'If thou turn away thy foot from the Sabbath, from doing thy pleasure on my holy day; and call the Sabbath a delight, the holy of the Lord, honourable; and shalt honour him, not doing thine own ways, nor finding thine own pleasure, nor speaking thine own words; then shalt thou delight thyself in the Lord; and I will cause thee to ride upon the high places of the earth, and feed thee with the heritage of Jacob thy father: for the mouth of the Lord hath spoken it.'"

There was something exceedingly pleasant in Mrs. Smith's way of repeating Bible verses; a sort of exclamatory style over some portions, her face beaming the while as if she were telling good news, and such astounding news as could hardly be believed at all, but for that last fact, "the mouth of the Lord hath spoken it."

My daughter Mary said to me once, that she

always marked a verse of Mrs. Smith's repeating
as something new that had just been put into
her Bible, for, however familiar, she was sure to
see it in a new way, after hearing the old lady
recite it.

No one responded to the verse this morning.
Almost nothing had been said about the manner of
resting ; yet each person present seemed to feel an
incongruity between Mrs. Jonas Smith's way and the
way which the mouth of the Lord had indicated.
That lady proceeded somewhat sharply with her
investigation as to who was going to church. The
host signified his willingness to escort such of his
guests as chose to attend. Laura and I were going ;
also one of the aristocratic aunts, and two of the
young ladies thought they should if they were
dressed in time. This induced a young gentleman
to promise to attend them. So, despite the doubt-
ful beginning, our party bade fare to be quite
large.

"I suppose it is too cold for you to venture out,
Maria ?" insinuated her sister-in-law, but she received
a brisk denial.

"Bless your heart! I haven't seen the weather in
more than fifty years that was too cold for me to go
to church. I can wrap up warm ; my cloak is as
warm as toast ; just right for such weather."

I confess to being very sorry that it was such a
queer-looking cloak.

Then came the question of distance. Laura asked
about that. Oh, the distance was a trifle, the host

said; not more than five minutes' ride on the cars; the red line at the corner passed their church.

"The cars!" repeated Mrs. Solomon Smith in tones of dismay; "I wonder now if they keep the cars agoing on Sunday?"

CHAPTER X.

"PERHAPS SHE IS NEARER RIGHT THAN SOME OF US."

"Of course," said Mr. Jonas Smith, in a shorter tone than a gentleman should use toward an old lady, and added, while two of the young people indulged in their inevitable giggle, "how would people get to and from church in large cities, if the street cars didn't run?"

"Oh, then they only run them just about church time?" said the old lady, in a relieved tone. "Well, I dunno but that's a good plan. Why not, as well as for folks to get out their own horses, and a good deal better for them that hasn't got any horses to get out! And do any considerable number of the drivers go to church?"

Whereupon the laugh became general among the younger portion, somewhat to Mr. Jonas' discomfiture; he had a dim idea that part of it might belong to him.

"Not much they don't!" volunteered one of the young men. "Why, madam, Sunday is their busiest day; they don't have time even to eat their dinners like Christians, but munch a cold bite as they drive along."

"But there isn't a meeting beginning all the time!" said Mrs. Smith, aghast. She was in thorough earnest; having fully believed that the cars were run solely for the accommodation of church-goers, there had been no covert sneer in her words.

"Meeting! No, that is the smallest part of their Sunday work; if they only took people to and from church, they could have half the day for whistling or sleeping; I am inclined to think they would spend it that way; for they have to begin work early and quit late; but they put on a double line of cars on some of the routes for Sunday, and keep them going steadily from morning till night."

"And where do all the people go to?"

"I don't know; everywhere; half of them go visiting, and some go to the Park, if it is pleasant enough, and some go to distant parts of the town on errands that they haven't time for on other days; lots of people go house-hunting on Sunday; stare up at the houses that they think they would like, and mark them for next day's use; for that matter, hundreds of them get the keys and survey premises without any scruples about it. Then a great army of hard-working people, boys and girls—factory hands, you know, and people of that class—ride for the pure fun of taking a ride, going somewhere, and having things a little different from other days; there are places enough to go to, and people enough to keep every carman as busy as a bee in a hive; that I know."

"Upon my word, Erskine," lisped one of the young

ladies, "you would make a good lecturer on moral reform; I had no idea you felt so deeply on the Sabbath question!"

The young man flushed, and laughed lightly as he said:

"You had no idea that I felt deeply on any subject, I presume. I am not surprised at that; but as to feeling, I am merely stating facts for Mrs. Smith's benefit; each person has a right to draw his own inferences."

"They are solemn facts," said Mrs. Smith, simply. "'And shalt honour him, not doing thine own ways, nor finding thine own pleasure.' That's the direction; and it seems a great many people are paying no attention to it: though 'the mouth of the Lord hath spoken it.' There's one plain thing, a Christian has no business on them cars on the Sabbath day."

Then one of the aristocratic aunts came to the front:

"My dear madam, you are not used to argument, I take it; you ignore the important fact that these rude pleasure-seekers, who as a rule belong to the lower classes, have nothing in common with us; and that because they choose to use the street-cars for purposes of their own, is no reason why we, who are on our way to the house of God, should not use the same conveyance in the cause of worship."

But Mrs. Smith shook her head.

"That won't do. 'Ye bring wrath on Israel by profaning the Sabbath,' that is what the Lord will

have to say, one of these days, to them Christians
that uphold such wrongdoing, and help along with
their money. Besides, I reckon the folks who go to
church don't go labelled, and the drivers and other
lookers-on have no means of telling whether they
are going to church or a-visiting."

"That is of very little consequence," declared the
aristocratic aunt. " What difference do you suppose
it makes to me what people think ? ' To his own
master he standeth or falleth.' That is Scripture,
too, I believe."

And she sat back with a severely complacent
smile, as if much gratified with herself for having
vindicated her side, and produced a Bible verse to
sustain her.

"That's true," said Mrs. Smith, in no wise
quenched. "That's true enough, so far as the judging of other folks is concerned ; the Lord wants to
do that himself, because he understands all the little
hidden things that we know nothing about ; but I
guess it don't apply to folks not caring what other
people think of 'em, because the same Lord told us
to be careful about that. ' Let not your good be evil
spoken of,' says he, and then he reminded us that we
had got to be known by our fruits ; and he says he
set us here to be lights, so that folks who looked at
us, and saw how we lived, would glorify him for it.
I guess it makes a sight of difference what the street-
car drivers think of us. I guess like enough the
Lord will ask us why we let our going to church on
his day be evil spoken of, by using evil means to get
there."

I

" I was not aware that I had pronounced the means evil," said the aristocratic aunt, and her voice was several degrees haughtier.

" Oh, well, that don't need any 'pronouncing' from human lips; it stands right over against the command, ' Remember the Sabbath day to keep it holy, not doing thine own ways, nor finding thine own pleasure.' Of course, anybody can see that them poor street-car drivers and conductors ain't keep- ing the Sabbath day holy; and they're doing their own ways, though like enough they don't see any other way to earn their bread; poor fellows, I suppose they ain't learned to trust the Lord; they don't have time to think about him. The trouble is when a Christian man or woman gets on them cars on the holy Sabbath day and rides a little while, they say to 'em, ' You car-drivers ain't of no account; *we've* nothing to do with your souls; it is your business to take us to church, we're going to worship God; whether *you* have any chance to worship him or not, is nothing to us.' Now, you see, the Lord said he had made of one blood all the nations of the earth, and he told us to love our neighbours as well as we did ourselves, and he made it pretty plain that even them drivers are our neighbours, whether they are on their way to Jericho or somewhere else. There's no getting away from our duty to them."

I could not determine whether Erskine was really interested, or whether Mrs. Smith's quaint ways amused him, and he wanted to draw her out by in- terposing an objection at this point:

"But, Mrs. Smith, the cars would run on Sabbath all the same, if none of the church people patronised them; not one-tenth part of their revenue comes from church-goers, I presume."

"That may all be true," said the old lady with assured tone; "but don't you see, young man, 'To his own master he standeth or falleth'? The Lord isn't going to ask *me* why some people helped rob him of his day by making the cars take them a-visiting on Sunday; them that go a-visiting will have to tell him their own story and answer for their doings as best they can; whatever *they* say won't alter the fact that he will say to me, 'Mrs. Solomon Smith, why did you help shut them poor fellows out of heaven, by putting in your example to help them break my laws? Didn't you know that to obey was better than sacrifice?'"

It was worthy of thought that, quaint and strange as this way of putting it was, something in the tone, or the words, or the influence of the Spirit whose breathings they were, hushed the group around the breakfast-table into decorous attention.

The questioner seemed satisfied; at least he pursued that portion of the subject no farther, but after a moment or so of silence asked:

"But what would you have people do? The fact remains that a great many, ladies at least, cannot get to church at all unless they ride on the cars. Do you think it would be right for them to habitually stay at home from church, when the street-cars pass their door every five minutes? Seems to me

I have heard a Bible verse about 'straining at a gnat and swallowing a camel'; wouldn't that apply ?"

Mrs. Smith laid down her knife and fork, and fixed penetrative grey eyes on the young man's face as she said :

"Suppose I hadn't a pair of shoes to my name, and suppose the Lord knew that I hadn't no way of earning any, and that I couldn't, no way that I could fix it, go to church without 'em, which do you suppose he would tell me to do, stay at home or steal *your* shoes and go ?"

In the midst of the general laugh which this sentence provoked, she added :

"You see, I believe that the folks who can't get to no church on Sunday, without helping somebody to break the Sabbath, and can't find any other place to live near by to a church, better tell the Lord all about it, and ask him what to do; seeing there's them two bars of his, that of course it ain't right to break down, 'Remember the Sabbath day to keep it holy,' and 'To obey is better than sacrifice.' I don't believe he looks upon his commandments as no bigger than gnats."

Even then, one of the sillier misses was not quenched, but had a tart question to put :

"Mrs. Smith, when you lived on that farm you were telling us about the other day, didn't you ride to church ? For my part I can't see the distinction between car-horses and farm-horses."

"Yes," said Mrs. Smith, taking a swallow of tea

from her saucer, "I rode to church every Sunday of my life. We got up early and did the necessary work and tended to the critters. We give them a better breakfast than usual, because it was the Sabbath, and packed our dinner in the basket to eat at noon, and filled the foot-stove with coals, and started, and when we got to the little white meeting-house, Solomon would drive into one of the sheds and tie the horses; and at noon he would get out their bag of oats, and set them to eat their Sunday dinner, and there they would stand and rest and eat. They always had an extra mess of oats, and if they didn't know it was Sunday, it wasn't because they didn't have a day of rest; other days they worked from sunrise to sunset, stepping spry, but Sundays it was only to take us to the Corners and back again; and neither Solomon nor I ever had to stay away from church on their account. Did you say, dear, that you didn't see no difference between that and riding on the street-cars?"

If the "dear" really hadn't seen the difference, she saw it now, and had wit enough to join in the laugh that followed at her expense.

Altogether, Laura was satisfied. Her old friend had come off in flying colours; whether or not her arguments were unanswerable, certainly no one had answered them.

"She is sharp," said Erskine, as we left the table, and he lingered beside Lida and her mother. "She is just as sharp as steel. It is fun to talk with her, but a fellow has to keep all his wits at work,

and then get worsted.   Perhaps she is nearer right
than some of us, too."

The most complacent listener at the breakfast-
table had been Mrs. Jonas Smith.   I could but watch
the satisfied expression of her face, and wonder a
little over the kind way in which she declared that
she believed in people following out their convictions of right, whether others agreed with them or
not.

"Bible verses seem to be our chief bill of fare
here this morning," she said, with a pleasant laugh;
"I remember one that brother Solomon was fond of
quoting when he was a young man, 'To him that
knoweth to do good, and doeth it not, to him it is
sin.'   I suppose it applies equally to those who think
things are wrong, and then do them.   I, for one,
respect Maria's scruples.   She is not used to the law-
less ways of a great city, and cannot be expected
to approve of them."

Whether Mrs. Solomon Smith was to be expected
to approve of Sabbath-breaking after she became
used to it, did not quite appear.

When we reached the parlours, the reason for her
tolerance came to the surface :

"You must take possession of the back parlour
this morning, Maria.   It will be deserted, and you
can have a nice, cosy time all to yourself.   Harris,
move the large green chair from the front parlour
over here by the register—the morning is unusually
cold.   I don't know whether there are any books
down here that you will care to read, but Lida shall

bring you a number from the library, and you can
select for yourself."

The picture must have looked inviting; Mrs.
Solomon Smith was fond of reading. She turned
beaming eyes on her sister-in-law, but answered
without hesitation:

"I don't believe I shall have any time this morning.
I've got a little bit of fixing to do, and it must be
most time to start for church."

"Oh!" If you have studied intonation very
much, you will be able to imagine how much that
"oh" expressed, without my trying to tell you. "I
did not suppose you would go to church this morning,
after all I have heard. You would have to ride on
the street-cars, you know."

"Bless your heart! no, I wouldn't; Jonas said it
wasn't more than five minutes' ride in the cars, and
I can walk as far as that would be without any
trouble. Oh, I shall go to church; a nice, bright
morning like this, and me feeling usually well and
strong; I couldn't think of staying away! Besides,
I promised Solomon I'd hear for him to-day; he is
uncommon fond of good solid preaching."

The easy-chair and the cosy corner and the tempting books were of no avail; the strong-hearted old
lady came downstairs, presently, shod in arctic
rubbers, which made her feet look nearly as large
again as usual, her long dark-green camlet cloak
securely buttoned from throat to feet, her neat black
velvet bonnet of a pattern that might almost have
dated back into her youth, and a strong cotton

umbrella to serve in lieu of a cane. It was still early, so none of the street-car party were visible. Several loungers who had chosen not to go to church at all, stood in parlour and hall, ready for any amusement that offered. Laura, in her handsome winter suit of velvet and silk, looked like a young princess beside her old friend. We had had but little talk together since breakfast.

"Mamma," she had said, with the little ring of determination which girls at nineteen like to put into their voices, "I am going to walk to church with auntie Smith."

"Are you ?" I said quietly; "then there will be three of us."

She came and wound both arms about me, in a caressing way that she had, as she said:

"You dear mamma, you always do such nice things ! And you do them so quietly, without any of the high pressure that I have to get up. I wish I could be more like you. Mamma, I was afraid you would go in the car; and after all that had been said, I could not endure to have you."

"Thank you, daughter," I said, and I could not help laughing a little.

The town in which we live does not boast of street-cars, and it so happens that the question of Sabbath-riding had never come up before her.

"I had not the slightest idea of riding to church. Your father and I settled that matter long ago, as inconsistent for us, at least ; and you know that even Mrs. Jonas Smith's decision was, 'To him that knoweth to do good, and doeth it not, to him it is sin.'"

"Mamma, why didn't you join in the discussion?"

"My dear, did you think our old friend stood in special need of help?"

She laughed brightly and said no more. Then we went downstairs to wait for our old lady.

CHAPTER XI.

*SAYS I: "I THINK THERE WAS AN UNBELIEVER
AROUND."*

I THINK it must have been a long five minutes' ride
on the street-cars, for it took us nearly half an
hour to walk it; but the church was reached at
last. A trifle late we were, and the Smith pew was
full with the gay party who had come thither by the
" red line."

We met Irving at the door, looking excessively
annoyed. We learned afterwards that he had called
to escort us to church, and Mrs. Jonas, in her vexation, had expressed herself more plainly than had
been agreeable to him.

" Upon my word !" he said, addressing himself to
Laura, I suppose because he did not dare to scold
me, " I think this is carrying philanthropy a little too
far. You are making yourself ridiculously conspicuous by this proceeding."

Laura was not in the mood to be scolded ; sensitive to ridicule as she was, it had taken considerable
moral courage to enable her to decide on her course
of action that morning. Once decided, however, she
was, like all persons who have to pass through a
struggle, nerved for the occasion ; so it was a very

haughty cousin who drew her arm away from his
detaining hand and said:

"We will not render you conspicuous, Irving, by
obliging you to accompany us. The sexton will
show us to a seat." And, before he could control
himself to reply, she had obeyed the motion of the
usher, and was moving down the long aisle, Mrs.
Smith and I meekly following. What became of
Irving I do not know. I was sorry for the boy.
Why will young people be so hard on each other?

It seemed to me a singular circumstance that the
usher should choose to give us a sitting in the pew
which was directly in front of Jonas Smith's own.
But a stranger circumstance followed. The lady
occupying the corner, who looked up with pleasant
face at our entrance, was none other than she of the
fur-lined circle, who had rejoiced over the gift of the
little book. She instantly recognised us. How could
she help it, with that green camlet cloak in the fore-
ground? Her face became radiant; and as Laura
had drawn back to let Mrs. Smith precede her, it
was the old lady's hand that she grasped with delight,
and a whispered welcome—church though it was.
That she was a woman of distinction was at once
apparent from the look on Jonas Smith's face. I
caught it as I turned to accept an offered book from
one of his party — astonishment, incredulity, perplexity, and a touch of dismay.

Perhaps I am, like Laura, growing uncharitable,
when I attribute the sudden, careful attention to his
sister-in-law's comfort, which he gave after service,

to the fact that one who was among the wealthiest patrons of the wealthy church had welcomed her as a friend. He tried to overcome Mrs. Solomon's scruples to the street-car.

"You ought not to walk," he said in a voice of extreme solicitude as we reached the hall. "The wind has risen, and I'm really afraid for the consequences if you undertake to walk against it."

"I'd be afraid for the consequences if I undertook to walk against the Lord's express command," she said with a good-humoured smile. "Don't you worry about me. My umbrella's stout, and so is my heart. I'll get home all right."

And she did, for our car acquaintance came toward us just then, holding out a hand to me as if I, too, were an old friend. She would be so glad to have us occupy the vacant seats in her carriage ; she came alone ; it would be no trouble at all ; she passed within a square of Mr. Smith's house ; nothing would give her greater pleasure than to serve her dear old friend, whom she recognised as of royal blood. So it transpired that Mr. Jonas Smith had the pleasure of seating his sister-in-law in the back seat of one of the finest carriages that drew up before the sanctuary, and tucking around her a brilliant, furry robe that represented much money—an all-important feature in his eyes. Then he and his waiting party betook themselves to the street-cars, while we rolled rapidly away.

Fairly at home in our own room, where we had escaped until the late dinner was served, Laura

arranged us to her own satisfaction; Mrs. Smith in
one easy-chair, I in another, then curled herself
among the pillows of the bed, prepared for comfort,
and began:

"Well, auntie Smith, how did you like the
church?"

"Why, it was beautiful," said Mrs. Solomon, with
animation. "I liked it. I always do like nice
churches, just as nice as folks can afford. I ain't
one of them kind that think the days when we used
foot-stoves for warming, or for freezing, and had no
cushions on the seats, and had high, old-fashioned
pulpits without any pretty fixings, were better than
these days or ought to come back again. In them
days we didn't carpet our own floors, nor cushion our
chairs. Times are changed, and I like the Lord's
house to keep pace with our own, at least. Look
how they did with the Temple. The Lord had the
best use for that. It came first, and I suppose if
the people had anything left, they could put some
of the pretty into their own homes, but not before
the Temple had all it needed. That ought to be
the rule now. I liked the church, child. The carpet
wa'n't thick enough to hurt my feelings. I believe
in making the church the very handsomest place
there is to go to; acting as though you loved it so,
you couldn't do too much for it. I liked the big
organ, too. The louder it rolled the better I was
pleased. It made me think of the 'ten thousand
times ten thousand, and thousands of thousands,'
and the 'sound of many waters.'"

"But, auntie, I meant the sermon; how did you like that?"

Silence for a minute, then a meditative "I dunno, child. Was it a sermon? You see, a sermon means more than just to stand up in a pulpit and talk. Solomon and I got to arguing about that once, and we didn't agree. He was kind of criticising—Solomon is tempted that way a good deal—and says he to me: 'Well, now, Maria, I'll look in the dictionary and see what's what.' We've got one of them great big dictionaries that knows most everything; I never did see a book like it! We had a little one, but my! it don't begin with this. Jessie, she sent it to us for a Thanksgiving present. That's what she said. It wa'n't Thanksgiving, and I dunno what she was thankful for just then; but she called it that. Solomon got up and went over to the stand, and hunted out the word *sermon*, and read it off to me; quite a long explanation, but this was part of it; that it was for the purpose of religious instruction. That's where Solomon and I didn't agree. I thought a talk about a verse of Scripture was a sermon, anyhow; but Solomon said there must be religious instruction in it. Now, Laura, I leave it to you: Was there any religious instruction in what we heard this morning?"

"Why, auntie," said Laura, greatly amused. "I thought it was all instruction from beginning to end. Don't you remember how many 'original readings' he gave us, and how learnedly he described what a miracle was, from a scientific standpoint, and the

physical, and mental, and moral, and I don't know
how many more kinds of impossibility that there
could be miracles at the present day? I think it
was as full of instruction as any sermon I have heard
this long while."

Mrs. Smith sat back among the cushions, and gave
a little sigh.

"Yes," she said, "there was instruction, but was
there religion? I don't know; I'm only an ignorant
old woman, and of course I haven't any right to pass
my opinion on a scholar like him; but I can't help
thinking that there might have been a different kind
of a sermon preached out of that text somehow; one
that would help me, you know. I ain't far enough
along to understand it; and like enough there was a
good many in the same fix."

"I don't doubt it in the least," observed Laura.
"I never expect to be far enough along to understand it."

"Well, now, you see, doesn't it seem a kind a pity?
such a nice text!" She repeated the words with a
sort of lingering, regretful tenderness: "'When Jesus
saw their faith, he said unto the sick of the palsy,
Son, thy sins be forgiven thee.'"

"Auntie," said Laura, as she raised herself on one
elbow to push another pillow under her head, "if you
were a minister, and had taken that text for a sermon to-day, what would you have said about it?"

"Bless your heart, child, you do have the wildest
notions! The idea of me being a minister and taking
a text! That would be enough if I was Solomon.

But I own I had the hardest kind of a time keeping my thoughts to listening to what he was saying this morning; they would go a roving off. You see, Solomon and I kind of studied over that story for a whole week, once, till it got to seeming about the wonderfullest one there was in the Bible. And I kept a-going over that Sabbath evening we talked so much about it, and a-thinking of what Solomon said, and then of what I said, and what he said to that, till I got away off from the minister in the pulpit, and says I to myself: ' Well, I declare, Mrs. Solomon Smith, won't you look pretty when you get home, and Solomon asks you about the sermon, a-saying, " Why, you and I was the preachers that morning! I can tell over what we said, but I dunno what Dr. Barmore said "; I guess you'll get sent to the city again to hear a sermon ! ' "

But Laura was not to be turned from her purpose by any side issues.

"That's just what I want to hear," she said earnestly. "Tell us just what you and Mr. Smith said."

Mrs. Smith laughed a cheery, pleased laugh.

" Dear me," she said; " it would take too long. We got most amazing interested in that story. It was a Sunday evening, and I remember we sat up till ten o'clock, and the fire went clean out while we talked it over."

" But I don't see what you found to say ?"

" Oh, there's enough to say, I tell you! Why, you see, there's wonderful things in it. We just happened to read it that night; it wa'n't in the line of our regular reading, but I got interested in it as I was looking over the book to find the place, and says I:

" ' Solomon, just think of it; there came such a crowd to hear him preach that they stood all around the door, and there wasn't room for any more.'

" ' When was that ?' says Solomon.

" ' Why, that time in Capernaum, after he had cured the leper, you know. I suppose they had heard of that,' says I, ' and so came post-haste to see what would happen next.'

" ' I don't wonder at it,' says Solomon. ' If they had known what they was about they would have crowded after him so that there wouldn't have been room for them in the streets. The wonderfullest thing about it all was that they let him go through the world as he did, travelling around, kind of home-less, and without a great many friends that amounted to much. It makes me kind of mad when I think of it,' says Solomon, and he leaned over and poked the coals.

" Solomon always pokes the coals when he gets excited; no matter if the fire is burning just as bright as it can, them coals have got to be poked But I went on with my reading, and says I :

" ' This was the time they brought the man that had the palsy, you know ; four of his friends brought him. What a time they must have had a get-ting of him started ! I wonder if he had a wife, and if she put in and helped and went along, or stayed at home and waited and watched to see what would come of it ? I suppose there was a great deal of talk before they started,' says I ; and says Solomon :

" ' Yes, I suppose they came up to it by degrees like. First, one of 'em said, Jesus of Nazareth is here again, and they say he has been doing wonderful things, curing the leprosy, and all that. And then, like enough, he looked at the sick man and said, I wish *he* could see him. And I think maybe somebody shook his head and said, Oh, there ain't no hope for him! Whoever heard of the palsy being cured?'

"Then I put in a word. Says I: 'Yes, and I dare say there was somebody to throw cold water on the idea by saying they didn't believe a word of all these doings. It was a likely story that Jesus of Nazareth could cure diseases that the learned doctors couldn't touch! Why, he was only a carpenter's son! What advantages had he?'

"Solomon laughed, and, says he: 'You always think there's a croaker around, don't you, Maria?'

"Says I: 'I think there was an unbeliever around. There seemed to be more of them than of any other kind of folks when he was here. But go on,' says I, 'I like to hear what you think they did.' Well, he went on to say he thought they worked up the notion, little by little, of taking the man down to the meeting. He said he hadn't much doubt that it didn't come to them on the sudden, but they kept a-wishing, and a-wishing, and hearing of wonderful things, and turning of it over in their minds, how the two could be got together, until finally one of them up and said: 'Let's take him down there on a bed! I'll carry one end, if you'll take the other.' And he said he reckoned after they had overcome all the objections and got started, and got to pretty near the door, and found they could not get in, some was for turning around and going back. Says I: 'Yes,

I can hear them; they said there was no use; he couldn't be got into such a crowd as that, and it wa'n't a mite likely it would do any good anyway.'

" But Solomon said he had no idea that them four men who was carrying the bed said any such thing. Says he:

" 'I believe their faith kept agrowing stronger with every step they took. Because, don't you see, they *acted* on what faith they had. And if it wa'n't any bigger than a grain of mustard-seed when they started, it got a pretty good growth by the time they got to the meeting; and when the folks began to say to them that they had done all they could, and had better just take the poor fellow home as quiet as possible, I have an idea that them men shook their heads and said: He shall be got to Jesus now, if we have to tear this house down to do it. And that gives one of them a thought, and, says he: Boys, this kind of roof comes off easy; let's lift it, and let him down right into the midst of them. I'll tell you what it is, I believe *he* can cure him. And then I think the others nodded their heads, and said: So do I, and I. Somehow I've kept feeling it stronger and stronger since we come along. Because,' says Solomon, 'you see it says he *saw* their faith; so they must have had it. I reckon, too, that the sick man looked at them and smiled all over his face. He felt the faith growing up in his heart fast. What do you s'pose them Pharisees thought when they see that bed coming down through the roof?' says Solomon; and says I:

" ' Why, it's easy enough to tell what *they* thought. Says they: If here don't come a bed, and that wretched sinner who was took with the palsy so long ago is on it. What a ridiculous thing! As if everybody didn't know that palsy couldn't be cured, and as if this miserable fellow was worth curing, anyhow. Such fanatics! That's what comes of letting this fellow preach and draw crowds around him!'

"Now I want to tell you just what Solomon said to me then, because I remember it very particular. Says he:

"'Maria'—and his voice sounded kind of strange —'Maria, don't you think it is most like being irreverent to speak of the Lord Jesus and call him "this fellow"?'

"For a minute I was beat; not that I thought I'd done anything wrong; but it struck me all of a sudden as being awful. Says I:

"'Solomon Smith, I do. I think it was dreadful! dreadful! It was all of a piece with the crown of thorns, and the spitting in his face, and saying: Aha! aha! But don't you know they did it? As for this fellow, they said, we know not from whence he is. I was only telling you what I thought more than likely they said. Not that I would say it for ten thousand worlds. I ain't a Pharisee.' And says Solomon:

"'That's true, Maria;' and he gave the coals a poke."

CHAPTER XII.

"Go on, please," said Laura, as Mrs. Smith paused in meditative mood.

She laughed pleasantly.

"Well, I dunno as there is much to go on about, child; you see, it was just our talk. Solomon said he'd a give most anything to be there when that man hopped up and picked up his bed and walked out; he said he guessed the crowd made way for him. Then I said I most wondered that when Jesus told him to arise and take up his bed and go home, that he didn't say: 'Why, I can't walk! I've got the palsy; I ain't stirred a step in two years!' But Solomon shook his head; 'No,' he said, ' by that time the little stream of faith had got to be a river, and the man felt it plunging along all through his body, and *knew* he could walk.' And then says he, 'Only think, Maria, what was walking and carrying of his bed, compared with what he got! "Thy sins are forgiven thee." 'Oh, my!' says he, 'seems to me if I could hear him say that to me, I should jump right up and down, and shout so they could hear me down at the Corners.' Says I, 'Why, Solomon! Haven't you heard him? I can hear him for you, just as plain! Sometimes for

myself I'm kind of in doubt, but I never am for you.'
Then Solomon he laughed a little while he says to
me : ' Hast thou faith ? have it to thyself,' and then
we had our little joke about 'wresting Scripture,'
and—why, the fact is, child, if I should keep on
talking till supper-time, I couldn't begin to tell you
all we said ; but you see it wasn't a sermon."

"I don't know," said Laura ; "seems to me it was
the kind of sermon that I should like to hear."

"Well, I don't deny we found it profitable to us—
we are only common folks, you know.   Solomon had
me notice what the effect of this man's faith was
on the crowd.   They was all amazed, you know, and
glorified God, and said, 'We never saw anything
like this before in our lives.'   And says he, I ' s'pose
if we had growin' faith like a grain of mustard seed,
that doesn't stay a grain, after it is planted, but
grows up into a tree ; if we was like that, we would
keep amazing folks all the time ; they would say
they never saw the like ; and they would have to
glorify God whether they wanted to or not.   The
trouble is, we ain't mustard trees at all, but poor
little dwarf plants ; we don't die outright, and that's
about all that can be said of us.'   But I kept a-going
back to that wife at home—I made up my mind
he had a wife—and I saw her a-sitting by the window, watching with her heart in her mouth.   I knew
just exactly how she felt.   I think she had a little
faith, just a shred ; that kind of imitation stuff that
we name faith.   I think maybe she said : 'Sho!
what an idiot I am for expecting that anybody can
cure him !   Haven't the doctors told me this long
time that there' wasn't any hope ?   It was real silly

of me to consent to his going; just as like as not
the excitement will make him worse. But then
there was Peter's mother-in-law; she was very sick;
I saw her myself, and I thought she couldn't get
well; and that very afternoon I heard of her going
around the house, helping to get supper for Jesus.
But then, a fever ain't the palsy.' That's the way
I run on to Solomon. Of course I didn't *know*
things was actually that way, but then they might
have been, and it's more than likely they was; and
it didn't do no harm anyhow; just made it all seem
more real and natural to me, and Solomon said he
liked it."

"So do we," said Laura, laughing, yet reaching for
her handkerchief. "What did you think she said
when she heard the news?"

"Why, I kind of thought that as he walked home
carrying his bed, a great crowd followed him, and
the boys kept shouting—there were boys along, you
may be sure, and it ain't no ways likely that they
kept still—and I thought, maybe she looked out of
the window to see what was to pay, and says she:
'What *can* all that crowd be for? What's happened
now? They act as though they was coming here;
and who is that they are crowding around. Why,
if that—it can't be!—and yet it is, I'd know *him*
anywhere; he's walking just as straight and fast as
ever he did in his life, and he's carrying his bed!'
Well, then we went to arguing about her. Solomon
thought like enough she fainted; but I didn't. I
thought she rushed out and joined that crowd, and
got hold of his arm somehow, and took one end of
that bed; and the way they all got into that house

again I don't believe none of 'em know to this day.
After that we got to talking about which of them all
we would like to have been, and Solomon said, next
to being the man himself, with all his sins forgiven,
he would like to have been one of the four who
helped take him to Jesus. Then says he : 'Only
hear us, Maria, two old simpletons ! Just as if we
couldn't hear his voice to-day if we wanted to—and
hadn't heard it many a time, for that matter—and
just as though we couldn't keep bringing our friends
to him all the time ; no crowd to hinder our getting
in ; no roof to tear down before we can get to him,
except the roof of our pride and unbelief.' 'Yes,'
says I, 'and, for the matter of that, we need to take
ourselves to him to get cured from the palsy. It's
a kind of palsy that keeps our hands, and feet, and
tongues from doing what they ought to a great deal
of the time. The palsy is incurable to this day,
except by that same Jesus of Nazareth. It is a
good thing he is the same yesterday, to-day, and for
ever.' "

"And yet we cannot take our friends to him to
be cured of bodily disease," Laura said, and her voice
was tremulous ; I knew she was thinking of a dear
friend over whose case human physicians had passed
adverse judgment. Mrs. Smith's eyes grew brighter,
and she sat erect. "I should like to know why
not," she said with energy ; "I can't find any place
in the Bible where it says he has lost his power
over the bodies, or lost his willingness to help us.
According to my notion, not a body gets over a
sickness or an accident unless he wills to have it
so. If the doctors did it, they'd always do it, and

there wouldn't be no use in anybody dying. Of
course, he uses means; that's no more than he always
did. I wonder if he didn't make clay and put it on
the blind man's eyes, and tell the man with the
withered hand to stretch it forth, and call on the
people to roll away the stone from Lazarus' grave.
I do suppose he could have rolled that stone away
himself, without any of their help, if he had wanted
to, but he was willing to let them put in their means,
just as he is now; folks talks as if 'means' was
something that they got up for themselves without
any of his help! I wonder where they got their
brains, and their plants, and minerals, and the land
knows what not, to work with? I suppose they all
come by chance."

"But, auntie, didn't you hear Dr. Barmore say
that the age of miracles was long past?"

"Yes," said Mrs. Smith, settling back among the
cushions, "but I don't know how he found out; I
don't find no such verse in the Bible; we talked up
that very thing, Solomon and I. He asked me if I
thought Jesus often cured people like that nowadays,
and I said I didn't know as he *often* did it; that the
world nowadays was very much like that country in
which he couldn't do many mighty works because
of their unbelief; 'but,' says I, ' we know he sometimes does such works.' Well, Solomon had just been
down to the city; he went with a drove, and was
coming back by the boat, and he got belated, and the
boat went off and left him, and there wa'n't no way
but to stay in the city over Sunday, or else ride on
the cars all night and get home Sunday morning;
of course he couldn't do that, so he stayed; and he

went to hear a D. D. preach, and, says he, 'Maria, that minister that I heard last Sunday said there wasn't any miracles nowadays.'

"'What is a miracle?' says I: and he was still for a minute, and then he said he reckoned we'd better ask the big book; so he turned to it again, and we learned the definition by heart: 'An event or effect contrary to the established constitution and course of things, or a deviation from the known laws of nature.'" She recited the large-worded sentence carefully, as a schoolboy recites a difficult paragraph in history.

"Well, we had to study over that answer and hunt out the meaning of two or three words, but by-and-by we got it pretty well simmered down, that a miracle was something different from what was happening all the time, and something that human beings couldn't do; but it didn't seem to me that that proved anything. Who would be more likely than God to do something different if he chose? And as to the established course of things, who established 'em; who made the laws of nature, I'd like to know? that man this morning talked about 'the laws of nature' and 'the established order of events' as though he had established them himself, or some of them scientific men he talked about had done it, and even God hadn't a right to touch 'em.

"But I ain't going to criticise him; I can't, because I didn't understand half the time what he was driving at; it might all have been true what he meant, and I suppose likely he knows what he meant, but I'm beat if I do. I couldn't help wishing he would prophesy a little; don't you know, dear, how

Paul says 'he that speaketh in an unknown tongue edifieth himself; but he that prophesieth, edifieth the Church?' Well, I got to thinking about that, and I kept on. Says Paul, 'Except ye utter words by the tongue, easy to be understood, how shall it be known what is spoken?' Ye shall speak into the air! Paul knew plenty of languages; one of the things he thanked God for was that he spoke with tongues more than any of 'em; but says he: 'In the Church I had rather speak five words with my understanding, that by my voice I might teach others also, than ten thousand words in an unknown tongue.'"

"But, auntie, do you really believe that people are *ever* cured nowadays as suddenly as that man was?"

"Why not, child? Because it would be a miracle? I ain't afraid of that; you see, a miracle is just what it always was; if it is contrary to the established order of things now, why, it was then; and if God went contrary to the established order of things eighteen hundred years ago, he is able to do it now; and there's only one thing that will make me believe that he never does it, and that would be a Bible verse that said right out, in plain words, that there wa'n't to be any more things contrary to the established order. But then, I'm only an ignorant old woman; I don't pretend to know. Maybe they ain't miracles; maybe they ought to be called by different names. But I know this: Did you ever hear about a girl named Jennie Smith? She ain't no kin of mine, one way of looking at it, and another way she is a blood relation, for her Elder Brother is mine, too, and he has gone to get some mansions in

our Father's house ready for us. Well, this that
I'm going to tell you I know to be a fact, and them
that dispute it don't know what they are talking
about. She lay on her back for seventeen whole
years! On her back! Dear me! that don't tell the
sixteenth part of it; she lay on a wheeled cot, with
one of her poor limbs bolted down in it, and the suf-
ferings she bore I don't know as anybody could
believe. I don't really, unless they knew her, and
knew about the suffering all along as I did, and heard
her sweet, patient voice, and knew how the Lord
sustained her, and helped her to use her poor weak
hands, and her clear, strong brain, to support her
mother and sisters. Folks talk about sick people
using will-power to make them well—there's a good
deal in it, too; I believe in the will, and I believe
in using it good and strong when a body feels sick
and nervous, and kind of tired of life; but when I
tell anyone about Jennie Smith, and then he goes to
preaching will-power to me, I feel like saying: Bless
your poor little wizened-up heart! It took more will-
power for that poor young thing to get herself through
one hour of pain and privation and trouble generally,
without screaming all the time, and ending up in a
lunatic asylum, than you ever used in all your life,
or ever will use, because you ain't got the will to
make the power out of. Well, how I am running
on! The long and short of it is, that one night,
after she had been serving him beautifully on her
back all these years, and after the very best doctors
in the country had said she never could hope to sit
up again, much less stand on her feet, this same
Jesus of Nazareth, who cured the sick man of the

palsy, and who said of himself that he was ‘ the same
yesterday, to-day, and for ever,’ set her on her feet in
a minute of time, and she has been travelling around
on them ever since, working for him with all her
might ; and a great many folks when they see her
and hear her, and know what she was, glorify God
and say we never saw it after this fashion, and a
great many others say, ‘ Give the doctors and the
will-power and anything else you can think of the
praise, for as for this fellow, we know not from
whence he is.’ It is pieces of the old stories over
again. They don’t mean it, you know ; they haven’t
a notion—some of them—of dishonouring God, but
they are most dreadful ’fraid the glory will be given
to him. Last summer, when I was gone to that
Convention, I met a man who had heard of Jennie
Smith, and when he found I knew her as well as I
know you, and had been a friend for years, he went
to cross-questioning of me with all his might ; he
was a minister, too—one of them kind that knows
all there is to know, and, says he, crossing one shining boot over the other, and looking wise and
benevolent :

“ ‘ I haven’t the least doubt, my dear madam, that
every word you say is true, neither do I, like some
others, doubt the sincerity of the young woman.
What I think is this : she was a Christian woman,
with great faith in God, and the hope that he might
one day cure her kept buoying her up, and her
prayers and those of her friends strengthened that
hope, and on this night in particular, as she heard
her friends praying, she made a tremendous effort of
will, and arose to her feet, and found that she could

walk! Naturally enough she attributed it to miraculous power, whereas, if she had made the same resolve and the same effort long before, the result would have been the same. It is all as simple to an analytical mind as a, b, c, and can be explained, you see, without assailing the estimable young woman's character.'

"'Ahem,' says I, 'Doctor Wisely, didn't I hear you telling, this noon, about the time you had when you was getting up from that eight months' sickness—how weak and feeble you was, and how you had forgotten how to walk, and had to learn over again, just like a child, and how the doctors wouldn't let you take but three steps in the forenoon and three steps in the afternoon for quite a spell?'

"'That is all true, madam,' says he, as bland as could be, and he wa'n't analytical enough to see where he was bringing himself to, and says I:

"'Well, could you tell us how comes that a young woman that hadn't walked a step in seventeen years, hadn't even sat up in bed, should get up and walk across the floor as steady as you can to-day, and should get down on her knees, as natural as you can, and should go up and downstairs the next day, and go where she liked, and do what she liked, just as anybody would? Maybe you can analyse the reason why her will-power worked on them muscles of hers after they had been idle for seventeen years, and your will-power wasn't strong enough to help you out, in walking straight, after six months of idleness.'

"Well, he put the left foot down on the floor, and put the right one over it, and got out his handkerchief and shook it, and coughed and wiped his glasses, and, at last, says he:

"'That is certainly a very extraordinary statement, if it is true!'

"Says I: 'Humph! Now I should think it was a very extraordinary statement if it wasn't true! To think of me, an old woman who has been for forty years the wife of Solomon Smith, whose word is as good as his bond, everybody knows, to set up here telling lies about a woman that she has known and loved for ten years, would be pretty extraordinary, *I* think.'"

"Auntie," said Laura, sitting upright, "do you mean that this girl or woman actually walked, all in a minute, and kept on walking! I never heard of such a thing in my life!"

"Well, I mean just that. It seems a great wonder, now I think of it, that I never told you about her before; but, then, dear me! there's so many things to tell; you see, it all happened before I knew *you* very well. I'll tell you what it is, child: you must read her books, two of 'em, then you'll know the whole wonderful story. The first one is named *The Valley of Baca.* She wrote that when she was on her back, and always expected to be till she got wings; but when she got out of the valley, why, of course, she had to tell the rest of the story, and so she wrote *From Baca to Beulah.*"

And at that moment came the summons to the dining-room, and our remarkable after-service meeting was concluded.

CHAPTER XIII.

"I DO DISLIKE SCENES."

FROM the dinner-table nearly all of the guests lounged into the back parlour, and disposed of themselves in various attitudes indicating listless weariness. One, bolder than the rest, admitted that she did not know what to do with herself on Sundays. She did wish there was some public place to go to that wasn't wicked—with a little deprecating laugh over this last; in summer she was nearly always at some seaside resort, and of course everybody went to the beach, but papa had a notion that it wasn't quite the thing to take Sunday walks in the city; she was sure she could never see why. There was but faint response to these murmurings, most of the guests seeming really too bored to attempt reply.

Mrs. Solomon Smith had followed us with alacrity when we proposed taking seats in the parlour; but I fancy her idea of a family gathering in a Sabbath twilight was different from this. She looked around her doubtfully, as little ripples of talk started from one group and another, all frivolous, aimless, and some of it lacking in the spirit of charity. Those who had been to church seemed voluble only over certain elegant toilets, generally in disapproval of the taste displayed in colour or design.

"Wasn't there any sermon?" questioned Mrs. Smith, at last, breaking in upon Effie Van Horne's adjective-abounding description of Mrs. Germain Terry's new suit—"so ridiculously gay for a widow of less than a year!"

Miss Effie had chosen a sanctuary at a greater distance than the rest of us, and so was reporting for the benefit of her friends.

"A sermon!" she said, startled and thrown off her course a trifle. "Why, yes, of course; there is always a sermon on Sabbath morning, unfortunately; I'm sure I wish there were not. I think a choral service once in a while would be a great improvement on the dry sermon. They are always so lengthy; at least Dr. Doriland's are. I timed him this morning, and he preached exactly thirty-eight minutes and a half. Don't you think that is entirely too long for a sermon?"

She did not address Mrs. Smith, but Erskine.

"Depends entirely on the matter of the sermon," he answered her, with a somewhat embarrassed laugh.

Miss Effie's silliness seemed to be especially trying to him that evening. But she was one of those persons who fail to discover that they are annoying people.

"Do you think so?" she said, with delicious childishness. "Now I think all sermons are equally dull and stupid. Whoever heard of a minister selecting an interesting theme to preach about?"

Mrs. Smith turned kind eyes on the silly girl.

"Didn't you ever hear a sermon about heaven, my dear?" she said sympathetically. "And don't you think the story of the beautiful city where there is

L

no night any more, and no trouble, and no tears, and no saying good-bye, and no dying, is just as interesting as it can be ?"

Miss Effie toyed with the ribbons of her sash, and blushed a little as she said :

" Oh, well, heaven is nice enough to think about, I suppose, for those who like to.   I never tried it much ; I like this world too well to care to change. I am not one of your croakers, always crying out against the world as an awful place ; that's the reason I don't like sermons ; they always make out that the world is a snare and a delusion, and I think it is a perfectly lovely place."

The kind old eyes still beamed, and her voice was bright.

" I think so too, and I've lived here a good many more years than you have, and shed a good many tears, too ; but I like the world ; I think Jesus liked it very much.   He came to redeem it, you see ; so it must be beautiful to him.   But then, we can't always stay here, and our friends don't stay.   One by one they go off to that other country.   I've got more there than here, and much as I like the world, my heart gets all in a flutter when I think of going up to my other home."

I could but notice Erskine.   He stood near Mrs. Smith, his eyes on the carpet, his hands toying with his watch-chain, but every feature of the expressive face spoke of a roused heart, or conscience, I could not be sure which.   As for Miss Effie, she shivered visibly.

" Oh, dear !" she said, " how perfectly doleful we are getting !   Talking about dying when we are all so

young, and ought to be as happy as birds. The night
before a wedding, too. It is a bad omen. Lida, do
play something lively and cheer us up!"

During this conversation Lida had been seated at
the piano, Irving bending over her, and the two were
trying snatches of song. "Sacred song," they called
it, out of courtesy for the day, but to my ears, and I
feel sure to Mrs. Smith's, it really sounded, some of
it, more like dancing-tunes than anything sacred.
At Effie's appeal she laughingly played a few gay
strains, which moved one of the gentlemen to join
her with a whistling accompaniment, and Miss Effie
declared that she could not keep her feet still.

After that the talk drifted into even more frivolous
channels than before, as if Satan, alarmed at this little
rift in the cloud of worldliness in which he was
enveloping us all, had redoubled his efforts to arrest
anything like serious thought. Laura looked im-
ploringly at me, and murmured her desire to escape.
Poor Mrs. Solomon, I suppose, thought of her cold
room, and leaned her weary old head back in her
easy-chair and closed her eyes. I think she went
back to the little brown house in the Hollow, and
rested her hand on Solomon's chair, and listened to
the music of his voice.

Watching my nephew as he hovered around the
maiden of his choice, I wondered whether, when her
head was grey and her face wrinkled like Mrs.
Solomon Smith's, there would be that fellowship
between them, that oneness of thought, and plan,
and purpose, that brightened the little brown house
at the Hollow.

The wonderment saddened me somewhat. There

were times when these two young things seemed to
me to be building their future on a very sandy
foundation. The talk flowed on, the dividing line
between Sabbath fitness and positive, undisguised
worldliness growing dimmer and dimmer. Among
other things, projects for the evening were discussed.
There was a concert, but it was so far down-town,
and required "too much dressing for people who
were to attend a wedding" the next day. So Miss
Effie said.

The statement roused Mrs. Smith, and opened her
eyes.

"A concert!" she repeated, in a bewildered way,
as if imagining that she might be dreaming. "Why,
isn't it Sunday yet?"

"Unfortunately, it is," said Miss Effie, tartly.
"If it were not, there would be ever so many nice
things to do."

"But did they really have concerts on Sunday
nights?" the dear, puzzled old lady wanted to know.

"Of course!" Miss Effie felt herself compelled
to reply, since the question was directed to her,
and no one volunteered an answer in her place.
"Why should they not? What more appropriate
way of spending Sunday evening than in singing
sacred music?"

"And do they have praying?" queried Mrs.
Smith, which question not only convulsed Miss
Effie, but several others of her stamp; and Lida's
cheeks crimsoned with shame over her aunt's ignorance.

For almost the first time since we had been
guests in the house, I gave attention to Harris Smith.

He frowned so distinctly on the rudeness of the young ladies, and made so prompt an answer:

"No, aunt Maria, they don't have praying, and their so-called sacred music is nothing that you would recognise by that name. It is about as sacred as that which my sister Lida is giving you at this moment. What they do have is a great deal of dressing and talking and flirting—why, a regular Monday night performance, with the same 'sacred' attached to it to catch the young and foolish."

"Like yourself, for instance," retorted Miss Effie, who was at all times divided between her desire to receive the exclusive attentions of Harris, and to attach young Erskine to her train. "I believe you are a frequent attendant. Do you come in the list of those recently caught?"

"By no means," with a very low bow of mock-deference. "I was referring to the lambs of the flock; it is well understood that I am nothing but a goat; never made any pretence of being anything else, and therefore belong to the devil, without being caught: he did not have to waste any special effort over me."

"Harris," said his mother, reprovingly, "you are growing irreverent."

Whereupon Harris laughed immoderately; his face had heretofore been grave enough.

"Upon my word, mother," he said, when he could speak, "it is the first time I ever heard anybody accused of irreverence towards his Satanic majesty!"

His mother chose to ignore this, but said:

"What is the matter with you young people to-night? There seems to be an element of discord.

I never knew you all to get on so unamiably together."

"There has been an element of discord introduced
into this house," muttered the little bride, in what
was certainly a very loud undertone. "I'm glad that
I am not to breathe the same atmosphere much
longer. Irving, you are very good; I don't know
how you endure her at all."

Irving laughed pleasantly, and made some gallant
remark about his being able to endure anything just
now; there was not enough, in all the old aunts
which all the country towns in the world could produce, to affect his happiness. Then Mrs. Smith
suddenly sat upright in her chair, and, at this inop-
portune moment, addressed the bride-elect:

"Elizabeth, give us some good old-fashioned hymn
tunes, won't you, and set all these young folks to
singing? I'd like to hear them sing 'Thus far the
Lord hath led me on,' or something sweet and tender,
like that. Come now, just to please your old
auntie."

But "Elizabeth" had a naughty frown on her
pretty face, and whirled herself away from the piano
with the pettish remark that she had never learned
to play psalms; she didn't consider a piano suited to
them anyway.

Now it so chanced, whether from thoughtlessness or
because they supposed that a young lady from the
country would not be a proficient at the piano, my
Laura had not been asked to play; it also chanced
that she was by far the most skilful performer in the
house. We recognised quite early in her life, that
she had marked musical talent, and we had culti-

vated it as thoroughly as we could. As for her
voice, it was simply remarkable. Irving must have
remembered it as a boy, but he had not mentioned music to her since we came; indeed, Irving,
naturally enough, had but little thought but for his
bride.

I suppose Laura had been a trifle piqued, as girls
will be, by the utter indifference of her new acquaintances, and lately had kept perversely in the
background whenever there was a call for music.

Indignation over Mrs. Solomon Smith's treatment,
however, called her promptly to the front.

"Auntie Smith, I will play and sing the hymn
you want," she said decisively, and moved to the
vacated music-stool.

Erskine sprang forward to attend her, which item
seemed to annoy poor little Effie and take from her
every remnant of good breeding. Her really pretty
face was spoiled by a sneer as she murmured to
Harris, "Now we shall see what musical prodigies
the country can produce." There was not time for
more before Laura's voice filled the room:

> "Thus far the Lord hath led me on,
>   Thus far his power prolongs my days,
> And every evening shall make known
>   Some fresh memorial of his grace."

Were I not her mother, I might be tempted to a
description of the tenderness and pathos and power
with which she rendered that grand old hymn. The
first line hushed the chattering groups into astonished silence. On the second verse Erskine joined
her, a rich, full bass, which of course added to the

charm. It was not strange that other voices than Mrs. Smith's clamoured for more when the music ceased. But Laura turned decisively away from the piano.

" I sang it for auntie Smith," she said, coldly. " I keep my voice for her and a few of my special friends."

But Mrs. Solomon Smith had a word for her:

" Laura, my dear, you will not refuse to sing the gospel for any one's asking. Maybe it is the Lord Jesus himself asking you to witness for him. I make no doubt that he gave you your voice for that very purpose; and yours too, young man."

This last to Erskine, who answered only by a grave bow, while Laura, with subdued face, turned back to the piano.

One and another and another favourite were called for, Mrs. Jonas Smith graciously adding her voice to the appeals; a musical genius right in her home was something to be proud over. I fancy Mrs. Jonas gave some regretful sighs to the thought that it was Sabbath evening, and none of her friends who had musical daughters or nieces or guests, would be likely to see her triumph.

Mrs. Solomon Smith, who, without knowing that Laura's voice was very unusual, has known for years that she greatly enjoyed it, drew out from the storehouse of her memory old, long-cherished hymns, and sat back with closed eyes and enjoyed her Sabbath at last.

Among other sweet, quaint ones that filled the gay parlour that evening was what few people sing now :

> " Jesus died on Calvary's mountain,
>   Long time ago ;
> Now he calls me to confess him
>   Before I go.

> " My past life, all vile and hateful,
>   He saved from sin ;
> I should be the most ungrateful
>   Not to own him."

" I wonder," said Mrs. Smith, breaking the hush that for a moment filled the room at the close of this verse, " I do wonder, now, if there's any of the folks in this room that he is calling to confess him for things he did for 'em long ago, and they don't want to do it ? Seems to me as if there might be one or two. How I wish you could all make up your minds to own him as your best friend, the lover of your souls."

I have rarely seen such silence as there was in that room then. We could fairly hear the heart-beats. Even the pretty Lida, after a first startled look to see what Irving would think, and what others of her fashionable friends thought, let the anxious look fade out somewhat from her face, and leave an almost wistful expression in its place. But it was the young man, Erskine, who broke the silence:

" I'm one," he said, in a voice that, though husky, was strong. " He did save my vile and hateful life years ago ; lifted me up from the depths, and I promised then to confess him always and everywhere ; and I have shamefully broken the pledge, until now hardly anyone recognises me as one who ever belonged to him. I feel as though he had justly cast me off ! "

"Return unto me, and I will return unto you, saith the Lord."

It was Mrs. Smith's clear, quiet voice that broke in upon the almost painful hush following this sentence. She trusted her voice to no words of hers, but poured like a healing balm upon a wound the gracious message of the Lord himself.

I thought then, as I have often thought before and since, that he stayed always very near to Mrs. Smith, and verified to her the promise:

"Thine ears shall hear a word behind thee, saying, This is the way, walk ye in it."

"If we had stayed in there three minutes more we should have had a prayer-meeting and an anxious seat."

This was what the silly Effie said, as a summons to the dining-room for a cup of coffee broke in upon the scene.

That same silly little voice said, an hour later:

"Don't you think Mr. Erskine has gone for his horses? He has the most elegant pair, and a perfect gem of a carriage. I suppose he will not be so wicked as to go anywhere but to church, after his curious speech to-night; but I do hope he will ask me to go along. I would be willing to be good all the evening, if I could have a ride after those horses. They only came last evening."

He came back with his handsome carriage, and came into the parlour, but he walked straight to Mrs. Solomon Smith's side, with this petition:

"Mrs. Smith, will you let me take you to a church where I think you will like to go to-night? I have a pair of very gentle horses and a close carriage."

And she rode away with him.

"The idea!" said Miss Effie, referring, not to the choice of a companion, but to the episode in the parlour. "Who knew that Erskine was such an eccentric being! For the matter of that, we are all church-members, I suppose. I am sure I am; but I do dislike scenes."

CHAPTER XIV.

"I HAVE TO STAY OUTSIDE, AND JUST WAIT."

IT was very late that night before the house settled into quiet. The temptation was evidently strong upon our hostess to do a hundred little preparatory things in view of the next's day's entertainment.

"It really seems as though I could not take time to sleep to-night," she said to me with a nervous laugh. "There are so many responsibilities resting upon me, and so many last things to do! Monday is a very trying day for a wedding. Some way, Sunday makes an awkward break in all the preparations."

She certainly rested very little that night. The various bridesmaids were also in a flutter of preparation. They discussed, in not very low tones, the last changes in the arrangements of flowers and other bridal decorations; examined their gloves and laces, and I'm inclined to think Effie Van Horne even went so far as to slip into her white robe once more, to be sure that it was absolutely perfect.

Laura turned in her bed and groaned, and patted her pillow, and wished they would all try sleeping for awhile, and give her a chance. At last they did seem to conclude to leave the excitements until Monday, and quiet settled down upon us.

I hardly know how long it lasted, certainly not more than an hour or two, when the slamming of doors and the hurrying of feet commenced again.

"Oh, dear!" Laura said, sleepily. "It can't be possible that it is morning! Mamma, don't you get people up so early, and make such a commotion when my wedding-day comes." Then she opened her eyes wide. "That is auntie Smith's voice," she said.

Quiet and clear it came up to us; a tone of decision and command:

"Sarah, stop crying, and shut the door. That is the very worst thing you can do for her. Run down and hurry up the hot water and send me some vinegar! Has Jonas gone himself for the doctor?"

"Something has happened!" we both said at once, and in a moment we were dressing.

Something had happened, indeed. The nervous irritability of the fair young bride-elect, which had so grown upon her for the last day or two as to be noticed by all the guests, proved to be something more than excitement. After an hour of restless sleep she had awakened in a burning fever, and was already talking so incoherently that it was impossible to determine whether she knew in the least who she was, or what she wanted. Then began a scene of unparalleled confusion.

The violent ringing of bells, the distracted hurrying to and fro of many feet, the calls for this and that and the other possible remedy, the frantic appeals of her mother to each new frightened guest who appeared, as to whether it could be possible that Lida was dangerously sick, all combined to bewilder

most of us too hopelessly to be of any use. It was
here that Mrs. Solomon Smith's strong common-
sense and rigid self-control rose to meet the emergency, and served us well. She took command in
the sick-room herself; gently and firmly held her
ground against those who were eagerly crowding
around the bed; called Laura to help her with the
pillows which poor Lida was tossing wildly about;
gave me a bottle with the brief command: "Drop ten
drops of that into half a glass of water and hand it
to me quick!" and peremptorily ordered the frightened
mother away from the room until she could come
quietly. I have rarely seen a woman so completely
unnerved as was Mrs. Jonas Smith. I suppose she
had taken but little rest during the preceding two or
three weeks, and her nervous system was greatly
wrought upon by the weight of care, added to the
weight of pain which her mother-heart felt in parting
from her darling. She was very fond of Irving, very
proud of him, and seemed in every way to approve
of the marriage: and yet of course it was a hard
thing to think of her one little pretty daughter going
out from her old home, never again to be in it, a girl,
as she had been heretofore. My heart went out in
sympathy for the poor mother. But she certainly
was a worse than useless person in this emergency.
It seemed impossible for her to get control of herself. She wrung her hands in helpless terror; one
moment was sure that Lida was dying, right there,
before her eyes, and nothing being done; and the
next called on us fiercely to agree with her that it
was nothing in the world but a severe headache, and
Maria was making a great fuss about nothing. It

transpired that Mrs. Solomon Smith, in groping her way downstairs in search of a glass of water, had heard Lida's groans, and gone to her relief; while her worn-out mother, having but just gone to sleep, slept on unheeding.

What a day was that! I find that when I want an illustration of confusion and dismay and general bewilderment, my thoughts go back to that trying time. After what seemed like hours of waiting, the frightened father arrived with the family physician. He was one of those grave, reticent doctors, who waste as few words, and give as little information as possible; but that little in his case was to be trusted; so when I heard his verdict, given after a close and careful examination: "This is a sudden and severe attack of the fever which prevails in the southern portion of the city," my heart sank within me, for I had heard only the day before that the fever was increasing in violence. I followed the doctor into the hall, intent on learning his exact opinion. It was given me with all due gravity and reticence : rather it was drawn from him by careful cross-questioning.

" It is impossible to tell, madam, at this early stage of the disease, how it will progress or terminate.

" Yes; the fever is certainly not abating in violence, and the number of cases is on the increase."

" The suddenness of the attack is a feature of the disease."

" You are right, madam. It is never so sudden as it appears to unprofessional eyes, being preceded by hours, sometimes by days, of great nervous excitement."

"It is true that this case has commenced in an unusually violent form, and there are indications of great cerebral excitement."

"It is undoubtedly a contagious fever, and it is important to expose as few persons as possible."

"Oh yes; any person who has been near enough to the patient to get her breath, is more or less liable to the disease; still it is frequently the case that all so exposed escape. It is owing entirely to the condition of the system.

"I always have grave fears, madam, as to the result of such a fever; especially when, as in this case, the patient has a singularly delicate physical organisation."

On the whole, I turned from him with a heavy heart. I certainly had nothing very cheering to communicate to the mother; and there was in my heart a sharp pain on my own account. Had not my Laura already been several times "near enough to the patient to get her breath"?

Gradually we settled down to something like the system which prevails in a family of means, when sickness becomes a recognised fact. Yet it was in many respects the most trying day of all that we endured during this period of suffering. There were such sharp and trying contrasts. All over the house were hints, more or less apparent, of the expected festivity. Half-open doors revealed glimpses of soft, fleecy drapery, slippers, gloves, laces, flowers, perfumes. The large dining-room showed in the grey dawn of the early morning, preparations for special festival; the long table was extended, while closets left open in haste, showed rows of silver and china waiting to adorn it. In one closet the bridal cake had been set, already garnished with its wreaths of green, and beside it stood a half-empty mustard jar which had been seized upon to minister to the poor little sufferer upstairs, and then set down again in haste, as a more urgent call came. This is a fair sample of the incongruous confusions that prevailed throughout the usually well-ordered house.

The guests were simply panic-stricken; the story of possible contagion had spread in the unaccountable manner in which such stories always do; and the young ladies of the party were literally tossing their wedding finery into trunks, and distracting the already bewildered servants with urgent calls for carriages to be summoned at once, that they might catch early trains.

"There is no need for us to hasten," I said to Laura—and I'm afraid my tone was a regretful one as I said—"you have already been exposed, my dear, if there is any danger."

She turned upon me eyes that were almost fierce:

"Mamma," she said, "I would not go away now if I thought I should take the fever in the next hour, and could save myself by going. I think it is despicable to be in such a panic. Yesterday they were so fond of Lida that they hung around her from morning to night; to-day they think only of their precious selves!"

An indignant girl, indignant in a righteous cause, is almost a pretty sight. I did not have it in my

M

heart to scold her for her vehement words. There was little time for mere talk.

We dropped into grooves of labour before that day was done. Constantly people were arriving from the more remote suburbs of the city, guests of the house for the day, their wedding paraphernalia following hard after in express waggons. These all had to be met, and explanations made, and exclamations of dismay and condolence listened to, and hurried returns arranged for, to say nothing of lunches that in common decency must be prepared for some. Laura stepped into this distracting gap as readily as though she had been hostess and manager-in-chief of a household for years. She seemed to know by instinct just whose name to take up to Mrs. Smith, with special messages, or offers of aid, and who on no account to allow to penetrate beyond the decorum of the parlours.

Seeing the need for a head below stairs, I took upon myself the humble office of directing the servants as to lunches, breakfasts, and the like, trying to see that in their bewilderment they did not attempt two things at once, and accomplish neither.

As for Mrs. Solomon Smith, no professional nurse could have slipped into office with the ease and speed that she established herself in the sick-room. How many times during that first day did we have occasion to be grateful for her presence there!

The poor, frightened mother did not gain better control of herself as the hours passed, and it became evident that Lida's was undoubtedly a sick-room, and there were days and nights of intense anxiety to follow; she seemed simply overwhelmed. With all

her planning and preparing, the thought of sickness
had not once been entertained. Now that the actual
fact glared upon her, and brought in its train that
other awful thought of possible death, a funeral
instead of a bridal, she was utterly crushed; good
for nothing at Lida's bedside; she could not keep
from moaning and wringing her hands.

I have not said a word about my poor boy Irving.
How can I put on paper the record of his distress,
the photograph of his utterly miserable face? He
hovered outside the stricken chamber like a shadow.
The doctor, after having the state of the case explained to him, shook his head gravely over the
question of admitting Irving; counselled waiting for
a day, at least, until they should see how the disease
was going to develop; it might be of the utmost importance to keep him away from the room; in any
case it was needless exposure to probable danger.
We did not tell Irving that last; the poor fellow
would have rushed in, in spite of us, then, to show
his contempt of all possible danger as connected with
himself. "Wait for a day, at least!" the doctor
said, and he said it as if he did not know that under
some circumstances a day is an eternity. Before the
close of this day Irving had expected to have had
his wife by his side for ever. "Until death do us
part." I thought of the sentence that had floated up
to me amid the laughter of the marriage rehearsal.
Was it possible that the dread shadow was gliding
between them even then, and none of us had recognised it?

Before that first day was done, Irving had gone back
to something of his old, boyish manner with his

auntie, turning to me instinctively for comfort as a boy would to his mother. During the intervening five years we had grown apart as mother and son seldom do; but amid all the trouble, it gave me a little thrill of joy to note that the first touch of sorrow brought him back to me.

It is not my purpose to detail all the miseries of the days that followed. I could not if I would. Of course we calmed down from the first panic, and recognised the inevitable, as people always do; but still it was a strangely disorganised household.

It was a strange thing to me to note how few *friends* the Smiths had in their trouble; acquaintances in abundance — a perfect deluge of cards showered down upon them that first week; many came in person, expressing sympathy, sincere expressions, and as kindly put as they knew how, and yet the very dress in which they came, so bright and gay, and suggestive of the society engagements they were even then on their way to meet, left the impression of something incongruous about it all. Among the hundreds there was hardly one that the mother upstairs cared to hear about, and not one that she expressed a desire to see.

This mother the doctor had taken in hand with a sort of stern courtesy; had informed her that she was a fit subject for the fever, would be almost certain to have it if she spent much time in the sick-room; that she could do no good there, she was not calm enough; indeed, her presence was a positive injury to her daughter.

After that we did what we could to keep her from Lida's room. Of course she came and went, some-

times a hundred times in a day—so it seemed to us
—but it was true that she was too painfully nervous
to be trusted to do much for poor Lida, who did not
recognise her half the time, and therefore did not
mourn her absence. Such being the state of things,
Laura and I, the acquaintances of the day, slipped
into our places in the household, and did not as
much as mention to each other the idea of going
home.

"You are so good," would the poor mother say
to Laura, as she came quietly to her side with a
message from some caller requiring attention; "you
are so good to see all these people and dispose of
them. I cannot meet them, not one of them. Only
think under what circumstances I expected to meet
them all—when they came to congratulate my
darling—and now she is"—and the voice would falter
and drop into sobs.

Laura *was* good. I have rarely seen a girl of
nineteen show so much tact and wisdom and quiet
tenderness.

Mrs. Solomon Smith was a perfect tower of
strength. Every one, from the doctor down, de-
ferred to her. She was really the very perfection
of a nurse—quiet, calm, cheerful, quick of move-
ment, catching at a flash the meaning of the patient,
and the direction of the doctor; firm as a granite
boulder when the question at issue was recognised as
important, yielding to the last degree when it was
only a difference of opinion. The doctor even took
time to compliment her one morning as he waited in
the hall for admission.

"You have a remarkable nurse in there. She has

a faculty which not one nurse in a hundred possesses —that of being able to do as she is told. I have often observed that people who can do as they are told, are the only ones capable of telling others."

It was true. Mrs. Smith differed from him quite often. Her notions, some of them, were old-fashioned, and his were new. I could see it in her eyes that she did not quite approve; nevertheless, she swerved not one hair's-breadth from his directions; she recognised his responsibility, and his right to lead, and, like a soldier under orders, she obeyed.

The summer guests had all departed. Of Irving's special friends who had come from a distance to attend his wedding, only Erskine remained in the city. He called daily, sometimes twice a day; but Irving shrank from him. He seemed to shudder at the thought of meeting anyone who had been close to him in his happiness. Not the least of my duties was the trying to keep Irving from utter despair. It was very hard for him, as he said, to know nothing except what was doled out to him at intervals from the sick-room.

"It is different with you, auntie," he said pitifully. "You can go in and out, and see her constantly. You know just how she looks, and just what she says; and you can bathe her head, and do for her; and I have to stay outside, and just wait."

Poor boy! Is there any harder lot in life than to stay outside and wait?

CHAPTER XV.

THERE came a morning when anxiety and suspense reached their climax. Lida was in that dangerous state in which she recognised us all, knew, in a puzzled, excitable way, that much time had passed, that she was very sick, that people were alarmed about her—and, worse than all, she was fearfully alarmed about herself.

Her lucid moments were few, for she immediately puzzled and frightened herself back into delirium. The doctor took no pains to conceal his anxiety. For hours he watched over her, applying quieting remedies with no apparent effect, her excitement seeming to increase every moment.

At last he turned from her as if in despair:

"If she cannot in some way be quieted and put to sleep," he said, addressing her father, who had followed him from the room, "she cannot live but a few hours. Her strength is not equal to this terrible strain."

Terrible words these, when the skilful doctor admitted by them that his resources were exhausted. We were all in the room, or in the hall, near at hand. Irving, looking haggard enough to have been the patient himself, hovered in the background, the doctor having nervously ordered him to keep out of

sight. It seemed to me strange and unnatural that
Lida did not ask for Irving; did not mention him in
any way; and yet she remembered, at intervals,
about her past; for she had said to me but an hour
before: "I was to have been married. I wasn't, was
I? Why was it changed? Was I too sick? Oh,
dear, I'm very sick! I'm going to die! I know I'm
going to die!" This sentence she repeated again
and again, each time her voice growing louder, until
it became a wild and fearful cry. Then for a time
she would be utterly lost to us in the ravings of
delirium. This in turn would be followed by a sort
of stupor, and then another partially lucid interval.
But it was painfully noticeable that she grew mo-
mentarily weaker.

It was in one of the wildest of these paroxysms
that the doctor had turned away with his despairing
sentence.

"I do not see that I can do anything more for
her."

Indeed, the climax of her excitement seemed to
have arrived. She tossed from side to side, and
wailed her fearful cry: "I am going to die, and I'm
afraid! oh, I'm afraid!" until her mother lost, for a
few blessed moments, her agony in unconsciousness,
and was carried from the room. I could almost have
wished that the same relief might come to Irving.
His face was so drawn with pain and misery that I
felt my heart groaning for him. Still the agonised
cries went on, and still the doctor bent over her,
murmuring soothingly: "No one shall hurt you;
you are not going to die. Nothing shall harm you."
He might as well have talked to the wind that was

roaring fiercely outside. She gave as little heed. In the hall, a short time before, the doctor had asked, turning fiercely to Mrs. Smith, whom he had called out to consult:

"What has started her in this way? Surely we have no fanatic among us who has been cruel enough to try to talk religion to her!" his finely-cut lip curving into almost a sneer as he spoke the word.

Mrs. Smith made very quiet answer:

"I've only talked to the Lord about the poor lamb; not at all to her. I felt that she had not sense enough now to think about it, but he can think for her."

The stern-eyed doctor regarded her with a puzzled air, as if she were a creature from another world, speaking a different language from any with which he was familiar, then turned and went back to his patient without further questioning.

"Elizabeth," said the firm, quiet voice of her aunt, breaking in upon the dread wail of the child, a quiet voice, yet strong enough to rise above the shrill cry which Lida was making, "Elizabeth, I want you to be still, and listen to me! I've got something to tell you. If you'll be real still I'll tell it."

The fevered face turned toward her, and the blood-shot eyes were riveted for a moment upon her. The very name "Elizabeth," a name which she never heard from other lips, seemed to arrest her attention, and the quiet, kind old eyes bent on her, held her gaze.

"Are you God?" she asked, in an awe-stricken whisper.

Not a muscle of her aunt's face changed, her eyes lost none of their calm.

"No," she said, as if answering the most natural question in the world; "but I'm his messenger. He has sent a word to you that he wants you to think about."

"Did he say I was going to die?"

Nothing more pitifully eager than her tone can be imagined.

"No; he said ' I have loved her with an everlasting love.' Tell her this: 'Thy maker is thy husband.' Thy husband, Elizabeth! think of it. You have thought what that word means. I daresay you have thought about it a great deal; and he sent it to you on purpose so you would understand."

There came into the child's eyes that retrospective look which shows us that a mind is sweeping back over its past. Doubtless she had dwelt on that word "husband" with tender anticipation; she was so nearly a wife that the word had become very sweet to her. She had looked forward to saying, in fond, proud tones, "My husband!" The wild light began to die out of her eyes, which were still fixed upon her aunt, who had risen and was bending over her, holding her hand, and passing a soft, light touch over her forehead, as she said, over and over again in those low, firm tones, which conveyed a sense of strength:

"He says he has loved you with an everlasting love; he says I am to say to you that 'Thy Maker is thy husband.'"

She was certainly listening, and the doctor, watching her with keen, professional eye, telegraphed with significant gesture that her pulse was lessening.

Presently she spoke in a perfectly natural tone:

"But, aunt Maria, I haven't loved him. I haven't done anything for him."

The doctor's start of surprise to hear the low-keyed, natural voice, was so instantly followed by a frown at his own folly, and a startled glance toward Mrs. Smith, lest she too should break the soothing spell, that we realised more fully still the importance of the calm. Nothing could have been quieter or more prompt that her aunt's voice:

"Yes, he knows all about that, my lamb, still he sends the message. He wants you to love him; wants you to begin now."

"But I have wasted my life."

"Yes, maybe so. He knows; he is your Maker, you know, and now he bids me say that he will be your husband. Don't you think he can forgive anything after that? His love is everlasting. He wants yours now; not yesterday's, but to-day's."

"Aunt Maria, am I going to die?"

The doctor gave an emphatic start this time, and tried vigorously to arrest Mrs. Smith's attention, while he shook his head earnestly.

She did not for a moment remove her eyes from Lida's face, nor for a moment hesitate with her answer:

"I don't know, my lamb; he knows all about it; he didn't send you any word about that, only the other: 'I have loved her with an everlasting love;' and then that other: 'Thy maker is thy husband.'

What he wants to know is, if you will love him, and take him for your husband."

How much did the fever-wasted mind understand of the solemn and tender message ? Who can tell ? We waited, breathlessly, the doctor curiously: his professional anxiety was giving way to professional curiosity, to see how this new form of treatment would work. Two other physicians, also eminent, who had been called in council, and been unable to appear until now, tiptoed into the room, and waited, and were evidently curious ; and the quiet old voice went on repeating its tender message, over and over and over, and then the tender inquiry :

"Elizabeth, he wants to know if you will take him for your husband now ?"

"Yes," came in low, yet perfectly distinct tones, from the fever-parched lips. Not a note of the controlled voice changed as the dear old lady instantly answered :

"Then tell him so, my lamb ; just shut your eyes and speak to him ; he can hear, you know, if you speak ever so low. If you only think it in your heart he will hear you ; he hears you now ; but he will like the word direct from you." Back and forth went the soothing hand, making its slow, regular passes ; again and again the firm voice repeated the message : "I have loved thee with an everlasting love."

Slowly those restless, wide-open eyes, that had been wide open all through the long night, and all through the long day, thus far, lost their distressed look, the lids drooped lower and lower, the two small, wasted hands were clasped as a child's might have been who was saying—

"Now I lay me down to sleep."

The lips moved, but no sound from them was heard this side heaven. We stood in perfect hush around that bed—nothing to break it save that steady voice falling lower and lower, making no pause between the sentences, or repeated sentence, for she simply said those sublime words. And at last it became apparent to us all that for the first time in two weeks the child was sleeping a quiet, natural sleep, or else it was the sleep that knows no waking here.

Weeks afterwards we called that day the climax; but we did not know it at the time. We hovered with Lida apparently on the very confines of another world. Not that there had not been a decided change; the fever had spent its force; the trouble was, all that it seemed to have left behind was a small pale wreck, without power to rally its scattered forces and creep back into life again. Day after day she lay there like a snow wreath, too weak to speak, too weak to move so much as her small, wasted hands; just strength enough to turn her eyes from one to another and smile. But it was a blessed relief that she smiled. The look of terror which had blanched her face during those memorable and fearful hours, was gone. She was evidently at rest.

Whether it was that she was now too weak, too nearly slipped out of life to be other than at rest, we did not know; we feared, and we hoped, and we trembled.

"It is a kind of death-bed repentance," said Mrs. Solomon Smith to me, wiping her tired eyes, during one of those brief intervals in which she was off duty. "I've always been mortal 'fraid of them, and I am now. Poor little dove! she ought to have been got into the ark long ago."

"Do you think she is going to die?" Laura asked the question in an awe-stricken whisper. She thought so herself, or, perhaps it might be put, she feared so; but no one, since the change, had put it into words.

"I don't know, child," in a tired, half-hopeless voice; "there is so little of her left to die; it seems as if it would be so easy, so much easier just to shut her eyes and not open them again, that I feel kind of astonished every time I see them open. She thinks herself that she is going to die," continued Mrs. Smith; "she told me so last night, in the night."

"But she is very quiet and peaceful?"

"Oh, as quiet as a lamb. She spoke about getting married, and said she thought she was going to be the bride of Christ. I wouldn't let her talk, the doctor said I mustn't; but I was sorry afterwards; she wanted to; she had sweet things to tell me, she said; poor lamb!"

Generally, Mrs. Smith was cheerful. It was only occasionally, in the privacy of my room, that she allowed herself to sigh; but I saw that she had very little hope of Lida.

Sometimes it seemed to us that this lull was almost harder to bear than the excitement of constant suffering and constant attempts to do for our sick one had

been. There seemed nothing to do now but to wait.
What the doctor thought he kept to himself. He came
and went, twice, three times, occasionally four times,
during the day and night; but apparently doing
as little for her as the rest of us; just watching
and waiting. I began to grow very anxious for
Irving. His business furlough had been extended;
his place temporarily supplied, in fact. It was found
that even governments had hearts, and there was
nothing for him but to bear from hour to hour that
fearful strain. It was telling on him like a fit of
sickness He had grown almost as thin as Lida; his
face was quite as colourless; and now that the
strange calm had come to hers, was far more haggard.
Auntie Smith thought much of him; made many
journeys from the chamber of watching on his account; always appeared to him with a pleasant face
and an earnest—

"Keep up a good heart, my boy. The Lord reigns,
and he loves the child better than you do, and you
know how much that means. You may be sure he
will do his best for her."

She was left much alone with her patient. It was
the doctor's command that the weakened brain should
not be disturbed by different faces about her, and as
the mother's strength had almost entirely given out
since the first strain had been removed, and she had
dropped into the *rôle* of an invalid, it had been de-
creed that she must not exert herself for Lida at all.
So it fell to me to relieve Mrs. Solomon in her ministrations, and we two took sole charge. Laura would
have liked to establish herself there, but this I peremptorily refused; the child had cares enough all

around the disorganised household, without becoming nurse.

I hardly know when it was that the doctor's daily deliverances began to change slightly. I think it was Irving who first said to me, with lips so white that I remember I thought him fainting, that he believed the doctor was a little less hopeless.

After that I watched more closely, and gradually began to detect what seemed to me hopeful signs; these I communicated to Irving, feeling that he needed them to help him keep his reason. Little by little the story grew, until we were almost prepared one morning for Lida's own words, as her aunt bent over her:

"Auntie, I'm not to go to heaven yet, after all. I've been afraid to get well, for fear I should lose this—this sweet something, I don't know the name of it; but Jesus told me last night, in the night, that he was going to take care of me down here awhile; that he could do it just as easily here as in heaven, and I suppose he can."

It was that very morning that the doctor stopped in the hall, held out his hand to Irving, and said, with the nearest approach to emotion that I had ever seen in him:

"I congratulate you, young man! I believe good nursing has saved her. That aunt of hers is certainly a remarkable woman."

Then we had another form of excitement for a few minutes, and the doctor another patient. Irving fainted quite away, and the grim doctor, gone· back into the very depths of his grimness, worked over him in silence for several minutes.

From that time we got on steadily; not rapidly, it is true, but from day to day the gain was apparent.

Before the week had closed, it became evident that the frail girl who had so nearly crossed the dividing line between us and that other world was coming back to the things of this life. She asked for Irving, one morning, before the hour that the doctor allowed him to make his daily call, showed great satisfaction in his visit, and regret over his speedy departure. He came to me with a radiant face.

"It is Lida herself, auntie," he said eagerly; "for weeks she has seemed to me like an angel who was just waiting for wings to float away out of sight; but this morning she is *almost* herself."

After that the improvement was noticeably rapid. Irving visited her oftener and remained longer, and gradually it grew to be the thing for him to spend nearly half of the day by her side. Long talks they had together, broken frequently by admonitions from her watchful nurse to talk no more until she had slept, or eaten, or taken her drops. She was a sweet, quiet patient, ready to obey with a smile; not in the least impatient over the long waiting for strength; totally unlike her former self, although Irving joyously declared that she grew daily more like the Lida whom he had known.

"I am not like her," she said, with a quiet, confident smile, looking full in his eyes; "I'm not a bit like her, Irving, in ever so many things. When I get well you will find me changed."

Whether he understood her or not, I did not know at the time; but auntie Smith understood; there was a satisfied look in her tired old eyes.

N

"It is a genuine thing," she said to me afterwards. "I'm a faithless old body. I didn't seem to believe that the Lord could accept her on her sick-bed, or could tell any better than I, whether she really meant it or not; so he let her get well, to prove to me that he can take care of his own, living or dying. She means it, all through."

It was impossible not to see the change. It so puzzled and troubled her mother that she felt sure Lida was not so well as we thought, and worried herself into many a sick headache over the fear that her darling was going to slip away from her after all.

There was another whom it puzzled, and that was Laura. She did not say much, but I could see her watching, with curious eyes, the settled calm of Lida's face—so unlike the restless flutter of her life heretofore. The sweetness that grew with returning strength, the gentle effort to give as little trouble as possible, the unselfish thoughtfulness for others!

"Mamma," she said to me one day as we came together from Lida's room, "it is almost as if she had died and come to life again."

"She has," I told her, and I quoted the familiar verse about being made alive in Christ.

But Laura shook her head.

"I cannot understand such sudden changes, mamma; and besides, I don't expect them to last. Wait until society gets hold of her again."

And I wondered when my poor Laura would understand.

CHAPTER XVI

"AUNTIE ALWAYS SEES THINGS."

IF you like pretty home scenes, a glance into one of the upper rooms of Mr. Jonas Smith's house that winter evening would have given you pleasure. It was Lida's own pet room; a sort of sitting-room for mother and daughter, and any specially favoured guest, but called by courtesy Lida's. She was the central figure in it on the evening in question. Her plush-covered couch was drawn up before the grate, and herself in delicate blue wrapper, with soft laces at throat and wrists, looked, in the play of the firelight, like some fair bud picked from the greenhouse to blossom in mid-winter. Lida was certainly very pretty; prettier in her simple wrapper and quiet face than she had ever been before. Irving occupied a chair placed in just the right position for watching the varying expressions of her face. Her mother, but a few degrees farther removed from invalidism, luxuriated in the large, old-fashioned easy-chair, a footstool at her feet, her salts, and her fan, and other graceful appliances of convalescence on a little table at her side. Laura was in trim evening costume, her careful toilet telling as plainly as any other little thing that the cloud of care and anxiety had lifted, and there was time to arrange her hair in crimps once more, and wear something besides the plainest of dark dresses and linen collars. She was toying also with bright-coloured wools, amid which the lights and shadows from the fire played hide-and-seek in fantastic manner.

Perhaps, after all, the central figure of our family group was the great rocking-chair, in which rested the trim form and strong, plain face of Mrs. Solomon Smith. Her knitting lay idly on her lap, for Mrs. Smith was tired. She had been out all the afternoon, intent on her own plans, asking no escort through the great city from anyone. Indeed, there seemed to be no one to escort her. She did not deem it wise to have both of us away from the frail invalid. Laura still occupied her position as self-appointed hostess, and had innumerable callers to entertain, and Irving had returned to his post, and was labouring hard to atone for lost time, as well as in token of gratitude for unparalleled past kindnesses. There had been talk of sending for Erskine to accompany Mrs. Smith on her tour of observation, but she had scorned the idea.

"I shouldn't know what to do with a boy at my heels," she said earnestly. "My boys were all girls, you know, and I never was used to anybody but Solomon. You needn't be afraid of my getting lost. I don't believe I could get lost if I should try. I always bring up all right."

She carried her point, and went off in triumph on the street-car, her only companion the greenish umbrella, which did duty as a cane.

She had been gone for hours, and Laura was in a flutter to hear some of her experiences.

"Auntie always sees things," she said to Lida.

" She goes everywhere with her eyes open wide, and if you have been the same route a hundred times, it makes no difference ; she sees a hundred things that you never thought of."

Two doors opened from the room in which we were sitting. One was Lida's own, adorned with all the hundred little prettinesses which a girl of taste and means likes to gather around her. The door was ajar, and revealed glimpses of blue-and-white carpeting, and furniture done in blue-and-white panels, blue silk and white lace curtains at the windows—a very bower of beauty. The other door opened into the guest-chamber, which was a counterpart of Laura's and my beautiful room, across the hall, save that it was finished in even more excellent shades and tints, so Laura thought; and this room was now the private property of Mrs. Solomon Smith.

On the very first night that she had consented to leave her charge in experienced hands and take an entire night's rest, Mrs. Jonas Smith had called Laura, and said :

" My dear, will you see that aunt's room is in perfect order ? Have the heat turned on, and the gas lighted, and everything. I leave it to you to see that she is entirely comfortable. You know which her room is ? The one that opens to the left out of Lida's sitting-room. I have had her trunk brought there. She will naturally like to be near to Lida, and Lida will like to have her; so I took the liberty of changing her room."

It was a liberty which Laura certainly was very willing to pardon; and this was all that had been

said about auntie Smith's room.   I do not know that
Mrs. Jonas Smith understands to this day that we
knew any thing about the fireless attic-chamber.

We had arrived at the time when the whole house
delighted to do honour to the country relative.   It
was tardy hospitality, but we took the hint from the
dear old lady's own large heart, and never mentioned
the attic-chamber again.   The only comment that
Mrs. Solomon made, when Laura escorted her to her
new room, was to gaze about her with astonished
eyes, and say:

"Deary me!   I wouldn't mind having Solomon
see this room."

Laura said there was a little sigh at the close of
the sentence.   I doubt whether any of us realised
what a trial it was to the loyal old heart to lie down
in the midst of all this grandeur and think of Solomon in his loneliness.

"Come, auntie," Laura said after a little impatient
waiting for the clicking needles to commence.   (Laura
knew that when Mrs. Smith knitted, her tongue was
apt to keep time with her fingers.)   "Aren't you
rested enough to tell us about your afternoon ?   Lida
wants to hear of your adventures."

Then Lida's voice: "Oh, aunt Maria, I've been
waiting these two hours to hear all about it.   It is
so long since I have been on the street, you know."

"Bless your heart!" said Mrs. Solomon, "nothing
happened to me that would be worth your listening
to, I dare say.   I went and I came, and I got along
all right; though I must say there was more people
going the same way—and the opposite way, too, for
that matter—than was at all convenient.   I couldn't

help wishing that they had all stayed at home just
for one afternoon, and given me a chance. Still,
I'm back, and no bones broke; which, considering
what I've been through, is something wonderful."

"You ought to have waited until Saturday, and
then I could have taken care of you." This from
Irving, spoken in tones of genuine anxiety. He had
adopted the country aunt, with all his heart and
soul.

"Oh no," she said briskly, taking up her knitting;
"I got along first-rate; I didn't need a bit more
care than I had. Folks was real kind, considering
what a hurry they was in. I never see the beat of
city people for hurrying! And the women are as
bad as the men, I do say! One might have thought
that every mortal woman I met to-day had left a
baby at home tied in the high chair, and a mince-
pie burning up in the oven, by the way they crowded
and pushed and elbowed themselves along to get
into places first. I thought when I got into the
street-car there would be less of a crowd; but, dear
me! that was worse than anywhere else. Why,
there wa'n't even standing room left in one car, and
yet the people kept pouring in, and the conductor
would call out, 'Pass up to the front there, please!'
when we was standing as close as pickles in a jar.
I can't make out where all the folks was going to.
I asked a girl if there was any great meeting or any
thing special going on, but she was deaf, I guess;
she just tossed up her head, and made no answer."

I believe that at that moment Mrs. Jonas Smith
rejoiced in the invalidism that had kept her from
attending her sister-in-law. She was a wonderful

nurse, and they owed her an everlasting debt of
gratitude but if I am not greatly mistaken, the
stylish matron did not wish to pay it by accompanying her down town.

"Did you have to stand in the street-car, auntie?"
Laura asked.

"For a spell, I did, child, most of us had to.
There was two or three ladies on each side, who had
fixed themselves up in such a way that they couldn't
even get close to each other without danger of
crushing something, so they just spread themselves
out and took up pretty near all the room there was;
and the gentlemen that was with them took the
rest. I felt sorry for their manners, for I was the
only old one among 'em· and while I didn't grudge
them the seats, it looked kind of mean in them to
sit still and see me stand. I suppose I might have
pushed in, but I thought I wouldn't. I had my
revenge, though: the people kept crowding in, and
claiming the seats until they was crushed up about
as close as they could stand it. I stood there, a-
bobbing around; first I would land on one side,
right in the lap of one of the fine ladies, and I
wouldn't no more than ask her to excuse me, and
get my bunnit straightened out a little, then there
would come a dreadful jolt and I would bob over to
the other side; I stepped right on a fine young
gentleman's toe once. I felt most dreadful sorry for
him. I know it must have hurt, for he had a little
mincing boot on, too short and too narrow at the
toes; they hurt anyhow, I know they did, and
when my foot came down hard on them, it must
have been awful!

"I didn't blame him for looking savage at me, and not saying a word when I asked his pardon.

"At last a pretty child got in; she wasn't more than seventeen or eighteen, and she looked a little like you, Elizabeth, I noticed her particular on that account; she had more roses in her cheeks, to be sure, than you have just now; looked about as you will next summer when you and Irving come out to the Hollow, and drink new milk and hunt for fresh eggs."

Then there came roses into Lida's cheeks, and she laughed a happy little laugh. As for Irving, he both smiled and shuddered; he had so recently slipped from under the awful shadow that he still rejoiced with trembling.

"Well, she settled herself, with a good deal of pains, into the speck of a place which they made for her; she had a good many ruffles and puckers to look after, and her great fur sack was quite a spell getting tucked into place, but by-and-by she got fixed, and had time to look about her. Just then the car gave one of them horrid jolts that feel as though they had driven over one end of a blacksmith's shop, and broke the irons all to smash, and I like to have tumbled down quite; I most couldn't get my breath, it took me so by surprise; and them straps that they hang on to, was so high above me that I couldn't but just get hold of the tip end. 'For the land's sake!' says I, 'I wish somebody would stop this thing for me, and let me git out. I shall be all black and blue!' Well, my pretty little lady hopped up in a twinkling, and her eyes blazed about as yours do sometimes, Laura, and says she, 'Madam, take my seat, please; I do not mind standing in the least; and I am younger than you.' Of course I told her no, and I said I couldn't take her seat away, and all that, but she just pushed me with them gentle little hands of hers. I wa'n't hard to push; you see, the thing joggled so that I couldn't stand stiddy, and I would push one way about as easy as the other; before I knew it another bounce landed me right in the seat.

"Well, if you'll believe it, there was no less than three of them gentlemen sprang to their feet, and began a-coaxing of her to take their seat. They knew her, too. They called her Miss something or other, and they was very much in earnest; but that little thing straightened herself up, and stood as still in that tipsy car as if she had been on solid ground, and got hold of the strap somehow, I don't know how—I'm sure she was a little thing, but the strap seemed to kind of reach down for her to take hold of, and says she:

"'No, I thank you, gentlemen. I'm quite able to stand; much better able than the old lady was.'

"Then they glowered at me as if I was to blame; but I don't see how I could help their setting there and not thinking of offering me a seat any more than if they had been posts. I never see gentlemen more beat than they was. One of them took it so hard that he wouldn't set down again at all; so I had plenty of room. It was the one with the tight boots, too, and I wanted to ask him how his foot felt now, but I thought I better not."

Our pretty little Lida laughed so heartily over this story that it set her to coughing, and Mrs.

Solomon laid down her knitting in haste, and returned to her duties as nurse.

"I'd better keep my old tongue still," she said, in a tone of self-reproach, when quiet had been restored. "Laura, there, always sets me going with her questions, and I forgit where I am. Solomon is such a master-hand to listen, that he has about spoiled me. I talk right on like a mill-stream, once I start."

Then did Lida protest with all her little strength against the still tongue. She wanted to hear every bit about the afternoon. It was such fun, and if aunt Maria would go on, she would promise not to laugh any more, and not cough another speck.

"Why, there's nothing in life to go on about, child," said Mrs. Solomon, leaning forward to see to narrow her grey stocking. "I didn't have no adventures to speak of. I saw a great many wonderful sights, to be sure; but I suppose you've seen them a hundred times. I wasted a good deal of time trying to make up my mind to cross the streets. The way them women did rush along right into the horses' jaws, scared me 'most out of my senses. I couldn't have done it, if I hadn't got across till this time. Solomon is always so careful in driving across a street—looking right and left first, to see that there is no child nor woman crossing. I thought about it while I stood there. Thinks I to myself, 'It's a good thing Solomon ain't here with old Nan. He wouldn't git across the streets at all, for there's a woman and a child all the time; forty of 'em, for that matter.' I'm beat yet to know where they could all be going to. I got to the very thickest of it at one place. I knew half-an-hour before that I must get across somehow, soon; but I kept walking along and thinking that here wasn't a good place; and the next place was worse, and every step I took the thing got thicker, and so I turned around and went back a little, and it was thicker there than it was anywhere else; and says I at last: 'Well, now, Maria, what's the use? You've got to get across; take your life in your hand and go. You'll be took care of, if it's your duty to cross; and if it isn't, you hadn't ought to be took care of.' So I started.

"I hadn't taken two steps when I was sorry. I tried to jump back, but I found it looked worse behind me than it did ahead. There was a horse with his mouth open right at my bonnet; ready to swallow it, without paying any attention to the head in it, and exactly before me was a couple of them, pawing the ground, and tossing their heads, and just aching to step on me. I could see it in their eyes. 'For the land's sake,' says I, 'what'll I do? Just then there stepped up one of them blue-coated gentlemen with gilt buttons; a fine-looking man he was, and tall enough for me not to feel afraid of anything, you'd think, and says he, 'Walk right across, madam; I'll see you safely over.'

"Well, I made another dash, and sure enough he came alongside of me. But dear me! he couldn't be both sides at once, and that road seemed to stretch itself out like a piece of india-rubber; seems to me it is a mile across; I was most awful scared. I tried to dodge back again, but it wa'n't no use; by that time the opening through which I come had closed up, so there wasn't a sign of it to be seen.

" At that minute another blue-coated, gilt-buttoned man, taller and straighter if anything, and with a bigger stick than the first, came to the other side of me, and marched along holding up his club to them horses, and they just stepped back respectful, as if they knew they had found their master now, and wouldn't be allowed to bite any heads off; and I walked along right through the jam as nice as you please. I don't know how it was done. There wasn't any place to cross; just a jam of men, and women, and waggons, and horses, and more a-coming as far as you could see from both ways. But I got across.

"'It's a broad road, sure enough,' I said to the policeman, 'and they all look as though they was hurrying to destruction; I hope the feet of every one of them are really and truly in the narrow way, and that they'll all get safe home at last.' I couldn't help saying it, you see. It seemed such a kind of solemn picture of our lives, all rushing and pushing along, not taking time to stop and think whether they are going the right way or not.

"'How many of them will get home, do you suppose?' I asked the policeman, and he answered me quick and pleasantly:

"'Oh, they'll come out right. We have just such a crush as this every day, and rarely an accident.'

"'Yes,' says I, 'but I was wondering about the other home. How many of them will get home to heaven?'

" Then he looked at me for a minute, and says he;

"'That's a hard question, ma'am.   I can't tell.'

"'I hope you'll be there,' says I.

"But all he said to that was, 'Thank you!' spoken real gentle, and then he went to help some other scared body across."

CHAPTER XVII.

"IT makes a great difference if you see things with your own eyes," said Mrs. Smith, letting her knitting fall idly in her lap, and giving herself up to contemplation.

Laura looked up curiously; the observation was suggestive to her of all sorts of quaint ideas in her old friend's mind.

"What did you see, auntie?" she asked at last, having waited as long as her impatience would allow.

"Why, I was thinking about that great big store. I had heard about them; Jessie, she tried to make me understand. 'They keep everything, auntie,' she would say: 'everything you can think of.' But I didn't understand. 'Well,' says I, 'so does Job Turner. I was down at the Corners the other day, and I couldn't help noticing what a sight of things he had! Bars of soap enough to wash the whole town, you'd think; and spools of thread, all colours and all numbers, and calicoes, a splendid stock, and alpacas, and all that kind of goods; and then on the other side you could get molasses and herring and eggs, and anything you wanted. He keeps everything I can think of, and a great many things that I

can't think of.'   Jessie she laughed, and said it was
different from that; but she left off trying to make
me understand.   I thought of it to-day, and says I
to myself, no wonder she stopped telling me about
it; she saw that I was such an old goose that I
couldn't understand!   When I got into that great
big store, near where I had such a time crossing the
street, I was so astonished for a minute that I couldn't
think of a thing I came for; I just stood around
there and stared.   A whole village full of Job Turner's
stores might have been packed in there, and you
wouldn't have known it by the space they took up.
Another city, that's what it was, and enough sight
cleaner and quieter than the one I had just left.
' For the land's sake!' I said at last, to a clerk who
came up to me and bowed politely and asked me
what I wanted.   'If you had street-cars in here I
think it would be a great deal nicer than the city
outside.'   He laughed, and didn't seem to object to
my admiring it.   He said he had thought himself
that Sedan chairs would be an improvement.   I
knew all about them—read about their having them
at the Centennial; and I really think they would be
nice in that store; I wonder they don't have them."

"Did you go all around, and see the pretty
things?"   Lida asked, with the eagerness of one to
whom the outside world had been shut away for a
long time.

"Go around!   I guess I did.   I believe I must
have gone into every nook and corner of that store.
I rode on the elevator.   That's a nice invention.
I've read about them, too; and I never could quite
understand how they were; but I had it all explained

to me to-day; and it was a real pleasure to sit
there on a cushioned seat and go slipping softly and
swiftly up in the air. I thought it would be a
skittish kind of feeling, but it ain't a mite. ' I
wonder if flying will be a little bit like this ?' I
said to the young man who went up with me. I
don't know as I was exactly saying it to him,
either; I was kind of thinking out loud; but he
thought I asked him a question.

" ' Ma'am ?' he said, kind of astonished, and then I
thought I ought to explain. 'I was wondering,' I
said, 'if flying through the sky, and the clouds,
would be anything like this. You know we can't
seem to think how we are going to get our bodies
up to heaven. I can think of my soul being there,
but I've been puzzled often, wondering about my old
lumbering body, how it was going to get through the
clouds and all, and get up there; but maybe it will
be just as easy, when we come to see it and feel it,
as this going up is ; holding ourselves still, and being
lifted, without any power of our own. I suppose
that is it, and I'm glad I'm having a ride on an
elevator, because it somehow makes me remember
there are ways of getting me up without any of my
help. It seems that just common ropes and wheels
can do it, so when I get my Father's hand on the
ropes that he means to use, I guess I needn't worry.'
Well, that young man made a queer answer. He
laughed at first, as though it struck him as something
funny ; then his face got dark and sort of fierce-
looking, and he said if he was only sure of his soul
getting through all right, he wouldn't take time to
worry about his miserable body ; it might go to the

O

dogs for all he should care—it wa'n't nothing but a trouble to him anyhow. Then I looked at him close, and I saw that he looked sick and miserable, and had a hollow cough. It was plain enough that his body wasn't going to trouble him long. I spoke real gentle, I felt so sorry for the poor fellow. Says I: 'If I was you, I wouldn't worry a mite about either of 'em. They're just as safe in your Father's hands as that little bit of a bundle is in yours, and worth a hundred times more to him than all the velvets and jewels in this store. He paid a big price for them, and it's more than likely he'll take care of them. The thing for you to decide is, whether you want him to.'

"We had got out of the elevator by that time, and was walking down one of the elegant rooms. He looked about as gloomy as ever, and he gave a real troubled sigh as he said:

"'Oh, well, there's no use worrying; if a fellow is to be saved he will be; and if not, he can't help himself.'

"Says I: 'The first part of that is as true as the last part is as foolish. You might as well say if a fellow is to eat his dinner he will, and if he isn't he can't help himself. Now it is true enough, of course, that if he is to eat his dinner he will eat it; nobody disputes that; but if you fix up a nice dinner for him and he sets down before it, and shuts his mouth tight, and glowers at it, and refuses to swallow a crumb, you would be one of the first to say that he wouldn't get any dinner, and it was his own fault. Your Heavenly Father has spread the table for you, young man, and now it is your business to say whether you will eat the Bread of Life or push it away and go hungry.'

"Well, I hadn't a chance for another word. He sat me down before the thing I had asked to see, and said a word to the clerk to wait on me, and then he bowed to me and smiled, and said in a low voice, 'Thank you,' and away he went, coughing. Poor fellow! I hope he won't insist on going hungry."

The tears had gathered in Lida's eyes, but her face was smiling.

"Aunt Maria," she said, "how did you learn to be different from other people about these things?"

"Different, child! Why, how? I didn't have a good many of the advantages of other people when I was young; I suppose that makes a great difference."

"Oh, but I mean different in your talk about heaven, and—well, about religion. It seems so easy to you ; nearly all other people whom I have ever heard talk of these things, seemed to me to drag them in, as though they thought they ought to say them, but they didn't quite know how, and dreaded it awfully."

"Well," said Mrs. Solomon, thoughtfully seaming her stocking, "I don't know, child ; I've heard folks talk that way myself; I never could understand it ; I've puzzled over it a good deal, because I found them very folks could be glib enough about other things. Sometimes I've thought that the Bible explained it when it said, 'Out of the abundance of the heart the mouth speaketh.' At least I find, when I've been thinking about a thing until I'm all

full of it, I kind o' want to speak to somebody.
But then I'm a talkative old body, always was;
Solomon is to blame for some of that: he thinks a
good deal more than he talks, and he is amazing
fond of hearing me talk."

Over this last explanation we all laughed; albeit
I think not one of her audience but would have
been willing to testify that Solomon showed excellent sense.

Mrs. Smith's thoughts had already gone back to
the scenes at the store.

"I met one chap," she said, " who wa'n't a bit like
my nice young man that went up the elevator with
me. He was one of your giggly kind; now a giggly
girl is bad enough but a boy who laughs at nothing
all the time is about as small a specimen as you can
find, I think. It is just wonderful to me to think
how the Lord has patience with them all. It would
be so easy for him just to stoop down and wipe
them out! But then there would be the soul!
Dear me! What a pity we can't always remember
that! Now I come to think of it, I've been going
on in my mind about that silly little chap as though
he hadn't any soul; and it does seem as though his
must have been a small one. I wanted to look at
some lace; I kind of wanted a little bit of the real
stuff. When I was a young girl I knew a woman who
had worked in lace factories; she understood all
about the different kinds, and she could do it beautifully; all the fine ladies were after her to mend their
laces. I always did like lace, and I asked her a
thousand and one questions, and got to be pretty
wise about it· I could tell the real from the imita-

tion, away across a church, and can yet. Well, my
chap undertook to have some fun over me. He saw
I was old-fashioned, of course, and kind of queer-
looking by the side of all the fine ladies; I didn't
blame him for that. I got a glimpse of myself in
one of them big glasses, and either I, or the rest of
the women, must have looked funny to him, for we
wasn't a mite alike. But then he needn't have supposed that because I didn't have on a pleated dress
and a hundred yards of lace puckered around it,
that I didn't know lace when I saw it.

"'Oh yes, grandma,' says he. 'I've got just the
lace you want; a very choice pattern. Is it for
yourself, grandma?'

"I believe it made me feel rather cross to have
him call me grandma; I ought to have been glad,
instead, that he was no grandson of mine. I
answered him kind of short: 'It is for myself until
I give it to somebody else,' I said.

"'Just so,' he said—and he was ahead of me in
good-nature. 'Well, now, grandma, here's the very
thing; cheap as dirt, and an elegant width.' And
he showed me a lot of coarse cotton lace!

"'I told you I wanted the real,' says I.

"'Real!' says he, pretending to be astonished, 'why,
I assure you every thread of that is real; as much
so as any we've got in the store.'

"Says I: 'I don't doubt it; real cotton, every
thread of it.' Well, he bothered me in that kind of
way for quite a spell, showing me cotton laces of
half a dozen kinds, and imitation laces, calling this
machine-made stuff 'real valenciennes,' and this
cotton imitation 'real Spanish lace,' until I got out

of all sort of patience with him, and says I, at last,
'Look here, young man, you must get a most
enormous salary in this store; but I shouldn't think
the biggest salary they could offer would pay you
for lying at the rate you have to me.' Says I: 'Do
you know you have told ten lies in the last five
minutes?' I looked right at him, and the fellow
blushed a little, and the clerks standing near who
had been laughing in their sleeves at me all the time,
was just as ready to laugh at him a little—these
everlasting gigglers are never particular on which
side they laugh—and in about a minute I felt kind
of sorry for him; so I spoke a little more softly.
Says I: 'I don't bear you no ill-will, but for your
own sake, if I was you, I would get out of this habit
of telling lies. Now I knew real lace of almost
every kind you can think of long before you was
born, and it is real lace and no other that I'm after,
and if you've got any I'd like to see it.'

"Well, all of a sudden the giggling stopped, the
idle clerks turned to their counters, and my young
man had a very red face, and began to fumble among
the boxes. Pretty soon I understood it. There
come a new voice on the scene: 'Wilkins,' says he,
'what does the lady want?' It wasn't exactly a
stern voice, not cross, you know, but grave, and with
a kind of power in it. If I'd been the clerk I
wouldn't have liked to go contrary to a man with
such a voice as that. He asked the question right
over: 'Wilkins, what does the lady want?' in
exactly the same kind of voice, looking right at the
clerk, whose face by this time was as red as Laura's
worsteds, and then I turned and looked at the man.

" ' For the land's sake !' says I, and then he looked
at me, and his face lighted up as if I had been an
old friend, and he held out his hand and shook mine
just as if I was his aunt this minute, and he was
glad of it. Laura and Mrs. Leonard, I wonder if you
remember my telling you about a Sunday-school
convention where I went and took my niece Jessie,
and a nice young man who sat near us, and told me
things, and seated us often, and was around a good
deal after that ? Well, don't you believe this was
the very young man! Here he was, one of the
partners in that great big store ! After that it was
plain sailing for me. He just took charge of me
himself. I got my lace and everything else I wanted,
and then he took me all around and showed me
everything. I couldn't begin to tell you in a week
all I saw. But, dear me ! I suppose you have been
there dozens of times. One thing, though, I must tell
you about. It is very queer to me that I never heard
of it before ; never read a thing about it. You
understand it, Irving, I s'pose ? Why, them great
brass pipes that go wandering all over that store, as
large around as my arm. I saw them before Mr.
Webster came up ; in fact, I saw them the minute
I went into the store, and I'd been watching and
kind of puzzling over them all the time. I'd see the
clerks put money in a little box and chuck it up
through one of them brass pipes. Away it would
go out of sight, as if a spirit took hold of it the
minute it came near the brass ; and by-and-by it
would come back again, and have just the right
change in it for some one who stood waiting.

" Says I to myself, ' What kind of witch-work is

this? Where does the thing go to, and who gets it, and what does it all, anyway?' Well, when Mr. Webster began to show me around, I asked him the first thing, 'What are all them brass pipes for, and what makes them little boxes they put in fly away and come back again?'

"'Ah,' says he, 'let me take you to the fountain-head and show you about it.' So we went upstairs, away up to the centre of the building, and there, in a little kind of a round office, sat a dozen clerks, or more, and those great pipes that wandered over that building and struck off in every direction, came all together up here, and those little boxes with money and accounts in were continually shooting out in front of these clerks, and they would take them about as quick as lightning, and look at the account and make the change and shoot them back. I never see anything like that in all my life! I just stood still and thought; it made me feel kind of queer. I couldn't say a word. 'What it is?' Mr. Webster asked me, after he had waited a spell, and I suppose he thought I ought to speak.

"'Why,' says I, 'it comes over me all of a sudden, and almost takes my breath away. It makes me think of answering prayer. They are sending up their prayers from all over the store down there, and they come up to this centre and get attended to at once, and the answer goes back in all them different directions.' Well, he understands things— he is one of them men that flashes at what you mean, even if you're as awkward as a post in telling it, and says he, 'I see. That is a fact. But then it takes a dozen clerks to attend to these pipes up here. The figure isn't quite perfect, is it ?'

"'*Only* a dozen !' says I, 'for all them pipes that travel all over this big store ; and these are only young, foolish girls to do it ; and yet we feel sometimes as though the Lord couldn't possibly attend to all our prayers at once !' Then he laughed again, and says he, ' I see.'"

" That must be Earle Webster."

It was Mr. Jonas Smith who made this interrogatory remark ; he had come in during the talk, and was listening with as much eagerness as any of us. Yes, his sister-in-law explained, it was Earle Webster.

" He had a good many questions to ask me," she continued ; " how long I had been here, and where I was stopping, and when I told him I come on to attend my niece's wedding, he looked so kind of surprised, or queer, or something, that I said—and I don't know what made me—'It isn't Jessie ; it's another niece.' Then he laughed outright, and said he knew it wasn't Jessie ; and then he said he had heard from her lately, and she said I was here, and he had been trying to get hold of my address. And, well, he kind of got himself mixed up so, that at last, to get out straight, he had to tell me that I must get ready to go to Jessie's wedding in the spring. And there the sly little puss is going to marry *him ;* and she never once hinted to me who it was ! "

" Going to marry Earle Webster ! " There was no mistaking the astonishment in Mr. Jonas Smith's voice. "Well, Maria, you are to be congratulated, I declare; he is one of the finest young men in the city; one of the first in every way."

"Yes," said Mrs. Solomon, in quiet satisfaction; "I know he is as good as gold. I told him about that poor young fellow with the cough, and he was interested at once; he had me walk down the store and point him out, and said he would have a talk with him; he is a new clerk, it seems.

"One of the giggling clerks stood near where he had seated me while he went to attend to some business, and says he, 'I guess our grandmother has come, or our old aunt or somebody. Do you see how we are being escorted through the store and shown the lions?' Then the other said something I was glad to hear. 'Pshaw!' says he. 'It may be his washerwoman! Webster is the queerest rich man there is on the face of the earth.'

"Well, I thought I would help them along, and I turned around with that. Says I, 'Young man, you are right; I *am* a relation; I'm more than his aunt, or his grandmother; we both belong to the royal family, and are brother and sister to the King.'" ·

CHAPTER XVIII

MEDITATIONS THAT MEANT SOMETHING.

In due course of time we were in a sort of quiet bustle
in the Smith household. Not by any means such a
state of excitement as there was before sickness
came into our midst, yet we were getting ready for
the wedding.

Lida was still in becoming wrappers, and spent
most of her time on the couch, or in the easiest
chair. And yet we were all decided that the
marriage-ceremony should take place. There were
several good reasons for this: In the first place,
Irving had received intimation that business reasons
would soon take him South for several weeks ; and
in family conclave we had each declared that nothing could be better for Lida than to accompany
him. Besides, Mrs. Solomon was growing restive ;
she had never been so long away from Solomon since
their fortunes were joined ; and, bravely as she had
borne it, it was plain to us all that now she was
homesick.

As for the little bride, she was sure of one thing,
that "Aunt Maria" must be present at her wedding.
So, as I said, the bustle of preparation was upon us.
All the details were as unlike as possible those others,
when she had been almost a wife. The ceremony
was to take place in the little sitting-room upstairs,

and the bride was to be dressed in a white cashmere wrapper, instead of the white silk, with lace over-dress, that lay in the drawer. The physician had given it as his decided opinion that there should be an interval of several weeks between the marriage and the departure from home, in order to allow our invalid time to recover from the first excitement, before the fatigues of travel should be upon her; and on being consulted in regard to her dress, had given this brief and peremptory direction:

" Put her into the garment in which she can lie down the quickest, and be the most comfortable after the minister has done his part. By no means excite and exhaust her with a fussy toilet."

We prepared to obey his instructions literally. The only guests to be admitted were Erskine and Earle Webster. The latter had been a frequent caller since the day he had discovered Mrs. Solomon Smith in the store. Instead of all the pretty bridesmaids, who had so distractedly flown away when trouble came, Laura was to do duty, with Erskine as a helper. Therefore the circle of preparations was, of course, wonderfully narrowed; yet we contrived to get up a good degree of excitement. How is any one to avoid a certain amount of excitement in connection with that old story, which is yet always so new ?

It was on a bright winter afternoon, when every detail was complete, and we had only to wait with what quietness we could for twelve o'clock of the next morning, that Mrs. Solomon summoned me as her attendant on an excursion.

" Earle Webster wanted to go with me, and kind

of thought I better have him along to tend to things," she explained; "but I couldn't bring my mind to it; men is dreadful convenient sometimes, and then again they are really in the way; kind of flustrate you, you know, and make you believe that you want green, when you was sure half an hour beforehand, and will be sure for ever afterwards, that you didn't want green at all, but red. I always thought there was just about one man in life that I could stand when I went to buy anything, and that was Solomon. It's been a good thing for me that I had him and nobody else. You see, we began by understanding each other. 'Solomon,' I say to him, 'don't you think that is the thing to do?' and Solomon he looks it all over, and maybe he says, 'Well, no, Maria, I can't say I see it in that light at all; I think so-and-so would be enough sight the best.' Well, if it's about the farm, or the stock, or anything that he has a better right to know about than me, I think it over, and like enough I see at once that I was an old dunce; and I don't mind saying so, out and out. But then again, just as likely as not, I think just exactly what I did before, and then I say, 'Go ahead, Solomon, I don't agree with you a mite; but that's for you to settle.' But mind you, if it is about the house, or the garden, or the hens, or my clothes, or the part of Solomon's clothes that I manage, he is just as quick as I, and maybe a trifle quicker, to tell me to go ahead. 'So that I don't have to wear the thing,' he will say to me, with one of them grave smiles of his, if it happens to be a dress or a bunnit that we are discussing, 'why, it's all right.' And Solomon ain't one of them mean kind of folks that is always

puckering up their mouths and saying, 'I told you
so.' I don't believe he would say that, whatever I
did. And that's the way we manage. To my notion,
it is the only way, for two folks, who both have
brains, to be of one mind."

"Take notes, Laura," I said, laughing; for Laura
was looking at her with so intent a face that I was
curious to know how the quaint old lady's notions
impressed her. She flushed deeply and turned away,
making no answer. Among other matters that were
going on, during this unexpectedly long visit to the
city, my daughter Laura was being educated to certain views and positions that I felt sure would tell
in marked ways for her future.

When we were fairly in the street, Mrs. Smith
trotted along with brisk step and voluble tongue.

"I'm going after Elizabeth's wedding present," she
said, "and I don't believe you can guess what it is to
be."

I could not, indeed; and as it had been the subject
of Laura's curious surmisings, of course I was interested. I fancied that it would be something use-
ful, and not very costly, for a wise economy governed
all her personal expenses, and I did not believe she
would feel justified in setting the young couple a
lavish example; still she was evidently impressed
with the importance of her intended purchase.

"I've laid awake nights thinking about it," she
admitted, a bright flush of excitement on her dear
old face. "At first I couldn't see my way clear at
all, and it bothered me that I couldn't; and then,
when light began to dawn, as to how it could be
managed, why, I begun to bother my brains for fear

I had been too set in my way; and one time I give it all up, but it wouldn't *stay* give up. I'd no sooner get it fixed and settle down on something else, when it would come trotting back to me as though it wasn't fixed at all. Right in the middle of the night, too, it would come and stand by my bed, and wake me up all of a sudden, out of a sound sleep, and say, 'Here I am now, and I insist on being thought about; you just wake up, old woman, and tend to me.' I declare, I've been almost beat out with it some nights."

This was so funny a way of putting the story of my own trials by sleeplessness and perplexing thought, that I'm afraid my laugh was more merry than sympathetic; but I questioned with renewed interest as to what the troublesome object was.

"I'll just tell you," said Mrs. Smith, lowering her voice, as one about to make a confidential communication; "it's a horse and waggon. Now, *do* you think I'm an old goose?"

Amazement almost took from me the power of answering.

"Yes," she said, nodding her head and growing more satisfied evidently, with her decision every moment. "I've been all over it fifty times; you can't think of an objection that I haven't urged with all my might, just to see what the other side could say.

"I always do argue a thing out. Solomon ain't no hand to argue out loud; he just sets down a few square sentences, and lets it go; but I don't, and I've learned to argue to myself. Specially if it is a thing that I want to do pretty bad, I make the other side

of me take hold well, and I have a tough time before
I get the consent of myself to do it.

"Expense! Dear me, yes. I've considered over
every peck of oats that horse of theirs will ever eat;
I've figered them up a hundred times if I have once,
and a hundred ways, for the matter of that—they
never seemed willing to come out twice alike—and
I suppose I've wrote a quire of paper about it to
Solomon.

"But you see it is just like this: Anybody can
see that that child is going to need a good deal of
petting and taking care of for some time to come.
She needs to get out in the fresh air every day, and
stay out a good while. Now, how is she going to do
it in this tucked-up city, where everything is a whirl
and a jam, and there's such an awful noise that you
don't hardly know what your name is half the time?

"There's nice, pleasant places, parks, and quiet
roads, and little patches that look almost like the
country, if you can only get to them; but as for
racketing along in the street-cars to 'em, I'd about as
soon she would stay at home. What she needs is a
horse and waggon. And there's the getting to church.
I'd like to have the child begin right, and I think
she's disposed to; but how is she, in her weak state,
going to get to the church where she'll think she
ought to go, unless she rides on them commandment-
breaking cars? To be sure, there is the church near
by, but you can't expect full-grown wings on a young
bird. I shouldn't expect her to see her duty clear
to that, with nobody to help her.

"The more I thought about it, the more it seemed
to me that she ought to have a horse and waggon of

her own. Well, then I talked with Jonas, and he was just as taken with the notion as he could be; said he'd have got her one long ago if he could have afforded the money to buy it. Things don't look about the house as though he couldn't afford whatever he pleased, do they?

" But then appearances is deceitful; he ain't forehanded at all. He talked real confidential with me about the note, and the interest not being paid up, and all. He seemed to feel real bad, and I think he did. He has some queer notions; seems to think the living in style, and all that, is necessary to his business. Maybe it is; I'm only an old woman, but I don't believe it all the same, and I advised him to pay up his debts and let the looks go. I don't think he paid much attention to me; he was thinking about the horse and waggon.

" Well, he said he had a friend who had a stable on his place, and all conveniences for keeping a horse, and didn't keep any, and had a boy who could be hired for a trifle to take care of the horse, and harness it when it was wanted; and he wouldn't be charged barn-rent, because he had done the man a kindness now and then in a business way, and he would be glad to pay for it this way. It sounds queer to hear folks talk about paying for kindnesses, don't it? But Jonas means all right, and the long and short of it is, my mind is made up.

" Erskine and Earle Webster have both been on the look-out for me about a horse, and Erskine told me last night that he thought he had just the thing; so now I'm after the waggon this very afternoon. I didn't mean to put it off so long, but them two was

P

hard to suit with a horse, and I knew a waggon could be bought in a hurry."

"But are you going to get both horse and waggon?" I said, appalled before such lavish gifts, and wondering much whether she had any idea of the prices of these articles.

"No," she answered briskly. "The waggon is to be my present, but I've just been managing the business of getting a horse. That's Solomon's present. He sets a good deal of store by Elizabeth; she's his only brother's child, you know.

"Solomon is a master hand to come to conclusions; you know I told you what great long letters I wrote to him, going over all the arguments, and being about as much on one side as t'other? Well, this is every blessed word he wrote to me about it. He never writes long letters; Solomon thinks things, but he says he ain't good at getting them on to paper; says he: 'Maria, 'pears to me you're a little mixed. If Elizabeth needs a horse for her health, and if it will help keep her out of the way of temptation to doing wrong, and if Jonas and the young man are willing to have the expense of taking care of it, I should think the hull thing was in a nutshell, and there wa'n't no more use in talking.' And then he went on telling me about the school, and the new books in the library, and the present to the minister, and not another word about a horse or waggon! Did you ever see a straighter road to a conclusion than that?" and her sweet old face beamed with her pride in Solomon. Nevertheless, she proceeded to tell me what a careful and intelligent estimate she had made of the expense of keeping a horse, with stable rent, and attendance, counted out, and of the heavy expense of car-tickets to balance the other, and made it clear, at least to her own mind, that in the end the thing was an economy.

"Borrowing a stable and another man's boy won't always last," she said, with a little sniff of her practical nose. "Kindnesses that are being given as pay ain't of much account, and can't be depended on, but then who knows what may happen? Maybe Elizabeth will get strong, so she won't need a horse, and then they can sell him for a penny; or maybe the young man will prosper, and can afford to build a barn, and take time to look after his own horse; or maybe the horse will die, and so won't need to be looked after. What's the use of going ahead and borrowing trouble about it? I'm going to buy my waggon this very day, and here's one of the places Earle told me to come to."

Whereupon she halted before a six-story building, large enough to contain "waggons" for the million, and boldly pushed her way into the elegant ware-room, lined on every side with carriages, large and small, gold-mounted and plush-lined, as well as some of the plainer sort.

Many misgivings beset me. What sort of a "waggon" did the dear old lady think her pretty city flower would ride in! I recalled the plain, old-fashioned, two-seated spring-waggon in which Mr. and Mrs. Solomon Smith had rode to church ever since I had known them. Long ago all the paint had been washed from it, the wheels were large and clumsy, the box was high, and the whole appearance ungainly, yet I knew that Mrs. Smith was attached

to it, and considered it comfortable and quite good
enough.   Did some such idea present itself to her as
a part of Lida's outfit?   Why had she not allowed
Erskine or Earle Webster, or even Laura to accompany
her, that they might have tempered her enthusiasm
with their educated judgment?   For myself, I felt
powerless in her hands, being always aware that my
influence over her was as nothing compared with
Laura's.

There was one relieving thought, however, to my
anxieties.   The character of the establishment in
which we were rendered it all but impossible that
we should find other than the most unexceptionable
outfits.   It would probably end in utter dismay on
the benevolent old lady's part; I was sure she had
no relative ideas of the prices of the "waggons" of
which she so gaily talked.   There were so many,
and such beauties, on exhibition, that while we
waited for a disengaged pilot, we wandered different
ways, gazing with admiring eyes.

Presently one who proved to be a proprietor, came
first to me, and looking around for Mrs. Solomon,
she was nowhere to be seen; so explaining that I
was merely accompanying another, I still ventured
to inquire the price of the little buggy before which
I stood, one of the plainest in the great room, and
one which I even doubted whether Irving and Lida
would feel that they could climb into.   Yet I groaned
inwardly over the announcement that "that was a
second-hand affair, and could be sold for two hundred
dollars."

Two hundred dollars!   I was almost certain that
Mrs. Solomon expected to get the desire of her heart

for about fifty! And surely that would be a liberal
wedding gift from her, if she could but content herself with a lace collar, or a diamond ring, or a set of
handkerchiefs, as others did.

While we waited she came toward me, walking
rapidly, her face unusually flushed. "Well, I
declare!" she said, dropping into a vacant chair, and
ignoring the gentleman.

"I've had such a turn, I'm just about beat. Did
you notice that horse and waggon standing down by
that south door?"

I hadn't noticed it.

"Well, now before we go, I want you just to walk
down that way and look at him. Such a fiery fellow
I haven't seen since Solomon had a colt twenty years
ago that came near breaking our necks. There he
stands, right in the room. 'For pity's sake,' says I
to myself, 'if that ain't the *queerest* thing to let a
horse come into a room like this! What in the
world do they do that for?' There seemed to be a
kind of a road there, though, and I thought it was
the place where the horses were let in to draw out
the waggons; but to stand there without being tied
seemed to me a most dreadful dangerous thing. Oh,
you never see a horse look more as if he would like to
eat everybody up than that one does! I walked off
a little way from him. Thinks I to myself, if he
took a notion to kick—and he looks as if he would
like nothing better—he could reach me with them
heels of his. Well, I turned to look at something else, and when I looked back again, don't
you believe a woman stood as close to that horse
as you are to me, with her back to him at that!

My heart flew right into my mouth; I expected
to see her kicked to death every second. It took
me more than a minute, I do believe, to pluck up
courage to step back and try to warn her quietly like
to move on, so as not to scare that horse. It just
seemed to me that I couldn't take a step; and I don't
believe I should till this time if I hadn't just happened to think, what if worse came to worst, and
there was an accident, how ashamed Solomon would
be of me! Then I went back. And after all that,
don't you believe that horse was made of wood!"

I never heard anyone give a more hearty or
delighted laugh than did the gentleman who was
politely awaiting our wishes.

"So our trade-mark frightened you," he said, stepping towards Mrs. Smith. "That is a compliment to
his naturalness; but he ought to know better than
that, the scamp! However, you are not the only
one who has been cheated. The children invariably
run from him, and occasionally we catch the ladies."

Mrs. Smith had already recovered from the first
effects of her fright, and her eyes had assumed that
thoughtful, far-away expression, which told those
familiar with her that there was some curious associa-
tion of ideas working in her mind.

"Did you ever read *Pilgrim's Progress?*" she asked,
apparently observing the gentleman for the first time,
and addressing him suddenly. "I thought of it the
minute I found out that horse was made of wood.
What a time poor Fearful had over them lions, and
they was nothing but stone! That made me think
of the verse that the slothful man says when he
wants an excuse for not doing his duty. 'There's

a lion in the way,' he cries, you know. I wonder if half our crosses are made of wood? What do you think, sir? If we should step boldly up to them and try to do our best, do you suppose a good many of them would be as harmless as your horse?"

CHAPTER XIX.

LUMPS OF CLAY.

IF the wooden horse in question had suddenly been endowed with life, and kicked with real earnestness, I am not sure that the face of the gentleman before us could have expressed greater astonishment. It was evidently a new experience to be faced with a direct question as to *Pilgrim's Progress* and personal crosses.

"I'm afraid I'm not posted," he said, with an embarrassed laugh.

"Oh, but I suppose you are posted as to your own crosses?" with a keen, questioning look out of her grey eyes.

"Still, I suppose people's ideas of crosses might differ. For instance, what is yours?"

"Well," she said, meditatively, "my crosses are apt to be when I want to do something that the Lord thinks I better not. I'm dreadful strong-willed naturally, and he has to pull me up pretty strict sometimes to keep me from running all awry."

The gentleman laughed; yet his face flushed, and it was evident that he both understood and appropriated the definition of crosses. Then we gave ourselves to the business of the hour. We were still standing before the very plain second-hand buggy; but when Mrs. Smith signified her readiness to look at "waggons," she turned away from that one without a second glance.

"That doesn't look the least bit like it," she remarked confidently. "There's no use in wasting time on it."

The gentleman laughed pleasantly; he seemed to have discovered that he had an original character to deal with, who was worth studying. He remarked that if he only had a photograph of the sort of "waggon" she wanted, he presumed he could suit her in a much shorter time; but she paid no other attention to this broad hint that she should particularise, than to remark that she would pick it out pretty soon, then he could see the real thing, which was always better than a picture. She must have spent those wakeful hours of night to good purpose, for she marched down that long, long room, gazing with keen eyes on either side of her, rejecting some with a glance as too "large," others as "fussy," and others still as "not looking a bit like" the one she meant. She asked the price of none of them. Suddenly she came to a full stop before a little gem of a phaeton. What a beauty it was! Low, light, delicately finished, upholstered in a lovely soft grey, which had that singular pinky tint that reminds one of a summer sunset. Nothing in all that establishment was better suited to Lida's refined taste than the phaeton. Very few, I was sure, of the simpler ones represented more money. Yet it was not showy, only tasteful. Of course I was aware that exceedingly well-made, tasteful things are more expensive, the more quiet they are; but did Mrs. Smith know it?

The proprietor was evidently astonished at her

choice. He waited before her in respectful silence, while the keen-eyed old lady walked around it, felt of the cushions, examined the lining, asked sharp questions about the springs and the axles, and in various other ways evinced her knowledge of carriages.

Her questions were answered, but no additional information was vouchsafed; she was evidently being studied.

"What is the very best you could do for me if I was to count you out the money for this in clean new bills?"

The gentleman looked at her, looked through her, apparently, while she steadily returned his gaze with those penetrative grey eyes of hers. Meantime I had, with a sinking heart, discovered a card hanging in an obscure corner at the back, marked six hundred dollars! What would Mrs. Solomon think of that? Meantime she waited for her answer.

"Five hundred dollars," he said at last, forcing out the words with an explosive sound as if they almost hurt him.

I remembered afterwards that the wonder as to whether he had found one of his crosses in leaving off that other hundred, occurred to me. But I had not much time for moralising.

"I'll take it," said Mrs. Smith, in a composed tone, and she dropped into a chair, took out her old-fashioned well-filled pocket-book, and began to look over her papers.

In undoubted and undisguised astonishment the owner of the carriage watched her. I was hardly less astonished.

"I promised you clean bills," she said, glancing up, "but I reckon you'll have to go to the bank for that; I forgot he told me I mustn't carry so much money around the streets. I don't see why, though; people wouldn't be likely to bother an old woman. I've got a paper here that he said would do just as well as money."

It was curious to me to note the change on the face of the man before us. The surprised and interested look faded rapidly; in its place came one of suspicion—an air that said almost as plainly as words could have done : " O, ho ! my pious old lady, that's your dodge, is it ? I'm acquainted with it; but you almost deceived me with your grey eyes." Then she passed him up the cheque. Another lightning-like change of the expressive face; it was a bank cheque, and bore the name and firm of Earle Webster.

"This is as good as the cleanest bills you could bring," he said with great heartiness. And immediately the minor arrangements connected with the sale were entered into.

" Cheques is interesting things," said Mrs. Solomon, with a satisfied air. She still occupied the seat into which she had dropped when she made her decision, and her mind, though alert enough for the business in hand, was still wandering off into other channels of thought. I could see it in her eyes. "I never had much to do with 'em," she continued. "It didn't seem to me that a piece of paper could be as good as the money. A promise to pay, Earle said it was. 'But they don't know me, nor Solomon,' I told him. Says I, 'If they knew Solomon, I could understand how a promise to pay would be all right; for everybody believes Solomon.'"

"I'll fix it,' says he. 'They know me where you are going,' and he got out his bank-book, and wrote this paper. And the first thing you say when you look at it is, 'It's as good as the gold.' Ain't that interesting now? Makes me think right away of my Master. Suppose I get up to the gates of heaven? The angels don't know me, never heard of me, most likely; but I hand them my cheque signed by the Lord Jesus Christ. 'Ha!' says the angel, 'I know him,' and the gates swing open. I tell you what it is, sir, we want to look out for it that we have a right to use his name, don't we?"

The gentleman was visibly embarrassed, and at the same time singularly moved. He drew out his handkerchief suddenly, and coughed, and made vigorous use of it about his face for a moment, and said in an apologetic aside to me: "I had a good old mother once."

"I hope you've made sure of living with her by-and-by."

It was Mrs. Smith who spoke the words, in a quiet, matter-of-fact, indeed I might say, business-like tone. Then she gave herself fully to the business of managing in the best manner about the home-coming of her carriage; looked after her receipt, and attended to all the details in a thoroughly business way. It was evident that the man's respect for her increased every moment.

As for me, I went home a good deal bewildered. Solomon Smith's bank account must be much larger than people in his vicinity had ever imagined.

I hinted something of the feeling to his wife, and she answered me with a satisfied air to the effect that, being content with spring waggons in a place where a spring waggon would do just as well as any, had put them in a way to give a comfortable little carriage now and then to folks who needed. Which was a way of disposing of the entire subject of giving and receiving that it struck me would be more novel than agreeable to many.

What a nice little wedding it was! Not of the common sort at all. Not in the least like the one that Laura and I had come to attend. In fact, I think all the details might have been said to be unique. Nothing of the sadness which usually hovers in the background of marriages where one party is an invalid was apparent.

As a rule in such cases, the shadow of an approaching separation that shall last as long as life, is upon the company. With us, the shadow had been and was lifted. Lida was steadily progressing toward renewed health. Indeed, she had almost no drawbacks from the first. Even the sense of parting from the old ties, the going out from the childhood home, which had been strong on the mother at least before, had lost its sting. They had so nearly parted from her for the grave, that to be making preparations for her to go to the sunny South-land for a few weeks, and to look forward to her speedy return in health, had in it nothing but joy. So we were very joyful at the wedding. An exceedingly subdued joy, however. Each member of the company was on the alert to do and say that which would least fatigue and excite the bride. Truth to

tell, however, she appeared the quietest and calmest
of the group—her face pale, it is true, but wonderfully reposeful, her eyes bright, but with a steady,
rather than a fitful joy.

There had been no rehearsals of the ceremony,
though the position of each participant was as unlike
as possible to the usual one. Lida's voice, when she
pronounced at last the irrevocable "I do," was as
calm and self-controlled as though it was merely an
outward form of what had been done long ago.

It was Irving's face that paled, and his form that
trembled, as the minister spoke these solemn words:
"Until death do you part!" Death had so nearly
parted them! He had hardly yet stepped shiver-
ingly from the brink of the chasm. Still, he
controlled himself, and gave a swift, anxious look
down at the wife whose hand he clasped. Excitement would tell heavily on her strength. She smiled
back a reassuring answer. But his whole mind was
presently absorbed in getting her comfortably settled
on her sofa, and the bright-hued silk afghan thrown
over her. Then, lying there like a princess, with a
delicate pink beginning to flush her cheeks, we came
up one by one and kissed her.

"Bless the child!" said auntie Smith, bustling
about. "She is getting red cheeks now; a little bit
too red. We better slip away and leave her and her
husband to a little quiet."

Then her cheeks flamed. It was the first time she
had heard the new name. The feast was spread in
an adjoining room, the doctor forbidding the invalid
to descend the stairs, and even according a reluctant
consent to her joining us with the coffee and cream.

This, too, was utterly unlike the regulation wedding fare. A substantial mid-day meal, with plenty of wedding-cake and ices, to be sure, but by no means confined to these ephemeral dishes. Lida's doctor had become something more than a professional friend; we had seen so much of him, and he had been so constant and persistent in his efforts, even after his hopes of saving his patient were faint, that every member of the family had come to look on him as a friend. The frail little patient had evidently won a large place in his heart. He watched over her with almost fatherly care, and became peremptory, even savage, toward those who seemed to him to plan anything contrary to her best interests.

"There is just about as much strength there as there is in a cobweb!" he said sharply to Irving. "It is spunk, not strength, that keeps her up. Young man, you must remember that, and look out for her with the greatest care. Spunk will do a good deal, but somebody has to be behind it that has common sense to see that it isn't carried too far."

Whereupon Lida laughed. She had lost all fear of the grave and reticent doctor. Truth to tell, he had laid aside much of his professional reticence, though he was still grave enough.

"The doctor doesn't give me credit for a bit of common sense, Irving," she said gaily, "only spunk."

"You needn't put the 'only' before that word," he said, quickly. "If it had not been for that you would have slipped away from us sure."

Then a sweet gravity, as new as it was fascinating, came into Lida's face as she gently shook her head:

"It was not that which brought me back to life, doctor."

"No," said the doctor, "that's true. It was good nursing. Your aunt here is to have credit, if you succeed in being a credit to us. I've seen a good deal of nursing in my day, but I must say this went a little ahead. I tell you what it is, madam, if you want to stay in the city, I can keep you employed without the slightest trouble. Young man, you have her to thank for your bride to-day."

Irving turned an eager, grateful face towards Mrs. Smith, but she was looking at Lida, and the two exchanged fond smiles that said how well they understood each other, and how far from the truth the doctor was.

"I guess we all did the best we could," the old lady said, fixing earnest eyes on his face. "But the fact is, there was a greater than even you in that sick-room, doctor. The Lord touched her with his hand of power, as surely as he ever touched Simon's mother-in-law that time when Simon had the sense to go to prayer-meeting and bring Jesus home with him, instead of moping at home because his folks was sick."

Everybody laughed, the doctor with the rest, but his sharp eyes had a sarcastic gleam in them as he said:

"That is a very comfortable kind of faith; hold on to it by all means. At the same time, I wouldn't have given a row of pins for Mrs. Irving Leonard's life if you hadn't hung over her for about twenty-four hours without giving yourself time to eat, or sleep, or even think."

"You're mistaken there!" she said triumphantly.

" I thought all the time and I prayed every minute. I don't suppose the Lord had that child out of his thoughts once during that day and night. I didn't give him a chance!"

This sentence seemed to amuse the doctor again. He laughed outright, but added immediately:

" Well, all I can say is, the Lord chose excellent help to carry out his designs."

" Of course he did! Why shouldn't he, when he knows all about the ends as well as the beginnings of things? That's the reason he chose you. Don't you suppose he knew what he was about when he gave you your education, and set you to doctoring the people, and gave you a special talent for studying out what to do? I don't think he ever makes a mistake with his means any more than he did when he was on earth.

" Only, wouldn't it have been a queer thing if the lump of clay that he put on the eyes of that blind man had started up and said: 'Aha, see what I can do! I gave that blind man his sight!' I tell you what it is, the lumps of clay that he uses nowadays to help, have got tongues, and are everlastingly taking the praise to themselves. It's one of the marks of his great patience that he bears it so well. But I don't want to be one of them, doctor. I did the best I could, because I loved the child, and because my feet and hands and brain belong to him anyhow, and I'm bound to do the best I can with his tools wherever he sets me to work ; but as for claiming the honour, why, dear me, I wouldn't dare to do it. It's honour enough for a lifetime to be used. Some- times, doctor, I'm dreadful afraid that you don't know anything about the joy of being used by Him."

It was an aside sentence, intended only for the doctor's ears. Standing near him as I was, I heard it, and saw the sudden flush that mounted to his forehead, and noted the sudden huskiness of his voice as he said: "I wish I did, madam; I wish I did."

"Mamma," said Laura, as we packed one of the Southern-bound trunks together late that evening, "she is certainly very different; before she was so excited and nervous that it was almost impossible to do anything to please her; but she has been just as sweet as a snowdrop all through this trying time. There is a great difference; but oh, dear me! I know it won't last!"

It really seemed as though Laura was waiting with a sort of feverish anxiety for Lida to make a failure of it, in order that she might be justified in remaining as she was. It was evident that Mrs. Smith had the same thought. She turned from the closet where she was folding clothes for the trunk, and looked with those grave eyes of hers full at Laura, who seemed to have forgotten that she was in the room.

"Child," she said, the utmost earnestness in voice and manner, "whether that poor little girl downstairs makes out to live the sort of life you think she ought to or not, don't you think Jesus Christ lived it? Now, there's one thing I want to know: Did he ever say to you, 'Take Lida Smith for your pattern, and if she fails you are justified?'"

CHAPTER XX.

"MRS. SOLOMON SMITH, YOU'VE HELPED ALONG IN THIS NIGHT'S WORK."

OUR next excitement was of a totally different character. It came to us in the night, the third after
the marriage. We had lingered another day, at Lida's
earnest petition, to enjoy a ride in the new carriage,
with the new iron-grey pony, which, though a wicked-
looking little fellow, was said to be a model of
gentleness, sagacity, and speed, and which, during the
two days of our acquaintance, sustained his reputation.

What Mrs. Jonas Smith thought of the munificent
present to her daughter, she seemed unable to put
into words, but whatever attention she could think
of, to lavish on her sister-in-law, was promptly
bestowed.

As for Lida, her old auntie had come to love her
so dearly, that kisses and smiles were payment
enough.

"She is a grand diamond in the rough!" did
Irving say, in a burst of confidence, to Laura and
me. "Laura, I don't wonder that your eyes glowed
at my misunderstanding of her. It is positively an
astonishment that you didn't cut my acquaintance
entirely. But how was I to know that she was
such a splendid woman?"

"True enough," said Laura, speaking with animation, "how should you know? You seemed to have but one way of judging her, and that was by the cut of her cloak and the shape of her hat."

"I don't altogether like Irving, mamma"—this of course after he was gone—"he is so sort of flippant in his manner about everything; he was quite endurable while Lida was sick, but now that his anxiety is over, he seems to have room for nothing but nonsense and flattery. I'll tell you what it is, mamma, if Irving doesn't take care Lida will get away ahead of him; he needs the shadow of a tremendous trouble of some sort, in the background, to keep him in anything like a dignified state of mind."

I hardly knew whether to be annoyed or to laugh over this absurd estimate of a youthful man, by a very youthful woman. Still, there was food for thought in her words.

"If Irving really does need a continuous background of shadows, in order to bring him home at last, be sure his Lord knows it; some people will not answer Christ's call, daughter, unless he makes the path on which they persist in treading full of thorns?"

I spoke with unwonted gravity, for something in her face just then led me to wonder with sudden pain whether my Laura would continue to move along the broad highway until she was driven out of it by thorns. I think she caught my meaning, for she turned away hastily, and said in a tone that was almost petulant:

"I could never be driven into religion, mamma, and I doubt whether Irving could."

Was there defiance in the words ?

The house settled early into quiet that night.

We were to leave on the following day ; not early, as we must of necessity have done, if we made the trip in one day. Mr. Jonas Smith was called by business to a town located on our route, nearly half-way, and would be detained there at a hotel over-night, and the whole family urged that, instead of planning for a four-o'clock train, we should go at noon with the gentleman and remain overnight at the hotel. The decision was left to Mrs. Solomon, and I fancy more for the purpose of spending a quiet hour with her brother-in-law, to say to him a few words as opportunity offered, than for any fear of early rising, she agreed to the hotel plan.

It must have been some time after midnight that we in our room were awakened by peculiar sounds in the hall. I think we had been all more or less inclined to wakefulness, and to listening for unusual sounds, since the midnight alarm when Lida was taken sick ; so I roused without difficulty, and immediately arose to investigate.

" Laura, there is someone groaning downstairs, a man's voice. I think Mr. Smith or Irving must be ill; I'm going down to see, as soon as I can."

" Don't, mamma," said Laura, springing up on the instant ; " let me go," and she began rapid dressing. Meantime the strange sounds, mingled with something very like groans, continued.

Mrs. Smith was, as usual, in advance of us ; her room door opened at this point, and her voice was heard in the hall ; not a loud voice ; Mrs. Smith's tones were emphatic, clear-cut, readily understood, but never loud.

"Who's sick? Is that you, Jonas? What is the matter?"

Then Mr. Smith's voice:

"Don't for Heaven's sake let Sarah hear or Lida. Is the child's door shut? And yet I shall have to call Irving. Oh, God help me!"

Laura and I paused in our hurried toilets and looked at each other with blanched faces. Some dreadful accident must have happened. Harris had been driving gay horses, over which his mother had worried more than once, in the past week. Perhaps he had been brought home all mangled and bleeding, and the father was trying to shield the half-sick wife and frail daughter from the news as long as was possible.

"*We* can help, mamma," said Laura. "He needn't call Irving."

Then we hurried again.

Mrs. Solomon Smith, with one brief, quickly suppressed exclamation, had taken in the situation, whatever it was, and gone quietly downstairs. A moment more, and Laura opened our door and stepped into the hall. Then I heard Mr. Smith's voice again:

"Oh, Maria, for Heaven's sake don't let any of them come! It is awful enough, just with us."

"Go back!" It was Mrs. Solomon's quiet, strong voice of command to Laura, and the child, her face deathly pale, came back to me.

"I don't know," she said, in answer to my questioning look. "I can't see him, only a glimpse; he

seems lifeless. It is Harris; they are carrying him
into the back parlour. He must be dead, and that is
why they need no more help. Auntie Smith had
hold of his feet. Oh, mamma! mamma!" and she
burst into a perfect passion of weeping.

Certainly Mrs. Smith had done well in trying to
shield my child from any more unnerving sights
and sounds, and I blessed those two downstairs for
their thoughtfulness as I bent over Laura. I coaxed
her back to bed presently, half-dressed as she was.
It might be only a faint, I told her, doubtless was.
Mr. Smith was terribly alarmed, of course, yet
remembered the importance of keeping exciting news
from Lida, or his wife; and had probably reasoned
that the safest way was to keep the upper hall
perfectly quiet. I listened, meantime, for sounds
below, which should indicate that the doctor was
being summoned, or those other terrible helpers, if
indeed the young man should be past a physician's
care. But the utmost silence prevailed. I could
almost have imagined the whole thing a dream, but
for remembering how wide awake and strong-nerved
Mrs. Smith's voice had sounded. It might have
been ten minutes, or it might have been half an hour
afterwards—I could not judge of the time, it seemed
so long—that a low tap came at our door, and I.
answering it, admitted Mrs. Solomon. Her face was
very pale, but quiet, though her eyes gleamed with
a light that seemed something more than sorrow.

"Have you had a great scare here?" she questioned, "I don't wonder; I've been shaken as I never
was before. Is the child asleep?" with a glance
towards Laura.

"Auntie, is he dead?" asked Laura, suddenly turning and fixing wide-open, frightened eyes on her. "I saw him, I caught a glimpse of him, it was Harris. Is he dead?"

Mrs. Smith turned towards her those grave eyes, full now with solemn meaning, and said slowly, "Yes, child, he is—dead drunk."

"*Drunk!*" I repeated in dismay and a sort of terror, the very outspokenness of the word seeming to make it more terrible; for the moment to have one lying *drunk* in the house seemed infinitely worse than to say, "He is intoxicated."

"Drunk!" repeated Laura with a peculiar emphasis. I had never heard the word or the tone from her lips before.

"Yes," said Mrs. Solomon, "dead drunk. He knows just as little this minute about what is going on as his body will know when it is laid in the grave; and it is an awful sight! I never saw its like before, and I pray God I may never have to see it again. Oh! Solomon has often told me that I ought to go down on my knees and thank the Lord that ours were all girls, and kept safe from the worst temptations, but I never felt like it until this minute. Think what it was for that father to help drag him in like a beast over the elegant carpet, all mud and filth he was, just from the gutter! Oh dear!"

And the poor shocked old lady buried her face in her hands.

"Is this a new shock to the father?" I asked, after a few moments of troubled silence.

Mrs. Smith shook her head. "I guess not; I guess he has had a good many just such times as this.

But he promised, you see, and had reformed, so his father thought, and so poor Sarah thinks; and Jonas, he shrinks awfully from the mother knowing about it. But she will have to know; how can such things be kept from mothers? Oh dear, oh dear! Ain't that trouble, now? If that boy downstairs was mine, what could I do? Do you suppose I could bear it?"

I can never forget the drawn look, as of pain, on the old lady's face, as she waited almost appealingly for my answer.

"My dear friend," I said gently, "he is not yours, remember; the Lord gave you dear children who were at all times a comfort."

"So he did, so he did. And then he took them to his palace before me, so that I would have nothing to do but to hurry on after them as fast as I could. That is what I have always thought; but to-night I've been thinking that maybe I haven't understood the Lord. Maybe he gave me good, quiet, Christian girls, so that I would have time to help the mothers with boys; with boys who go astray; and then, maybe, when he saw that I did not understand, and would keep spending my time on my girls, that didn't really need it, he just took them into his own keeping; and even then I stupidly hurried along, the uppermost thought being that I was getting old, and that time was passing, and Solomon and I would soon be home with the children."

"Oh, auntie Smith! I'm sure you have spent your whole life, ever since I've known you, in trying to help other people." This reproachful protest came from the bed.

"No, I haven't, child; I've done a little at it now and then, when anybody stumbled right before my face and eyes, and I had to see 'em. But that's very different from going around looking after 'em. Even when the Lord set them right before me, I couldn't seem to see more than one at once. Here I've been in this house for weeks and weeks, and I dunno as I've thought three times about that boy downstairs. How shall I ever know what I might have said or done for him, that would have helped him? I tell you, when I see him lying there like a beast, instead of like a man made in the image of God, says I to myself: 'Mrs. Solomon Smith, you've helped along in this night's work just as like as not. There's more ways than one of helping; you've managed to give Satan a lift by just folding your hands and thanking the Lord you hadn't any boys, and made not the least move to keep this one out of the devil's clutches, just because he didn't happen to belong to you! It's my opinion that there's about as much mischief done in this world by folding our hands and thanking the Lord that our folks are not like other folks, as there is any other way.'"

It was a strange time for a lecture on the universal brotherhood of the race, or on the solemnity of human responsibility, and consequent accountability to God. Yet certainly I had never heard my old friend speak with such solemnity, nor seem so moved.

"I tell you," she said with energy, as she rose up to go, "we are all asleep. Everybody is asleep. It is high time we woke up and went to work."

"Mamma," said Laura, as the door closed after her, "if she is asleep, what do you suppose can be said of all the rest of the world?" Silence for a moment, and then this: "Mamma, do you suppose, according to auntie Smith, that I also am to blame for this trouble? For instance, I could have prevented this evening's work, I suppose. Harris asked me to ride with him, but I felt so utterly unequal to the undertaking that I declined. Am I to blame for to-night?"

I was prompt with my answer.

"No, daughter, no; that is the mistake which young people are apt to make. To ride with a young man of an evening may or may not be a wise thing to do. In this case I am decidedly of the opinion that you did right; but if it is all that a young girl can do towards holding a young man back from ruin, it amounts to very little indeed. To have been able to have exerted such a Christian influence over Harris as would have led him, possibly, to the Strong One for strength, might indeed have been his salvation. You know, dear, you did not try that."

She turned from me with manifest impatience.

"Mamma, you and auntie Smith think that there is nothing worth doing for people unless you can talk religion to them. What are those poor mortals to do who have none to talk about?"

"I don't think you mean just that, Laura. Neither of us believe that merely *talking* religion to people will do much good; but I confess that I do not see how, unless one *lives* religion, she is going to be able to help another to the only foundation that is absolutely safe to build upon."

Soon after that we settled into quiet, and tried with what skill we could to forget the scenes of the hour, and gather a little strength from what night there was left. Both of us, I think, were troubled with visions of the sleeping son and the waking father below-stairs.

We saw nothing of Harris the next morning, heard nothing of him. The father appeared much as usual, a trifle graver, perhaps, but I could not be sure, and from the smiling face of the mother I fancied that the family disgrace had been hidden from her; though much I marvelled as to how mother-eyes could be deceived. Amid hearty good-byes, and almost oppressive attentions, we left at last the house which we had entered as strangers. Especially interesting to me was Laura's parting with the child-wife. My daughter was never given to tears, but her eyes were dim when she turned away from Lida, and after a half-hour of utter silence on her part I heard only this:

"Mamma, fancy my loving the little thing, and hating to leave her! I never supposed that I could!"

Our journey was comparatively uneventful; only comparatively, however, and that word, I imagine, would not apply could we look into the future. There were quiet words dropped that day by our alert old friend, that I doubt not will bear fruit such as she will meet again in her Father's house. I think I have represented her to you as one strangely on the watch for opportunities, singularly ready with just the word that it seemed wisest to speak; but on this day, after her solemn declaration of the night before that everybody was "asleep", it was more distinctly noticeable than ever that she was intent upon her Master's business. Never obtrusive, almost never seeming to offend, being rarely repulsed, yet deftly slipping in her quiet, telling words where they must have been least expected.

In fact, I think she, more than any woman I ever knew, united those two peculiar characteristics of successful work: "Wise as a serpent, and harmless as a dove."

Mr. Smith proved a very careful and courteous attendant. Almost too careful, indeed, he fairly oppressed us with attentions, opening and closing our windows, arranging our blinds, folding and refolding our wraps, buying the daily papers, and offering us some of every dainty that passed through the train, pop-corn and fashion-books included. There seemed all the afternoon a nervous unrest about the man; I could not help thinking that he was trying to get rid of his own sorrowful thoughts, by inventing wants for us that he might busy himself in supplying. Arrived at our stopping-place for the night, we were packed into a carriage and taken whither he would, having all resigned ourselves to the feeling—which, however much of a veteran in travelling she may be, is always a luxury to a woman—that we were being taken care of, and need not think anything about routes or stopping-places or luggage.

The hotel was one of the princely sort, Mr. Jonas Smith being evidently one who never economised in travelling, and by seven o'clock we were divested of travel-stains, and seated at a cosy round table in the elegant dining-room, with well-trained waiters standing obsequiously by, ready to serve us with whatever we might select from the bill of fare.

It was here that occurred the next startling episode of what had, in the last few weeks, become an eventful life.

CHAPTER XXI.

"PRINCIPLES IS INCONVENIENT THINGS; I'LL OWN THAT."

AND what will you have, Maria?" Mr. Smith was saying, as Laura and I having stated our preference, he waited for his sister-in-law.

But "Maria" was engaged in an earnest, and to judge by her eyes, startled perusal of the bill of fare.

"Jonas, look there!" she said at last, laying the paper before him and pointing with her finger to the head-lines, which indicated that choice wines in every variety would be served to order.

"Yes," he said, in low tone, "of course, they all do that. What shall I order for you?"

"Jonas, you don't mean that? They don't all have them? In this great city there must surely be one temperance place where a body can eat and sleep without staining his conscience!"

The tone was low, almost pleading; still I think the nearest waiter caught it, and there was an amused smile on his face while he waited. Probably Jonas saw this. He answered hurriedly:

"There is no time to discuss such matters now, Maria. Don't you see we are already the subject of remark? Let me send your order; it is growing late. I am to meet my committee at eight o'clock."

"Then I must just go hungry, that's all. She spoke in a positive voice, yet one couldn't call it obstinate. There was too mournful a tone in it, as if she were fully conscious of all the perplexities and annoyances that the question at issue set in motion, and would fain have shrunk from it if she could. "I'm dreadful sorry, Jonas. If I'd dreamed of such a thing, I wouldn't have come this way. I don't like to put folks in unpleasant places, and make talk, and all that, not a bit; but as for eating my supper, or sleeping under a roof where they sell rum, or giving a cent of my money toward helping it along, I can't do it."

By this time the waiter was smiling broadly behind the napkin with which he vainly tried to hide his mouth. Mr. Jonas Smith was growing visibly annoyed.

"Don't be absurd!" he said, in a quick, irritable undertone, "we must have supper at once. Tea and toast, waiter, in addition to my other orders, and be quick about it."

"Not for me, Jonas." There was quietness in Mrs. Smith's voice, but there was also firmness. "Not a mouthful for me at this table. You don't understand. I can't do anything of that kind; it simply ain't right. None of Solomon's money must go toward helping the curse along, in any way, shape, or manner. We promised that to the Lord long ago; and a promise to him ain't to be broken for convenience, you know. I can go hungry, but I can't eat the bread of sin."

"What ridiculous nonsense!" Mr. Smith was unaffectedly angry now. "Just as if eating your

supper at this table either helped or hindered the
cause! I'll tell you what, Maria, fanaticism does
more to hinder than any other single thing."

"Maybe so," said Mrs. Smith, quietly. "Jonas,
what would you give to see Harris just such a fanatic
as I be?"

The father's face paled instantly, yet what were
we to do? Here we sat, waiting for our ordered
dinner, and one of our party refusing to touch it?
He turned toward us an appealing look, and I essayed
to help:

"I should certainly much prefer a temperance
house. Can we not go quietly to one?"

"And leave the supper we have ordered uneaten
and unpaid for?"

There was something very like a sneer in his voice,
yet he was so tired that I could excuse it. Mrs.
Smith saved me the trouble of answering:

"No, we wouldn't leave it unpaid for. We've
made 'em trouble in ignorance, and we'll pay 'em for
it. That's principle; but they'll know just why
we can't eat our suppers here; that's principle, too."

Mr. Smith looked as though if it were he hated
principle, and would have nothing to do with it;
but, after another moment or two of hesitation, he
rose abruptly, made his way to the cashier's desk,
held a hurried conversation with him, during which
time certain bills exchanged hands, then he came
back to us. And it was with haste and gloom that
we retreated from the elegant hotel. A somewhat
silent party rode through the streets of the city in
search of a temperance house. Mr. Jonas Smith did
not condescend to sit inside, but slammed the door

R

on us as if we were all equally in disgrace, and took
a seat with the driver.

The ride was not a long one, but the change, both
in location and appearance, was marked when we
again alighted before a hotel.   Perhaps you are accustomed to being a martyr to your temperance
principles and know all about the stuffy hall, and
small, not overclean, not well-kept rooms, all smelling more or less of food that had been cooked some
time, into which we were presently ushered.

"I hope you like it?"   Mr. Smith said to his
sister-in-law, with meek voice and savage eyes.

He was speaking of the room to which the
slovenly and somewhat surly waiter had brought us.
The main one, by no means immense in size, and the
one opening from it, not larger than the clothes-
presses in his own house.   The furniture was plain,
even to shabbiness; the carpet, that large-figured
abomination in red and green; altogether, though
the bedding was clean, and the necessaries to comfort were there, the air of cheapness which pervaded
everything evidently tried Mr. Smith's æsthetic taste
to the utmost.

"It will do," Mrs. Solomon said decisively, in
answer to his insinuation.   "It ain't so grand by
considerable as the one we left.   I suppose these
folks can't afford to be grand, they don't get any
help from rum.   And I don't suppose they have any
too much custom, either.   Folks don't go out of
their way, maybe, to find a temperance house.   It is
a good deal easier to go to the glittering places, and
ask no questions for conscience' sake.   Principles
is inconvenient things, I'll own that.   Solomon

and I have been bothered with ours a great many times."

"Well," said Mr. Smith, "everyone to his taste. I'm glad you like it. They say there will be some sort of a supper served for you soon. As for me, I must go without supper to-night and hurry right back to my appointment."

It was his parting thrust, and we were alone.

"But, auntie," said Laura, as she poured water from the broken-nosed pitcher, and exclaimed over its smallness, and yellowness, and brokenness, "is there any principle involved in having things look like this? Temperance people need not necessarily be stuffy, and dusty, and shabby. If they want custom, why don't they keep such a house as people will patronise?"

"Sometimes there's a good deal of principle in that very thing, child. A man has got to have the money to make a house elegant in the first place, and keep it so afterwards; and often he's got to earn the money before he can have it, and if his principles won't let him earn it by selling rum—which I have heard is altogether the quickest and easiest way—and if you and I ain't got principles enough to stand his broken-nosed pitchers, and cracked-look-ing glasses, so as to help him earn money for better things, why, he won't be likely to get on very fast. I like nice things, child, but I like clean consciences better. I'm sorry for Jonas, his principles ain't skin deep, anyhow, and his conscience is tough, and his stomach is tender, and he'll likely have a hard time of it here; I'm sorry for all of us for having made an uncomfortable time all round; it is the most uncomfortable time I ever remember to have had in my life, and I'd have given my best Alderney cow to get out of it; but I was in and I didn't know no way out; as true as you live, I didn't. I'm an old goose, maybe; an opinionated old foolish thing, but I couldn't no more set there and drink that tea out of a china cup, and stir it with a silver spoon, and think of that boy of Jonas' lying dead drunk in his father's parlour only last night, and me a sitting one side of him and his father the other a groaning out in agony every few minutes, and me helping to pay for the rum that went to make him so, than I could fly up through that chimney-hole this minute. I couldn't do it!"

She looked worn and haggard with the weight of her trouble, and with the trouble which she had made for others, which last was at all times harder for Mrs. Smith than anything that she had to bear for herself. I could feel that as she turned away from Laura's unanswering eyes and sighed heavily; she was thinking what a blessed haven of rest that little house in the Hollow would be to her, with Solomon at the hearth-side.

I did not know what to think of Laura; for the first time since we left home, she seemed to have deserted her old friend. Her eyes flashed their vexation, and she shut her lips tightly as though she had just enough self-control left to resolve to keep silence. One might have supposed that her whole heart was set in favour of the liquor traffic, instead of having been all her life an earnest temperance worker. I felt very much puzzled. I could not think that the luxuries of life had suddenly grown so important to

her that she could not dispense with them for one
night; for, like most sensible girls reared in comfortable and harmonising surroundings, she had not
given them such a high place that she could not
cheerfully, and even gleefully, share the annoyances
and discomforts of travel, or of anything that disturbed the usual routine.

Altogether, the rest of our journey was not pleasant. The breakfast did well enough; the steak
was somewhat tough, to be sure, and the coffee slightly
muddy, but if everything had not been made so uncomfortable by Mr. Smith's sarcasms and Laura's
silence, we should have gotten along nicely. As it
was, I was glad certainly to bid the gentleman good-
bye, and Mrs. Smith curled herself into a seat in the
car with a long-drawn sigh of relief, after his somewhat stiff good-bye to her.

Fancy a man saying good-bye stiffly to a woman
who had been what she had in his household, for
weary days and nights, week after week, simply
because by her conscientious scruples she disturbed
the luxury of one night's rest! I felt angry with
him, and provoked with Laura, and left her much to
herself.

As our train rolled into the familiar depôt, and
Mrs. Smith, peering from the window, caught a
glimpse of the high, old-fashioned waggon, plenti-
fully besprinkled with mud, and of Solomon, in
his much too long grey coat standing beside it,
watching eagerly the moving car windows, I shall
never forget the radiant face that turned to me, nor
the triumphant voice that said:

"There he is! the best sight that my old eyes have

seen in a year—it seems most a year, don't it? I declare for it, I hope it won't be made my duty to trot around this world any more without Solomon; I don't like it!"

I laughed, but Laura was persistently cold and silent. The child had never tried me so much in all her life put together, as she had during this journey.

I think I showed a little of this feeling as we talked over, with her father and Mary, the episode of the hotel; for Laura, without being directly censured, arose to the defensive.

"I don't care, mamma, I still think it was very silly and selfish in Mrs. Solomon, and I shall always think so. The idea that her money was helping along the sale of liquor just because she was stopping at a hotel and paying for just what she consumed, and nothing more. What had she to do with the liquor? She might as well refuse to stop in the world any longer, because there are rum-selling, and Sabbath-breaking, and I don't know what not. So long as she doesn't do it, and can't keep others from doing it, what is it to her?"

Now Laura was not usually so illogical as that; in fact, her father had often playfully told her that he ought to educate her for the bar; she would make her mark as a lawyer; and I was more surprised than I can tell you. Her reasoning seemed too absurd even to require an answer; so absurd, indeed, that Mary laughed, as she said pleasantly:

"Why, Laura! you are on exactly the opposite side from what I should have expected, and, besides, have certainly forgotten how to argue. Of course, it really is countenancing the sale of liquor in hotels

to patronise them ; in fact, it apparently accepts the
popular argument that first-class hotels cannot be
kept without the sale of liquor. And so we submit
to having liquor pay half of our first-classness.
Doesn't it, papa ?"

" Looks like it," said her father, sipping his coffee,
and evidently enjoying the argument of his daughters
too much to care to cut it short by helping them.
But Laura was excited.

" Well, they can't," she said sharply, ignoring her
father's remark. " Look at the condition of the
temperance hotels ; first-class, indeed ! I wish you
could have been with us last night. Even the
soaps were third-class, and the thin coating of silver
all worn from the spoons, and papa, you couldn't
cut the steak with a sharp knife even !"

" But what does that prove," persisted Mary,
" save that it is a humiliating truth that we are
allowing the poor fellows who drink liquor to pay
part of our bills ? I should think that that was helping along the liquor traffic with a vengeance ; and I
should think that if it is really so we would better
get along with third-class soaps, or take our own, and
even eat tough steak once in a while, or else patronise temperance houses so exclusively, and at such
good prices, that they can soon afford another state
of things."

" Does Malcolm stop at temperance houses wherever
he goes ?" was Laura's apparently irrelevant reply,
and Mary, with a slightly heightened colour, answered,
laughing, that she presumed not ; she imagined that
he had never given the matter any thought ; but she
would write to him about it immediately, and give

him auntie Smith's views; and she believed in his
temperance principles so thoroughly that she thought
him willing to give up toilet soap and tender steak
altogether, if necessary; and that it was one of the
advantages in having auntie Smith's conscience in
the world; it roused other people's.

But Laura persisted that she thought auntie Smith's
conscience altogether too tender in some directions,
and that she had shown herself to be obstinate and
selfish.

" Well, I think so, mamma," she said, with a
defiant little flash in her bright eyes, as she caught
my reproving look.   " She doesn't care for little
daintinesses herself, isn't, in fact, accustomed to
them as we are, and as her brother-in-law is, and so,
of course, there was nothing special for her to give
up.   She cares for just one person in this world, and
that is her Solomon, and so long as her conscience
doesn't touch him in any way, nor waste his money,
she is willing to ride into all sorts of discomforts,
and take other people with her, without caring how
hard it presses them.   I should like to see a question of conscience come up that would affect Solomon's
welfare in any way.   I think she would discover
that she is selfish in her crosses, and that in reality
she doesn't know much about them."

I couldn't understand Laura.   Her eyes were
bright, her cheeks burning, and her lips were quiver-
ing.   She was evidently strongly wrought upon, and
had apparently gone over entirely to the enemy's
side.   Mary looked at her wonderingly.

" One would think you were an anti-temperance
partisan," she said, " instead of being your grand-

father's pet scholar in 'no-licence' arguments. Laura,
I believe you caught the fever from Lida, and are
out of your head!" This last with a half-laugh.

But Laura did not smile.

"I am just as strong a temperance woman as ever
I was," she said firmly, "and I'm as strong as anybody ought to be. I simply try to keep common
sense on my side. And I say it is the man who
sells the liquor, and the man who drinks it, who are
to blame, and no others. All these side issues,
wandering around to see if our consciences are mixed
up with it, because we eat steak, and sleep on beds
in hotels, is all nonsense. It is just being fanatical.
I believe that the people who trouble themselves
about other people's consciences in this way are
just the ones who will 'strain at a gnat and swallow
a camel,' if the camel takes the shape that they
would like to swallow; and Mrs. Smith will do it as
quickly as any of them." Whereupon she abruptly
left the breakfast-table.

All day, pressed upon by many cares and responsibilities, growing out of my long absence from home,
there came this undertone of anxiety: "What can
have so disturbed and altered Laura?" That evening,
when we were alone together, my husband answered
the question with a single sentence:

"Has Laura told you how Norman has at last invested his surplus funds?"

"No. We have been so excited with weddings,
and sickness, and travelling, that we have had no
opportunity to speak of business together. How has
he?"

My tone was somewhat indifferent. What did I

care, really, how Norman Eastlake had invested his
surplus funds? He had money enough, too much;
indeed, I had often believed that he would be more
of a man if he had less.

"In hotel stock," said my husband significantly.
And then I understood Laura!

CHAPTER XXII

"AND BEHOLD, THEY WERE ENGAGED."

NORMAN EASTLAKE was my daughter Laura's intended husband. You can readily see how her father's announcement enlightened me. In a moment I saw it all—the poor child's sensitive attempt to think that what her friend did must be right, though at variance with all her previous views and teachings, and her determination to sustain him, and argue him out of the inconsistency. I could understand how Mrs. Smith's extreme action had wrought upon her nerves with its irritating question as to why that ignorant old woman should be able to reach conclusions of right and wrong that Norman with all his culture and logical education had failed to see. Of course he was right, and Mrs. Solomon wrong—it should be so!

As soon as I understood my poor child I was sorry for her, though I cannot say that I was greatly astonished at Norman's course.

The truth is that, could I have had things just as I would, Norman Eastlake was not the man whom I should have chosen for my son-in-law. I had never meant that he should occupy such a position. It had been a boy and girl friendship, not so very strongly marked. They liked to walk from school together, and were rivals in rhetoric and algebra. friendly rivals always; I thought that their interest in each other was nothing more than the natural result of belonging to the same classes, and being interested in the same pursuits.

When Norman went to college, I had been foolish enough to consent carelessly to their interchange of friendly letters. Her father had shook his head, and asked me if I thought it wise; but I had only laughed and assured him that Laura was just a gay child, and would correspond with him as joyously and as innocently as she would with her brother if she had one; and I remember that I added that Norman was a sentimental boy, who thought it would be a fine thing to get letters regularly from a pretty girl; it would give him a sense of manliness, which secretly I thought he needed.

So the years passed on, and before I fully realised that Laura had for ever laid aside her doll, and romped with her kitten no more, she came to me one day with glowing cheeks and speaking eyes, and a letter to show me—a special letter—she had always showed them to me, and they had been gay and careless enough, but this one was written after Laura had been spending a month with an aunt in the same town where Norman was at school, and behold, they were engaged! Norman had taken everything in his free and easy fashion. "They will be expecting it," he had said to Laura. "Of course your father and mother knew the end of all these things; they have as good as given their consent already, we need not trouble to be very formal."

Had we? Yes, I thought it all over afterwards, many a time afterwards. Norman was right; we

had allowed things to drift, exactly as though we had
expected they would go down just the channel that
they had ; and yet I never expected it, never meant
it, would have given much, very much, to have taken
it all back ; I had simply made the mistake that I
think many mothers are making now—that of calling
two young things "children," and letting them play
on together, long after the childishness had been in
a sense laid aside, and they were playing at man and
woman, without recognising it as play.

Well, what objection had we to Norman Eastlake ?
We asked each other the question—her father and I
—he, looking with troubled face into the coals, staring straight before him all that hour, and never by
word or look hinting to me that hateful "I told you
so," yet, do you think I forgot that he had ! Oh,
there were many objections ! Norman was of good
family ? Yes. He was a good-hearted, well-inten-
tioned fellow ? Yes. He was a fair scholar, and
would be likely to succeed fairly well in his profession ? Yes. He was rich ? Yes. Unhesitatingly I
answered all these questions to my heart in the
affirmative ; and yet I did not want him for Laura's
husband. Well, did I want anybody ? No, I didn't.
I recognised that, as in part, the trouble. Laura was
a child yet ; ought to have been. I resented her
being defrauded of her fresh young girlhood, and
being pushed thus early into the responsibilities of
life. Why couldn't they at least have been content
to remain boy and girl friends for a few years ?
Why must Norman suddenly go to imagining himself
a man ?

"Norman is a Christian ?" said Laura's father at

last, hesitatingly, with a curious upward inflection in
his voice.

I answered the questioning sentence with another.
" Is he ?"

" Why, Mary, you know he has been a professor of
religion ever since he was a little fellow !"

" I know it," I said, and if Laura had heard me I
suppose she would have resented the dreariness of
my tone. But therein lay one of my troubles;
Norman was by no means the sort of Christian that
I thought he ought to be; he was simply a free-
hearted, good-natured, easy-going, social young fellow,
lacking, I believed, in moral backbone. I had never
seen him tried, to be sure. His tastes did not run in
the line of dissipation; his friends did not happen
to be of the stamp that led him astray, and his reputation was therefore exceptionally good. I believe
in that word " therefore." I have put the hint of
how the matter stood in my own mind. I had not
unwavering confidence in Norman's self; his virtues
seemed to have happened around him, creatures of
circumstance, rather than of choice, based on con-
viction. I remember as long ago as when he united
with the Church, in company with a large number of
young people, just after a period of special religious
interest, it seemed to me rather that he came because
all the boys in his set were coming than because he
he had taken firm foothold on the Rock. I had all
along felt that little undertone of distrust, not of his
good intentions, but of the soil on which they were
growing. He had been a boy who was easily persuaded to go sleigh-riding, or rowing, as the case
might be, on prayer-meeting evening, if the other

boys were going, and almost equally easily persuaded
that it was not just the thing to do, if enough of the
others thought not, which little illustration just
serves to show his moral power. Imagine such a
one the husband of my Laura, with her quick, keen
insight into all questions, mental or moral. I had
small comfort in thinking that she could lead him,
for I believed that, like all weak natures, his was
also an obstinate one; it could take a position and
maintain it stoutly againt reason and common sense,
if the motive for doing so was sufficiently inviting.
Besides, I felt confident that Laura was not a woman
to lead her husband and live a happy life; she was
too strong-willed for that, in the better sense of that
word. I felt sure that, in order to respect him, she
must look up to him and believe in his superior
strength. Then how in the name of wonder was she
to be happy with the man of her choice? Over
this problem her father and I grieved much, after we
settled to the mournful truth that she was unques-
tionably a woman at heart, and that he was unques-
tionably the man of her choice. At last it became
apparent to us that it was to be done by shutting
her eyes and assuring herself that the strength was
there, and that she might lean on it. I hoped that
she mercifully did now know her eyes were shut. If
she could always live in a state of real blindness as
to Norman's character—provided my estimate of it
were correct—she might be a comparatively happy
woman. But there had, in the past year, been
several little episodes like this hotel affair, which
had told me only too clearly that Laura sometimes
saw painful things, even with closed eyes. The

Temperance question had been one on which I believed that Norman stood more squarely than on any other, for the reason that his father had been a pioneer in that direction in the dark days of the struggle, and Norman had admired his father; yet it will explain to you how little real confidence I had in the young man, that after the first start of surprise I asked my husband simply who it was who had succeeded in persuading Norman that very safe investments were made in hotel stock, and that morally it was all right.

After all, I don't think I have made this matter very plain. You see, you don't know Norman East-lake; if you did you would understand. There was really no ground for complaint; look at him outwardly from any standpoint that you chose, he was unexceptionable; and I was not sure, any of the time, but that the boy was a Christian, only a limping sort of one, if he chanced among cripples; and Laura was not even that. We could not appeal to her need for a higher type of Christian manhood, we could not appeal to anything; and when we hesitated and urged, there was nothing to argue that could be put into words, save that she, and he, too, for the matter of that, were so very young.

"We shall be growing older every day," she said gravely. "People grow old fast enough. And mamma, I know you don't like Norman—that is, you don't like him well enough to marry him—that is plain, I have seen it this long time. But there is this to be said about it: I do, and I'm the one, you know."

What could we answer?

So, for more than a year it had been an understood thing in our family that Laura was the promised wife of Norman Eastlake. He was an orphan, and was most unnecessarily wealthy.

There were always surplus funds coming in to torment him as to investment; and it was probably to escape the bore of looking any further that he had become half owner in one of the princely hotels in the city where he was studying his profession. Laura's father had heard of it through his lawyer, who had been engaged in the legal part of the business; but directly he mentioned it, I knew that Laura had heard it from Norman, and accepted it as the thing to do, or else Norman wouldn't have done it!

Because of the example of Christian life thus kept before her, I had been surprised that Laura had espoused Mrs. Smith's peculiar views on many subjects so heartily. My conclusion had been that she believed the difference in them to be largely one of development, and that Norman would grow into what was now Mrs. Smith's daily life.

This being the case, it was not difficult to understand what a shock the hotel enterprise had been to her. This was not development, surely! He had been pronounced enough on the entire temperance question when she saw him last; not exactly this phase of it, to be sure; and I believed that this would always be the difference between Laura's mind and Norman Eastlake's. Questions parallel to those already settled would by her be accepted as matters of course, while Norman would have to argue himself in or out of each new development, and would be likely to decide negatively about one, and affirmatively about the other of two phases which to Laura appeared as one and the same.

I plainly saw that the problem which she had now set herself was to convince her heart and her conscience that in this new departure Norman was right and Mrs. Smith absurdly wrong. I knew it was not yet settled, because her irritation still continued in full force. She argued at length with Mary that our dear old lady might be very good, but she was narrow-minded. Of course she was; why should she not be? All her life experiences had tended to make her so. Also, this wise woman of nineteen was convinced that the woman of sixty-five did not understand herself. She had never been tried in a direction that would press home. "Her children's graves," I ventured to hint; and the foolish child, who knew nothing about a mother's heart, said, Yes, but that was long ago; and she had been so busy about her energetic life that she really had not had time to miss them much, and she did not believe, any way, that they had ever been to her what some daughters were to mothers—she had given all her heart to Solomon, and had none left for others; and certainly for twenty years at least she had not had a ripple of personal trouble to disturb her; no wonder she was able to settle questions of conscience for all creation! I gave over trying to argue with Laura; what was the use?

Nevertheless, it was she who, one evening, after Norman, in a new dressing-gown of most becoming pattern, and gay slippers—the gift of a sister of one of his college friends—had lounged among us for two or three days, made a proposition that surprised me :

" Mamma, I want Norman to make the acquaintance of Mr. and Mrs. Smith. Suppose we go over there this evening for an hour ? They are original characters, Norman ; you will enjoy studying them.' And Norman gracefully declared that he could not conceive of himself as enjoying anything better than he did that easy-chair, with his feet on the hearthrug, and that delightful open grate fire to stare at, to say nothing of his companions ; at the same time he was ready to attend us to the ends of the earth if such was our pleasure.

Mary was at this time much absorbed in a missionary entertainment that was being got up by the Young Ladies' Band of our Church, she being President of said Band. On the evening in question there was a committee meeting and rehearsal at the other end of the town, and her father had attended her thither, and was to await her pleasure. Therefore I was thrown upon Laura and Norman for the evening , at least, Laura chose to so consider me, not being willing that her mother should sit alone, while she entertained her guest in the parlour. It was one of the pretty little ways in which my younger daughter differed from many young ladies of the present day.

I glanced up surprised at her suggestion. She had not been to call on Mrs. Smith since our return home, nearly six weeks before ; and though of course we had long since dropped all discussion in regard to the matter, I was aware that she had not grown reconciled to the old lady's tacit condemnation of

Norman's course. I remember I wondered whether she had in mind an argument on the subject of temperance, and temperance work, and temperance fanaticism, to be held in my neighbour's kitchen, in the course of which the neighbour should find herself silenced and convinced by the brilliant logic of the young man.

Whatever motive provoked the suggestion, I was glad to receive it, for I knew her absence and coldness had sadly hurt the heart of her true old friend who loved her dearly; and with alacrity I laid aside my sewing, assuring Norman that we had a special treat in store for him if he really did not remember Solomon Smith and his wife.

"I remember them perfectly," he said in his cultured drawl, which was growing upon him, and which I used to wonder that Laura, with her quick ways and her clear-cut tones, could endure.

"I remember the queer old waggon in which they rode to town on market days, and Sundays. It used to be associated in my juvenile mind with stories of the ark, and I was always contriving how to stow away the animals. I remember I decided that old Solomon himself would do for an ape, but I could never be sure whether I would have the old lady a species of monkey, or whether she belonged to the cat kind; she had a curious way of climbing over the wheel that suggested the feline tribe to me."

I hope he had not expected Laura to laugh; if he had, he was disappointed.

"They could not have been very old at that time," was her sole comment.

"Oh, they were, I assure you; they were always

old. As long ago as I can remember, they were quoted from as we quote the wise sayings of the oldest inhabitants. Mrs. Leonard, there is no reason why my knowledge of them should not be fresh and vivid. In the letters which I have been receiving from a certain person this winter, at least every third sentence began thus: 'Auntie Smith says.' It took me weeks to determine where she had found a new aunt; naturally I did not associate her with the days of Solomon. When light finally dawned upon me, I spent some anxious moments in wondering whether Laura also said 'Uncle Solomon' and whether I should be expected to learn such a formidable name."

Laura was still grave, and the flush on her cheeks plainly showed me that she was tried by all this banter.

"I think, Norman," she said with dignity, "that the utmost tax your nerves will receive in that direction will be to say, 'Mr. Smith.'"

There was a somewhat marked emphasis on the "Mr.," whereat Norman laughed, and then we three proceeded to the little brown house in the Hollow.

CHAPTER XXIII.

"SHO! THAT ARGUMENT UPSETS ITSELF!"

THERE was something wonderfully pleasant about Mrs. Smith's kitchen. In the strictest sense of the word, it was not a kitchen at all, all the rougher household work having been banished, with the large cook-stove, to a small outer room; but the Smiths liked the homely, old-fashioned name, and clung to it for this larger room.

A wonderfully bright rag-carpet adorned the floor, a carpet that was in truth an artistic study, the colours having been arranged with the greatest care, and with a special regard to brightness. The white-washed walls were hung with many pictures; some of them cheap prints, many of them really fine engravings, the hoarded treasures of years. They hung in cheap frames, or were merely tacked to the walls, but every one of them, whether cheap or fine, was in itself a treasure. Then the chairs were as unlike as possible to the usual kitchen furniture—in fact, as my Mary said, they were unlike themselves. No two were mates, and yet they were not an incongruous happening of different patterns. Each one was a study.

Solomon's special property was a somewhat high, wide-seated, wooden-backed creature, with spring castors in front, and none at the back, which gave it

a curious, swinging motion. It was upholstered in a
brilliant cushion of small and intricate patchwork,
containing—so Mrs. Smith triumphantly informed
me once—a bit of every woollen dress she ever wore
from the time she was a year-old baby, and Solomon
remembered those in which he used to draw her to
school on his sled.

Her chair was a low-seated, high-backed arm-
rocker, upholstered also with home work, but in sober
hue, being decorous stripes of grey and black woollen,
fashioned of strips from Solomon's worn-out coats
and pantaloons.

Then there was my special chair, a flag-bottomed
rocker of the olden style, with a peculiarly easy back,
and a gay cushion stuffed with feathers from Mrs.
Smith's own geese, and covered with bright strips of
her own knitting.

Laura's favourite, a white-flagged, green-painted
little sewing-chair, sat up pert and sparkling against
the wall, one or two respectable, broad-banded, very
old-fashioned "splints" keeping it company.

The Smiths, like ourselves, were very fond of open-
grate fires, and clung to them as late in the season
as the weather would admit. But, unlike ourselves,
they were blessed with an old-fashioned fireplace,
wherein the traditional black-log could blaze and
snap and sparkle as in the olden time. I never
wondered over Solomon's fondness for poking the
coals—he had such a royal chance in that great wide-
mouthed fireplace.

Into this cosy room, with a bed of coals and
brands in just the right state for poking, we were
ushered on that spring evening. The small, square

stand, just large enough to hold the lamp and a book
or two, besides the Bible which always lay on it, and
generally open, was drawn quite near to the hearth,
"just for the sake of being sociable," Mrs. Smith
said.   I had heard her remark that she felt sorry for
the fireplace when spring grew late.   It kind of
seemed to her it must know that its shining was
over, and that it must lie in blackness and shadow
for a long, long time.   "We sit close up to it as
long as we can, and make its last fires as bright as
the spring weather will anyways stand," she had
said with a half-regretful smile.

There they sat together; Solomon in his chair on
the hearth, his comfortably slippered feet spread out
on the bright, braided mat, which was almost thick
enough to serve as a footstool; his wife just opposite
him, not so far away but that she could lean forward, on occasion, and rest an emphatic hand on his
knee; her inevitable knitting in her lap, but a book
in her hand, and an *Evangelist* which had apparently
just slipped from her lap to the floor.

I remember thinking, as I took my special chair,
that the whole bright, homely scene would make a
picture for an artist.   My Laura had an artist soul,
and I could see her eyes brighten and soften with
the beauty of it all; but those other eyes saw a re-
flection of the ape and monkey caricature which he
had tried to draw for us, I suppose.   At least, they
showed no appreciation of the sweet homeliness to
which we had introduced him.   I do not think I ever
liked my prospective son-in-law less than I did that
evening.

We were most cordially received.   Mrs. Smith's

homely old face glowed genially over the sight of
Laura at her hearthstone again; yet, with the rare
tact which was so marked a trait in her character, she
made no comment on the length of time that the
child had stayed away.

She was equally cordial in receiving Norman, and
told him with a smile which should have redeemed
her face from all ugliness in his eyes, that she used
to know his father well, and a better man never
lived in the town.

"You've got his eyes," she said earnestly, "and I
hope and trust you have his good heart."

He was pleasant enough, though he thanked her
with too much ceremoniousness for her good opinion
of his father, and disclaimed all expectation—I had
almost said all intention—of ever being so good a
man as his father.

Then Mrs. Smith, brimful of talk, as usual, went
back to the subject that had evidently occupied her
thoughts when we came:

"I was just taking dips into the New Version,
and Solomon and I was talking over some of the
changes. We hadn't had it but a little while. I
brought it home with me, you know." (This to
Laura.) "Well, sir, and what do you think of the
New Version?"

I waited somewhat curiously for Norman's answer.
I had not enough faith in his religious life to believe that he had made a very careful study of either
the new or the old version for some time; but he
was a man who always had opinions to express,
whether or not he had them at hand to live by.

"I think," he said with promptness, "that it represents a great deal of time and money wasted, which might have been used to better advantage."

Mrs. Smith was evidently astonished at the answer.

"Why? Do you now?" she said eagerly. "I can't think it. I have been awaiting for that book to come out as eager as a little girl for a new dolly. Seemed to me I couldn't wait till they got it ready, though as it happened I did, and a good while after. The Lord filled my hands so full of work of one kind and another that I hadn't time for no new versions; but when I got hold of it I was tickled. Seems to me that whatever makes the Bibles a mite plainer to plain people can't be a waste of time or money, can it?"

"But has it made it any plainer?" queried Norman. "I don't know of anything in it that amounts to much in the way of plainness, I'm sure."

And again I could not help wondering whether he really knew what was in it.

"Oh, I do," the old lady said, in quiet positiveness. "We've found some things, haven't we, Solomon? When you come in we had just been talking about the Lord's Prayer. Now, I s'pose if there is any one thing we ought to understand pretty well, it's them verses of the prayer we've been praying ever since we got in and out of our cradles; and yet I don't think I understood it till I got hold of the New Version. I've about held my breath over that prayer a good many times; in a kind of a scare, you know. The fact is, I've been a peppery body all my life. There's Solomon knows I could go off as quick as a lucifer match; quicker a good

deal than the worthless things they make now-
days."

"Oh, now, Maria, sho!"

These were the first words that Solomon had
uttered since he had given us greeting. After this
effort he leaned forward and poked the firebrand so
effectually that it sent up a shower of sparks.

"It's so," said his wife. "That's been my thorn
in the flesh all my life, and will be something of a
thorn, I'm afraid, as long as I have any flesh ; and by
streaks I find it most awful hard to forgive folks ;
mean, snakey folks, you know, that slip around
doing slimy things. Not to me specially, though
I've borne my share of slime in my day, but kind of
general slipping around, doing of things that you
hate. You know what I mean.

"Well, I've come to that before now, many a
time, when I've just had to hold my breath and
think : 'Forgive us our debts as we forgive our
debtors ?' Says I, 'Hold on, Mrs. Solomon Smith,
do you really want that ? Are you sure you want
the Lord to forgive you just exactly as you've forgive
Susan Barker ?'

"She was a young woman that tried me most
awful in her time ; for about two years she was a
regular thorn. She's been in heaven these dozen
years ; I've no kind of doubt of it. I was with her
when she went, and I knew the Lord sent his angels,
and they was waiting all around there before she
died. Think of me having hard work to forgive
her, just because she had made some mistakes, said
things here and there she no business to, and gone
quite a while without takin' of 'em back ! and I act-

ing as though I'd never done nothing wrong in my
life, couldn't see my way clear to forgiving her!
But that's just the kind of mean creatures we are.

"Well, many's the time she's given me a stab,
right on my knees, and I'd wait, and I'd have to
own up: 'No, Lord, I don't believe I can do it; I
believe I want a better forgiveness from you than
I've give to her. I feel kind of grouty this minute
when I think of her;' and there was days at a time
when I'd slip around that prayer, all on account of
Susan Barker. And she wa'n't the only one, either.
There was times when I had quite a number of
them that didn't do right, or say right, and seemed
to be bothering around me as sure as I got down on
my knees to pray that particular prayer!"

Over this frank statement Norman roared. He
was entirely capable of seeing the ludicrous side of
a question.

"But I'm utterly unable to see what the New
Version has to do with this trouble," he said, as
soon as he could command his voice.

"Why, don't you see what I did? I had just
sense enough to know that it would be an awful
thing to pray to God to forgive me as I'd forgiven
my botherers, if I hadn't done my part just right;
and so I thought I could make it all right by slipping around the Lord's Prayer, and making up one
of my own, and leaving them out of it altogether,
till I got ready to right down out and out forgive
them in the fashion that I saw plain enough the
Lord must forgive me, if it was going to do me any
good. But now look at the New Version: 'Forgive
us our debts as we also have forgiven our debtors.'

Don't you see that shows the work is all done? It
is just plain sailing: 'Lord, I've forgiven Susan
Barker the best I know how; now forgive me.'

"I don't know as I make my meaning plain; but
it is most dreadful plain to me that there's no slipping around it. The Lord's Prayer don't make us
ask the Lord to treat us just exactly as we have done
our enemies, but it says in plain English, 'We've
done our best. We forgive them before we come to
our knees.'

"I dunno as you see through it. I'm not good at
making other folks understand; but I know if I'd
had the New Version while I was on thorns with
Susan Barker, I'd have understood that leaving out
the Lord's Prayer didn't do no good; that he expected us to forgive before we come to him with
any prayer at all about anything else. And if we
hadn't done it, and couldn't do it, every living thing
we had a right to pray about was: 'Lord, give me
the heart to forgive them;' and let that be settled
before we talked to him about forgiving us. Then
I am glad, for one, that they put Satan into that
prayer."

"Put Satan into it!" repeated Norman, with an
astonished stare, and then going off into a perfect
roar of laughter, while Laura exclaimed as to what
her friend could mean.

"Why, yes, child, put him there himself in so
many words: 'Lead us not into temptation, but
deliver us from evil;' that's the way we've prayed it,
you know. 'Now, I'm an ignorant old woman, and
didn't understand it; and that's what I say, the
New Version is good for such as me—I couldn't

seem to make it mean anything but this: 'Lead us
not into temptation, but if we do succeed in getting
in in spite of you, why, deliver us from the evil of
it. That don't sound reverent, maybe. I mean it
reverent, but I didn't understand it. Now I pray:
'Lead us not into temptation, but deliver us from
the evil one. Him that's for ever after us, going
around like a roaring lion, and liking nothing in life
so much as to lead us right into the thickest temptation he can. Deliver us from him.' 'Amen,' I say,
with all my heart; and when I speak him right out
on my knees to Christ, and recognise him as an
awful enemy, I seem to sense the thing that for this
purpose was the Son of Man manifested to destroy
the works of the devil, and I somehow feel surer
that he can do it. But now there's something I
want to ask you. I saw the other day, in a paper,
that some folks thought it was a kind of triumph
for the infidels and scoffers that we had got out a
New Version, and I don't see how it can be. What
does that mean?"

"It is true," said Norman briskly—the young man
liked to impart information as well as any person I
ever saw—"you see it plainly proves what they have
been saying all along, that our old Bible is full of
errors, and that we have outgrown it, and are dis-
satisfied with it. 'And,' say they, 'in a few years
you will have outgrown this New Version, and you
will need another, and another; and the thing will
go on, as man increases in knowledge, until he gets a
Bible to suit him.' And there is altogether too much
truth in the thing to have it in any sense agreeable to
thinking people.

" That is my objection. The fact is, we didn't
need a New Version ; the old one was good enough.
There are a few changes, which, as you say, make
things plainer, but those have been explained again
and again by commentaries ; and to put an argument
into the mouths of infidels that we had outgrown
our old Bible and had to have a new one made for
us, has overbalanced all the good that the slight
changes might have done."

Norman delivered this lecture with the air of one
who had settled an important question for all time.
Mrs. Smith was leaning forward in an attitude of
fixed and eager attention. Her lips moved several
times, as one who had a great deal to say, and was
burning with the desire to say it, yet she did not
interrupt him.

" Sho ! that argument upsets itself ! knocks it
endwise." It was the slow, grave voice of Solomon
that said this. " We need a New Version to show
them folks that we don't want a new Bible, and
haven't got one, and can't get it. Don't you see
you've said yourself that the changes don't amount
to nothing, only to make things a little plainer than
they was before ? Here's them infidels been a
harping ever since I could read, and I dunno how
much before, about our Bible being full of mistakes ;
not to be trusted ; you couldn't meet a little popinjay
just out of college but he would try to sputter to you
about the 'original,' and the dreadful mistakes in
our translation. Now here we've had the smartest
scholars we could find in the world at work for the
best part of their lives, doing the thing all over
again, and what have they made out ? Why, there

ain't a doctrine changed a hair's breadth ! The road to heaven and the road to hell is just as straight in the New Version as it is in the old ; and the way to escape the one place and get to the other is the same old way, and Jesus Christ is the beginning, and middle, and end of it all, just as he always was, and there ain't an honest infidel among 'em but can see it ; and if he goes to harping about not being satisfied with the old Bible, and wanting of a new one, he shows that he's a fool right on the face of his own argument." Whereupon a perfect shower of sparks went up from the hitherto smouldering firebrand at his feet.

Mrs. Smith bestowed admiring glances on her husband as he sat back from the poking, and even Norman seemed roused out of his good-natured condescension to realise that Solomon Smith, however much he might resemble an ape, had let some sparks of good, plain common sense out into the room.

Laura moved restlessly in her chair. She believed in the New Version, she supposed that most educated people did. It was a surprise to her to learn that Norman did not ; though if she had known him as well as I did she would have understood that, for all he had said, he might believe in it, or what was more probable, he might not have given it any thought. He had just been, parrot-like, repeating words that he had heard from others. The thing that had not been pleasant to Laura was to see him worsted in argument by a plain old man.

I thought it time for a change of subject.

"What news do you find in the paper ?" I asked Mrs. Solomon, indicating by a glance the *Evangelist* at her feet.

CHAPTER XXIV.

"*THEY UP AND CALLED HIM A FANATIC.*"

" WHY," said Mrs. Solomon, stooping to pick up the paper, " this is old news. I didn't have my paper while I was away, you know, and I've been reading up. To-day I come across an article which made me kind of mad, and I've been reading it over again, to Solomon, this evening. It is written by a man named Smyth. He ain't no relation of mine, for he spells his name with a 'y.' I'm glad enough that I don't have to claim him, for, to tell you the truth, I don't altogether like him. He writes real interesting, too, but for a smart man as he seems to be, he says rather queer things. I wonder if you've seen this ? It is about most everything, and among the rest, communion wine. He says it won't greatly afflict his soul if he never sees another word on the threadbare subject. According to his notion, the Lord used whatever wine happened to be handy, either good or bad, when he had the supper with his disciples, and he does hope that the whole subject of what kind of wine to use at the sacrament may have rest for the next thousand years. Now ain't that kind of queer talk for a smart man ? "

" It is talk that is much needed," declared Norman, springing vigorously to the combat. " Our fanatical temperance friends have done what they

T

could to injure the cause. We have need of strong words and pronounced opinions from level heads."

"But it don't appear to me that this man's head is exactly level. He is an out and out temperance man. He goes on to talk about the folly of the other side, and he makes it plain enough that the folks who try to make a principle of using the other kind of wine are idiots, and then he kind of knocks things over by saying a little against his own views."

"The strongest logicians we have," quoth Norman, "are those who can see both sides of a question. In fact, that is the foundation-stone of all true argument; any other method is fanatical ranting. Have you been troubled about that important question of what wine to use at communion?"

There was an air of good-humoured tolerance about the self-possessed speaker, which would have been amusing, if it had not been provoking. Mrs. Smith took it meekly.

"No," she said, reaching for her knitting, and making the shining needles fly. "I've never been troubled since I've settled the question. It is about thirteen years since I made up my mind that a thing which poisoned the body, and killed the soul, couldn't be a fit emblem of the life of that soul in Christ, and of his undying and purifying love, and so I refused to drink it; much as I love his table, I'd go without the emblems from now till I could eat them anew in my Father's kingdom, before I'd take fermented stuff into my mouth. You didn't know I had a trial of it, did you?" (This sentence addressed to me.) "That time I went with Jonas to church, after Lida was sitting up. It was communion, you know. Well, if you'll believe it, I smelled the wine before they had got within three seats of me. Do you remember our poor Mr. Marshall who went to ruin because he couldn't let wine alone ? That smell just brought me face to face with him, and his dead wife, and all his awful trouble; he a bending over her dead body and crying like a child; and his breath smelling of liquor, then, so you couldn't get away from it. There he came right along with that communion wine down the aisle. And that made me think of the other memories that some others must have, mixed in with the smell; poor fathers, you know, and mothers, and wives, with their sons and husbands gone wrong. Do you s'pose I'd touch that cup? Not for its weight in gold. Says I to myself, ' Mrs. Solomon Smith, you need purer and holier memories than that at the table of your Lord. I sat up straight and let that cup pass right by me, and shook my head. My pledge reads not to touch, nor taste, nor handle, and I wa'n't going to break it in the house of God. What right had they to tempt me to do it, I'd like to know ?"

Norman's face wore its superior smile.

" And so, my friend, you missed the communion ! What a pity ! If you had read your namesake's argument on the folly of having two kinds of wine, which you say yourself is an unanswerable argument, it might have relieved you."

" No, I didn't miss my communion, young man. The Lord can commune with his children without the help of a drop of wine, though I own it was a trial to me to have man put a bar up between my right to use the emblem of his own planning. But

you don't understand what I said about this article.
I suppose I muddled it; I'm a master hand at mud-
dling things. It is all on the other side. He says
if you undertake to make out that folks must use
intoxicating wine at the Lord's table, because he
used it when he was on earth, then you are bound
to make out that they must use bread without any
yeast in it, for the same reason; and it ought to be
used, even if it gave all the Christians in the land
dyspepsia, for dyspeptics can go to heaven while
drunkards can't. · He's sharp, you see, and sharp on
the right side too. I don't believe, mind you, that
the Saviour used a drop of the stuff that makes
drunkards, but even if he did, that don't prove that
we ought to do it now, unless it proves, as this
writer says, that we ought to use heavy bread."

"Oh," said Norman, sitting back discomfited,
"that's his dodge, is it ? I don't see but he is strongly
enough on your side; why are you quarrelling with
him ?"

"Just because he can't seem to stay 'level-headed';
I like folks to be square and consistent; it shows
they may be honest, you know, even if they are not
on what you call the right side. But I never could
understand how a body could be on both sides. You
know I told you how he said he hoped the 'threadbare' subject would be left to rest for a 'thousand
years,' and he goes on to hint that the way to do is
for each church to do as it likes, and then he says—
wait, let me read the very words: 'It is a terrible
fact that men have relapsed into drunkenness from
taking intoxicating wine on sacramental occasions !'
Now, if that is so, what business has he or anybody

else who loves the Lord Jesus Christ, and the souls
he died to save, to let the subject rest? It is just
that that made me mad. I say a man who can
write like that, and prove things as he has proved
them, has no business to let the thing rest for a thousand years, or one year. If it puts one soul in peril,
it ain't threadbare, and no Christian has a right to
say it!"

The strong old eyes grew bright with earnestness,
and the shining needles clicked very fast. Mrs.
Smith had mounted one of her hobbies. A bright
red spot was burning on Laura's cheek. Norman
was lounging back in the splint chair she had given
him, and was surveying Mrs. Smith with mild curiosity. He did not attempt to answer her; I believe
he was too entirely indifferent to the whole subject
to care to.

"I believe in temperance," he said pleasantly.
"But I repeat, as I said before, I think that fanaticism on the subject is to be deplored and avoided; it
does harm."

"Oh, I suppose so," was Mrs. Smith's meek reply.
"Though I looked out the word in the dictionary
the other day; there's been such a big talk lately
about fanaticism in one way and another, that I
wanted to know just exactly what the thing was,
and it wasn't half so dreadful as I supposed. 'A very
great enthusiasm for a subject,' says Webster, and
I'm sure I don't see why we need care how enthusi-
astic folks get over a good cause. To be sure, Webster
said that the schemes of fanatical folks are apt to
run away with their judgment, or something of that
sort; and I s'pose it's so. I s'pose some of the ways

that temperance folks have worked was lacking in judgment, maybe; but then it don't seem to me that it takes a great deal of judgment to decide that when there's good, pure, unfermented wine, made a purpose for the Lord's table, that can be had by taking a little trouble, and spending a little money, we better have it than to have the poison stuff that some folks think is wicked. I don't see much of what you call fanatics about that. I'll tell you what I've thought sometimes, as true as you live, and that is, that 'fanatical' is a word that some people have got in a habit of using when they want to do a thing that others don't think is right; if somebody tells them of it, they up and say he is a fanatic. I dare say Herod and Herodias thought that John the Baptist was a first-class fanatic. There's another thing I think is queer, and that is the way that money will blind folks' eyes. There's that tavern down at the Corners, you know what a low-lived place it has always been, Mrs. Leonard? Well, they are trying to reform it, you know; they are getting up a stock concern, and they want Solomon to go in and take two or three shares, and says he, 'If you will make it a temperance house, and write out the papers so it can't never be used for anything else but a temperance house, I'll take all the stock you want me to.' Do you believe they would do it! They up and called him a fanatic right away. It was that day that I looked out the meaning of the word, and I ain't liked the sound of it too well ever since."

She was as innocent as a child. She knew absolutely nothing about Norman's hotel stock. It was simply one of those strange "happenings" of which this world of ours is full. The blood flamed over poor Laura's face, reaching to her very temples ; but Norman laughed serenely. The second-rate " tavern" at the Corners might be very disreputable stock; he was not prepared to say that it wasn't; he was entirely willing that Solomon Smith should think it was, but his logical mind saw no connection whatever between investing a few hundred dollars in the tavern at the Corners, and having those hundred multiplied by many thousands, invested in the St. Pierre, with its massive, many - storied walls and its aristocratic finishings.

Was it harder or easier for Laura that he was so obtuse ? He seemed disinclined to pursue the subject of temperance further. There was no opportunity for displaying his powers of oratory ; he was not annoyed by the narrow view which this old couple took in regard to all these matters; he was simply indifferent; they were at liberty to think exactly what they pleased, so long as they did not disturb him, and he was not easily disturbed. One further thrust which Mrs. Smith gave, which did actually bring a flush to his cheek : " I know you agree with me in that," she said, referring to the investment, " for you was brought up to it. Twenty years ago, don't you remember, Solomon, they wanted his father to build a hotel here, a real good one, and let it to Timothy Doyle ? and they represented to him that there was more money to be made by it than in any other way. And says he, ' Gentlemen, I don't do it; none of my money shall be spotted with rum. I'll keep it clean from that curse, whatever else I do.' That was your own father, young man, and I heard him say them very words. That's something to be proud of. You see, it wasn't then as it is now, a kind of a matter of course with Christian people; he was way ahead of the times."

Norman laughed, albeit his face, as I said, was flushed. "The world moves," he said, "and people's views change." Then he turned entirely away from the subject, as one who thought it was worn out, and would have no more of it. And Laura looked as though she was wearied with all subjects. I was trying to determine in my mind whether a suggestion to go home would be too abrupt, when Solomon Smith, who had been utterly silent during the last discussion, and, indeed, had worn a look that indicated him as thinking gravely about something else, now made known the subject of his thoughts in slow, serious tones:

"Job Simmons is sick."

"Is that so?" questioned his wife, forgetting alike her stocking and her guests, and ready with instant sympathy in face and voice. "How did you hear? Much sick?"

"Dreadful sick, I guess. In a bad way, the doctor said; I met him when I was coming from the cross roads."

"He had the doctor! Then they must think he's bad. What appears to be the matter?"

Solomon Smith leaned forward, reached for the tongs, carefully laid two smouldering bits of stick that had fallen apart in such close connection that a friendly blaze sprang up between them, restored the tongs to their corner, and sat back in his chair before he made slow answer:

" He's got the fever."

" Not the fever they are having in the city !"

" I expect that's the fever."

" Really," interrupted Norman, in a more interested tone than he had used before that evening, " I hope that wretched fever isn't going to break out among your poor people here ; it has been very fatal in the lower portion of the city ; hardly a case recovered, one of the physicians told me. I was panic-stricken, Laura, when I heard of your being with a fever patient ; I thought at first it was the same disease."

Mrs. Smith did not seem to hear his ; her knitting still lay in her lap and she was looking at her husband in a thoroughly startled way that seemed singular to me, knowing, as I did, how free from panic her nature was.

" But what will Job do for care ?" she asked at last.

" Yes," said Solomon, " there's the rub."

Then I :

" Why, isn't his wife a capable woman ?"

" She ain't any woman at all to speak of," said Mrs. Smith, not sharply, but as if she were stating a recognised and undeniable fact. " What little there was of her before is about took out with the chills she's been having this spring ; they live in a low, marshy place, and the cellar is damp ; and they're poor ; poorer than usual this spring ; they can't hire no help, and I dunno as there'd be anybody to hire if they could ; folks is dreadful panic-struck about that fever ; Miss Perkins was telling me to-day that she wouldn't go into it a bit quicker than she would into small-pox. I don't know as she's to blame ;

they do say that folks that are over it, taking care of the sick, are pretty near certain to get it, and she's got children to think about. Solomon, what are they doing now down to Job's ?"

"They're doing just about as bad as they can. Nobody's there, only Jim Beers, and he ain't no good in sickness, you know."

Then there was a moment of silence, not of idleness, for we were all engaged with the fire. Solomon reached for the tongs, and poked, and poked, and relaid, with skilful touches, until from the dying embers there burst a glow of beauty, and the flames shot up to the low ceiling and set all the pictures in frames of gold. When he once more laid aside the tongs he put his old worn hands on his knees and looked straight into his wife's grey eyes, and said:

" Maria, I suppose I ought to go."

It seems to me I can feel yet the stillness that there was for a moment; I can almost hear the great sigh which broke it, and the quiet words :

" Solomon, I don't know but you are right." Then after another moment, " Who's to stay with him to-night ?"

" There's nobody to stay unless I be."

" Then did you think of going to-night ?"

" Well, there 'tis ; there he lies alone upstairs in that uncomfortable room, and there *she* is downstairs, with the child and the chills ; and here I be sitting by the fire."

" Did you tell the doctor, Solomon ?"

" I told him you and me would talk the thing over; and that Job would likely be took care of somehow."

I could not keep my eyes away from poor Laura's white, startled face; one might almost have supposed that Job Simmons was her dear friend, and to think of him as ill and suffering put her in mortal terror. Across my mind there flashed her, of late, often-repeated hint, or it might almost be called challenge, that she should like to see Mrs. Smith tried with anything that in the remotest degree touched *her* Solomon, that she might be made to realise what a cross was. I wondered if Laura thought she was being put to the test, and whether there occurred to the child the possibility that it might be in part for her sake. Had she a dim feeling that, perhaps, the Lord had said to her, "Hast thou considered my servant, Mrs. Solomon Smith? that there is none like her in the earth; a perfect and an upright woman, one that feareth God and escheweth evil?" Was she dimly conscious that in spirit she might have answered, "Doth she fear God for nought? Hast thou not made a hedge about her, and about her house, and about all that she hath on every side?"

"Solomon," said Mrs. Smith, a whole minute of silence and consideration having passed, "there's that beef broth, hadn't I better put it in a pail, and you warm it in the night to hearten you up; and maybe Job can take a spoonful of it. And do you think you could manage the big blue comforter? *They* haven't got a comfortable spot for a watcher to lie down and rest between times."

CHAPTER XXV.

"THEM SMITHS AIN'T OF THE COMMON KIND."

THE days that followed were full of unrest. There were some things on which we settled. One was that Job Simmons was very alarmingly ill, stricken with the fever which had proved so serious in a neighbouring city; and from the first the disease took that fierce hold upon him which it is apt to on the over-worked and ill-fed poor. Another fixed point was, that Solomon Smith, without talk, other than that which he may have had with his wife, took up his abode at the run-down farm where the Simmons family struggled, and did not come home at all. What little sleeping he managed to secure was done on a cot stretched by Job's bed-side. His wife—Solomon's, not Job's—saw to it that he had food of the best carefully prepared.

"Well," she used to explain, with a thoughtful air, and the far-away look in her eyes, when questioned as to why her husband should have felt called upon to leave his home, and his work, to look after one who was no kin to him, "Job Simmons had to be took care of, you know; it wouldn't do to leave him there suffering, and you know what she is, she can't take care of nobody—and Solomon said there wasn't anybody to be had, for love or money, so far as we knew, and so there was nothing else to do; don't you see?"

No, they didn't see. Very few people would have seen a clear, plain, matter-of-fact duty before them, and taken it up, in the way that Solomon Smith and his wife did it.

We, his neighbours and friends, made certain efforts to help. We said to one another that he was too old a man to undergo such constant fatigue and loss of rest, and efforts were made to secure a paid substitute. But it was a sickly spring, and nurses were in demand, and it was soon discovered that Solomon Smith was right; neither love nor money could secure a watcher for Job Simmons, except that surely it was love which had already secured him a faithful and patient nurse. Not such a love as we give to our kindred; not that which grows out of similarity of tastes, and plans, and aims. Job Simmons was a good, well-meaning, plodding, unfortunate, rather stupid soul, with a genius for losing his crops in critical seasons, and making poor bargains at all seasons, and getting sick on very slight provocation. He and Solomon Smith could not really be said to have much in common; yet love held the latter steadily at the sick bedside—the love embodied in the commission: "Inasmuch as ye have done it unto one of the least of these, my brethren, ye have done it unto me." Yes, Job was one of the "brethren." As the days passed, and the struggle with life and death grew fiercer, we who talked over poor Job's case at home, used to say, with half-drawn sighs, that there was great comfort in remembering that if he should die, which seemed probable, he would enter into rest; and certainly his laborious life had known no earthly rest.

Meantime, one of the most restless waiters, watching as an outsider to see how all this was to end, was my Laura. She seemed shocked over the good man's going into the midst of danger, to nurse one who was nothing to him. It almost seemed as if she resented the unselfish Christian spirit which had taken him to this place of fatigue and danger. So strangely miserable was she over it all, that I think there were times when she longed to accuse Mrs. Smith of caring nothing for her husband, because she did not urge his staying away. But for one who had so persistently declared that the dear old lady's one idea in life was her husband, this mode of fault-finding would hardly do.

"He will not get the fever, mamma," she said to me one day, and she said it impatiently. We were speaking of Solomon Smith; "I am not afraid that he will get it. Such people never do. They live a charmed life; they can do wonderful things, bear fatigue, and go through trials and dangers and never get touched."

"What sort of people, Laura?"

"Oh, a few specially favoured ones. Just a very few who are shielded from all life's bitternesses."

We were quite alone, and I felt that I must speak plainly.

"Daughter," I said, has your life been such a bitter one hitherto, that you are moved to envy Mr. and Mrs. Smith their brighter lot?"

She flushed under the question, and I think realised the folly of her words as they sounded to me; though I knew, better than she thought I did, about the real unrest of her heart.

"Dear child," I said, and I am sure I spoke with tenderness, for my heart felt very gentle with the poor young thing; "isn't it time you gave over the folly of trying to account for your old friend's strong, true, unselfish Christian character on any other ground than that of one whose life is hid with Christ in God? You have tried to change her into a narrow-minded, selfish, fanatical old woman. Have you succeeded? You are waiting, apparently, to see whether poor, weak, little Lida will prove to have a strong enough hold on Christ to lead her safely through life's temptations, or whether your cousin Irving's influence will pull her down; if the latter is the case, you seem to imagine that you will thus, in some way, be relieved from personal responsibility. I used to think that you entirely believed in our poor old friend, but I see I am mistaken. Satan is tempting you to throw aside her love, and the respect you have had for her, and name her Christian life self-will and ignorance. But, daughter, suppose he succeeds, and you cast aside our dear old lady's true living as worthless, and suppose poor Lida makes a failure of it, what then? Do you remember the question Mrs. Smith asked you, that evening, after Lida's marriage? Didn't she ask whether you thought the Lord Jesus Christ made a failure of life? Don't you sometimes hear his voice asking: 'What is that to thee? Follow thou me.'"

She was weeping bitterly by this time. She interrupted me suddenly:

"It is not that," she said; "mamma, you do not understand. I do not distrust her religion; I never said so. You know I respect her, mamma; but she may make mistakes ; no one is perfect ; and I—I do not want to think she is right about all questions ; that is, I do not want to think her opinions and actions are the result of her Christian experience, because—well, if what she lives is Christianity, it condemns other lives too much ; I do not want them condemned."

How well I understood the miserable type of Christian living which that term "other lives" covered ! Norman Eastlake had been gone for some days, but the shadow of his sham religion hung all over her ; she could not get away from it. Constantly the old argument was being gone over in her heart : " If these two old people are right about this about that, about a dozen things which he directly condemns by word and act, then I must condemn his life as unworthy of his profession, and that I will not do !"

I felt the necessity for treading very carefully during these days. Evidently my daughter was being called upon to make grave decisions, such as would perhaps influence all her future. I could not get away from the feeling that she was, perhaps without fully realising it, being called upon to decide between Christ and Norman Eastlake. Yet I did not dare to tell her so. In trying to influence her, I felt myself at a very great disadvantage, because she recognised my unspoken disapproval of the young man. During the conversation to which I have referred, I quoted this verse : " He that taketh not up his cross, and followeth after me, is not worthy of me." It was in answer to her confession that Mrs. Smith's life put to blush other lives, and Norman's name had not been mentioned between us; but she instantly answered me with a burst of tears, and these words:

" Oh, mamma, I know you do not like Norman, you never have; and I'm afraid you never will. It is very hard on him, and it is very hard on me; but I shall never give him up."

" Has anybody asked you to do so, daughter?" I asked her, and it was all that I could trust myself to say.

Meantime the days went by, and the struggle between life and death, in that shabby farm-house just out of town, went on. Presently, contrary to the expectations of everyone, the attending physician included, it became apparent that Job Simmons— little wizened-up, half-alive man that he was—was to come off victor. He was getting well. His sickly wife told me it herself, with a wan smile, and a sentence about Solomon Smith which had more energy in it than I had judged her capable of.

"Them Smiths," she said, "ain't of the common kind, I tell you; if there was more folks of their sort the world would be a good enough place to live in, and I'd just as soon live in it as not. But I tell you you might go a thousand miles, in all directions, and never see their like again."

I repeated the eulogy at our family tea-table, and drew from Laura first a laugh and then a burning blush.

" What is the matter with the child?" her father asked me that same evening. " She doesn't seem like herself; she hasn't, in fact, since you came home; and it has been worse since Norman went away."

I had to confess to him that I was afraid our

daughter was struggling with her own convictions of
right. This belief grew upon me; for one evening,
when we were alone, and I, in much fear and trembling, and I doubt not with much bungling, was trying to speak a word in answer, that should not do
more harm than good, she burst forth suddenly with
this:

"Mamma, I do not want to be a Christian; I cannot be one, indeed; I should be a fanatic; I should
carry things to extremes, I am certain of it; and
that would spoil my life. Oh, mamma, don't you
know it would?"

I had no answer ready, and she went on hurriedly:

"Almost all the time we were away I thought
about it; I admired auntie Smith, but I thought
many of her views were peculiar and old-fashioned
—the outgrowth of her rugged nature; and—I do not
mean to be disrespectful—but I thought that both
you and papa had been brought up under peculiarly
strict influences, and held some views as a result
that could not be expected from young people; still
I thought that young Christians would develop in
that direction as they grew older. I admired the
development, and I used to say to myself that when
I was an old woman I would be, not a gentle low-
voiced woman like you, but noisy and rugged, and
pronounced in my ways. You know I cannot be
like you, mamma, so then I used to think I would
be like auntie Smith; but when Lida became so
changed, I could not help seeing that she was already
growing like you; young as she is, mamma; she is
taking up advanced questions of Christian life, and

settling them as you would; not as young people do; she is not waiting to grow old; I can see it in her letters, she is moving right on; and stranger than that, she is taking Irving with her.

"Besides, there was Erskine, you know, a professor of religion, and not a bit better than the rest of them, not so good, I have often thought, as many who made no profession; but all that is changed. I hear a great deal about him in one way and another, and he is actually growing like auntie Smith! Mamma, you don't understand it, but I cannot be such a Christian as that; it would make my life miserable; and I cannot be any other kind, for I see that it is the only right way. I know you cannot imagine what I mean, but I understand myself."

It seemed to me there was but one answer to this question, and though with troubled voice, I gave it:

"I comprehend you, I think, daughter, fully; and I can only say to you what I have said before, ' He that taketh not up his cross and followeth after me, is not worthy of me.' "

There came presently a new element of disturbance into her life. She came to me one evening with an open letter from Erskine, a long, cordial, genial letter, detailing work that he was doing, and work that he was planning, seeming to expect her approval as a matter of course: and there was such an air of breezy energy about it all, and such evident ignorance of the fact that he was doing any more or any different from what a disciple of Christ would do of course, that I understood what the child meant by telling me that he was growing like Mrs. Solomon Smith. The young man had repudiated utterly

those former days of profession ; he believed them to
be mere *profession,* and felt sure that he had known
nothing of the love of Christ as a renewing power,
until after his meeting with Mrs. Smith. He dated
his conversion from the evening in which he took
her in his carriage to church. This was not Erskine's
first letter, but it was the longest and most communi-
cative, and had that about it which made me understand why Laura sought her mother in perplexity.

"I don't know what to do, mamma, I enjoy his
letters, of course ; any person of sense might ; and I
like him ; his friendship is worth having ; but—and
he may mean nothing at all but friendship, probably
does not ; and yet, mamma, don't you know what I
mean ? You always know what I mean before I say
it."

"I understand you, dear," I said, "and if I were
you I would be entirely frank with Erskine, he is a
good, sensible young man ; let him know that you
enjoy his sense and his letters, just as a young lady
engaged to be married might enjoy the friendship of
a dozen good men."

"But how could I tell him ? It would seem to
him as though I was afraid he thought more of me
than merely as a friend ; and I have no reason to do
so. I couldn't do that, mamma !" and her cheeks
flushed over it.

But I assured her that I thought she could.
Erskine had been too intimately associated with us
as a member of the same family, and as a special
friend of Irving's, for us to treat him other than
as a valued friend ; if her belief was correct, that
he thought of her only as a pleasant acquaintance

to whom he would like occasionally to write a
friendly letter, her frank confidence reposed in him
could do no harm, but good; and if, on the other
hand, there was a possibility that he was growing
interested in her, frankness might save much future
harm.

All the time, I think, I was talking more for
Laura's sake than Erskine's; I found myself nourishing the hope that her eyes were being opened to
the contrast which his character presented beside
Norman Eastlake's.

It was not that I would have counselled her to the
breaking of solemn pledges, unless, indeed, she
reached the point where she herself felt it would be
wrong to keep them; but if she were to realise in
bitterness some day that she had made a mistake, I
prayed God that the knowledge might not come too
late.

I am not one of those who believe that a bad
promise should be kept; nor would I ever counsel
one to go to the marriage altar with solemn pledges
on her lips to which her heart said nay. That is
simply adding sin to sin; and the way out of sin is
not to shut ones eyes and add another. At the same
time, I hold a promise as a very sacred thing, so
sacred that the necessity for breaking it should be
mourned, and wept, and prayed over; so sacred that,
before it is made at all, every step of the way in
which it leads should be looked over on one's knees.
The remedy lies not in adhering to false vows and so
making a mockery of life, but in being so careful, so
conscientious, so earnest, that the first mistake is not
made.

I turned almost with a sigh from the fact that there was no wavering about Laura; she was so sure indeed that, however unhappy Norman's peculiar views might make her, she belonged to him, that she did not even understand my probing. But as the days passed, and Job Simmons crept out among us again, and Solomon Smith came home, and life at the little brown house in the Hollow settled into its wonted calm, much of Laura's nervousness began to wear away. The period of anxiety lest our old friend should take the fever was past, and the doctor said cheerily, that his good constitution and good wife had brought him safely through; and Laura seemed satisfied to go back, in a degree, at least, to her old warm feeling for Mrs. Smith; vexing questions were dropping into the background. She seemed growing content to let Norman have his type of religion, and the Smiths theirs, and for herself, to do without any.

No Christian mother needs to be told that my heart was not at rest. Laura was the child of many prayers. I did not believe that the dear Lord would let her make such a disastrous compromise with Satan as to try to stand on neutral ground because one type of Christian life was too strongly marked for her to be willing to take up its crosses, and the other too weak to command her respect. The solemn question was: How would he lead this poor foolish lamb into his pasture?

CHAPTER XXVI.

"THERE WASN'T ANYTHING ELSE TO DO."

" THINGS that folks plan for never happen." This
Mrs. Smith said to me one lovely spring morning,
when I had walked over to see her, and plan for
more fresh eggs. She said it with a grateful smile
playing around her mouth and a satisfied look in her
eyes. " Now, there's Solomon, I really did think he
would get the fever. I laid awake nights to get
ready for it. I planned who to get to look after the
house and the critter, and I hunted up the bundles
of old linen and things, such as is wanted in sickness,
and whenever I sent any round to Job Simmons, I
laid some out for Solomon. And whenever the
doctor asked for this or that about the house for
Job's comfort, I set right about getting it ready for
Solomon. After he come home I put things straight
every night regular, without saying anything to him,
you know, so that if he should be took before morning I'd know just where to lay my hand on everything. If ever I planned, and fixed, and fussed out
anything, it was the way I'd do for him when he
had the fever; and he ain't no signs of it about
him! I must say I think it is wonderful, broke of
his rest as he was, and lifting hard, and puttering
all day as well as all night. Ain't it wonderful now

that he escaped ? It is the Lord's mercy. I wish I knew how to be grateful enough."

Poor old lady ! All the time the shadows were gathering around her so softly and sweetly that she did not perceive them. At least she let none of us know it if she did.

"Solomon was kind of tuckered out to-night, and I coaxed him up to stay at home," she said to me one evening after prayer-meeting, as she was getting into our carriage to ride home, having walked the mile and a half thither. "He ain't quite so strong as usual, somehow. The warm weather is coming on pretty early, you see ; and then he's had such a hard pull, it stands to reason it will take him a while to get over it."

One Sunday she came to church all day without him.

"Solomon ain't sick, and he ain't well," she said in answer to inquiries. "I dunno exactly what ails him ; tuckered out, I call it. He don't seem to have no strength to spare ; and no wonder, he used it up a good ways ahead. I tell him that by fall he'll catch up, if he is careful, and be all right. You see, Solomon is older than he was"—spoken in a half-confidential tone, as if it were an admission that she made reluctantly, and would like as little said about it as possible—"and, of course, watching and care tells on him."

It was a very unusual thing to see Solomon Smith's seat in church vacant. It gave me a strange sort of pang to look at the old lady sitting alone. If there had been a stalwart son or a cheery-faced daughter beside her, it would have been different.

Not long thereafter we went, Laura and I, to take
our friend a loaf of a new kind of corn bread Mary
had been learning to make. We found her in the
neat kitchen, which, in its summer dress of fresh
whitewash, and green, sweet-smelling boughs in the
fireplace, and a pot of June roses smiling from the
mantelpiece, looked in its way quite as inviting as
the more glowing attire in which winter found it.
Mrs. Smith had a way of her own of marking the
seasons. The red curtains which glowed all winter
at her kitchen windows were replaced by plain
white ones; white tidies, carefully stitched into
place with cord, covered the wools with which the
favourite chairs were upholstered. Even the floor-
mats were of a lighter, more subdued hue, and in
various ways the mistress of the house had made
her abode say, " It is summer."

On this day the door leading into the large and
roomy summer sleeping-room, which generally stood
open in the afternoon, revealing glimpses of a very
chamber of peace, was closed. Mrs. Smith, glancing
toward it, lowered her voice : " Solomon has gone to
lie down. He is having a nice long nap, and he
needs it. He went out in the lower field this morning for about an hour, and I never see anybody look
so tired as he did when he come in. I coaxed him
to lie down right away, and he did, and this afternoon he went of his own accord and laid down
again. He ain't been no hand to take a nap in the
daytime, but he'd ought to. When folks get to be
his age they need it, I think."

I did not want to be a Job's comforter, but I
could not help saying :

"Do you think your husband seems as well as usual this summer?"

She laid down the seam she was sewing, and looked at me with grave, earnest eyes for a moment before she answered:

"Well, now, he don't, that's a fact; but I don't think strange of it. The doctor thinks he ain't quite right. He wants him to take a tonic. He's been talking to me about it this very morning. I was out in the yard when he rode by, and I wanted to know how that Adams boy is, so I stopped him, and then I was saying that Solomon wasn't real chirk, and he said he told him more than a week ago he ought to take beer, or porter, or some of them things. But land! Solomon won't. I know as well as I want to, that he won't; and I ain't the one to coax him to either.

"I don't mean," she hastened to explain, catching a glimpse of the dissent and disapproval in Laura's eyes, "that I would be opposed to it if we thought it was necessary. Solomon wouldn't either. I suppose we would about as soon take that as any other poison, if it seemed to be the thing to do; but, you see, we both believe that other tonics will do just as well, and not have the same objection to 'em that these have."

"But," said Laura, belligerence in every tone, "I should suppose that you would be willing to accept a physician's opinion. You say the doctor advised it. Surely he ought to be supposed to know what should be done!"

"Well, I don't know," speaking thoughtfully. "You see, child, there's doctors and doctors, and you

can't believe in 'em all, for they contradict each
other about every earthly thing, and if you undertake
to follow one man's notions, you may comfort yourself with the thought that you are going right contrary to the notions of another, who is just as smart,
and has as good a chance of knowing as the first one.
I don't see anything for it but to study up some
things and decide for yourself; and that's just what
we've done a good while ago about this tonic business.
Fact is, you've got to study it up.   It belongs to the
temperance question, and we read everything we
could get hold of on both sides, and we talked with
some that know a good deal, and one day when I
was in New York, a year or so ago—that time I
went to take care of my niece's cousin, you know—I
happened across that big doctor that everybody
praises and runs to consult—at least, them that can
get money enough.   A lady that boarded in this
house where my niece's cousin lived, was relation to
him, and she thought a great deal of Fanny—that's
the cousin—and she sent for him to come and see her
when she was at the worst; and he come, and he was
as good as though he hadn't been great at all.   He
come two or three times, and one day, when he sat
waiting to go upstairs, I had a chance, and I up and
asked him his opinion about tonics.   Well, he come
down on the hull thing stronger than I thought any
of them ever did.   He said he believed the hull
system of prescribing rum for strengthening medicine
was of the devil, and brought forth the devil's fruits
in nine cases out of ten.   Them was his very words.
They was pretty strong, I thought; but coming from
him, wa'n't they worth thinking about?   Solomon

and I thought them over, and put one thing and
another together that we heard here and there, and
we made up our minds that we didn't believe in rum
tonics and couldn't take 'em.   So you see I ain't the
one to coax him to back down on that.   Why, this
very doctor, this morning, owned that there was
other things that he supposed would do about as
well, only they was harder to get, and more expensive.   'As far as that goes, doctor,' says I, 'Solomon
and I agreed a good while ago to obey the Lord even
if it was expensive now and then.'   I said them very
words.   It seemed a queer thing to me to be talking
about expense, when I was talking about right and
wrong, and the danger of doing harm to folks' souls."

"Auntie Smith," interrupted Laura, "do you really
mean that you are afraid if your husband took a tonic
of some sort, for a few weeks while he is run down,
he might become a drunkard?"

"No, child; I dunno as I can say I'm the least
mite afraid of it; I ought to be, I suppose, for the
Bible warns us against that very thing: 'Let him
that thinketh he standeth, take heed least he fall,' it
says.   But I can't help, somehow, feeling so sure of
Solomon's standing that I haven't a speck of fear;
but I'll tell you what we are both afraid of, and that
is his influence.   There is folks that don't stand
firm; it's all you can do to keep 'em up, with all the
props you can put around them; pledges and
examples, and all that.   'Shall the weak brother
perish for whom Christ died?'   That's the verse that
comes bowsing out at me the minute I think about
Solomon swallowing a drop of the stuff.   You see,
child, it has all been up lately and had itself talked

over. As soon as the fever left Job Simmons the doctor began to talk tonic to him; says he to Solomon : ' The man will die in spite of you, if he doesn't have brandy every little while. I don't know how he's going to get it. It's expensive stuff, but he'll slip through our fingers if he doesn't have it.' Well, Solomon went straight to Job about it. Poor Job, you know, was away down in the gutter in his younger days ; and Solomon he told him just what the doctor said. He didn't feel that he ought to take the responsibility of doing any other way : and says he, ' It ain't the expense, Job, that needn't stand in the way a minute ; what you need you're to have ; and the doctor says if you don't have brandy you may die ; now what do you say ?' And Solomon says he'll never forget the way in which Job looked at him out of them great sunken eyes. Says he : ' Then, Solomon, I'll die ; I will so ; not a drop of brandy for me !' Some folks say Job ain't got much spunk ; but if he hasn't he's got grace ; for it took some, I guess, to get him through that place with his wife a-crying over him and the doctor telling what would happen. Not a drop of brandy did he take ; and the doctor himself says he never see any one come up faster ; and yet he goes and prescribes the tonic again the first thing !'"

Laura arose at once ; she was ready to go home. I did not know it then, but long afterwards I saw the letter that she had received that morning ; one sentence was as follows :

" I'm rather under the weather just now ; nothing to signify, a little run down with irregular hours and over-exertion. The city has been pretty gay this

spring; several weddings in high life, and matters of
that sort have rather knocked me up; but you have
no cause for anxiety; the doctor says I will be all
right in a few weeks.   He prescribes a glass of old
ale on rising, and perhaps after each meal.   I shall
not need so much as that, I presume, but I am trying
the prescription sparingly, with excellent results
already."

I think about the time that Mrs. Smith quoted
poor Job Simmons' words : "Then, Solomon, I'll die ;
I will, so; not a drop of brandy for me!" those con-
trasting words stung her.

After that the shadows deepened rapidly.   Solomon Smith took no tonic—at least of an alcoholic
nature.   Indeed, before three more days had passed
it became apparent to the doctor that he needed
more than a tonic.   There came speedily a morning
in which, essaying to rise with the dawn, as usual,
Solomon Smith fell back with something very like
a groan, and owned that he felt too weak and miserable to move.   His alert wife moved skilfully, and
in a very brief space of time tried to rally his strength
with a bit of nourishing broth, while she waited for
the doctor, for whom she had quietly sent a messenger.

She spoke cheerily both to him and the doctor
when he came.   It was an uncommon weak kind of
morning; she didn't feel near as chirk as usual herself, and Solomon had overdone the day before; he
would be all right in a little while, she guessed; but
she had thought it safest to call the doctor.

She said much the same two days later, when I
spent an hour with her.

" Solomon was getting a rest. He needed it, had needed it all the spring ; and folks like him couldn't rest unless the Lord took them gently and laid them on their backs. He didn't suffer any to speak of, had no pain ; he was just tuckered out.'

Her face was bright while she talked, and she kept her needle going busily, finishing a garment for her husband that she fancied would be cooler and more comfortable for him. Meantime he slept.

" He sleeps a good deal," she said brightly ; " I think that shows he needs it. Being tired is a dreadful kind of feeling, and nothing will do for it so quick as sleep."

There was nothing we could do to help her ; she was sufficient to the occasion. So there was no object in lingering. Cheerful, our hostess certainly was, but as certainly she was quiet ; her usually busy tongue was hushed, and her brain engaged with the effort to keep all the outside world quiet, and to hear the first sound which came from that sick-room. We went away feeling that, although on the surface nothing looked like it, still it was a sick-room.

When we met the doctor and stopped to inquire as to the state of things, he shook his head gravely.

" Yonder is a wonderful nurse, Mrs. Leonard, but she can't nurse her husband back into strength."

" Mamma, what does he mean ?" said Laura, her face white. " Does he think that Mr. Smith is going to die ?"

I didn't know what he meant, but I was afraid, and I told Laura so. She seemed wonderfully shaken by our fears ; more so than it seemed to me her interest in our friends would account for. She talked about it a great deal, and went about with a white, anxious face.

"It will kill auntie Smith, I think," she said to Mary, "she is so utterly deceived, or else we are. I dare say we are the ones who are frightened, after all; she doesn't think him sick; and why shouldn't she know better than the rest of us? But if he should be really sick it will be a dreadful shock to her. She is so entirely unprepared for it. Mamma, you do not think he can be going to die, do you?"

I did not know. I hardly knew what to think. He was not a man to give up and lie down weakly and fancy himself sick. But as the days passed, he certainly did not gain in strength; and yet he had no fever and no pain. What was the matter with him?

"Worn out," the doctor said, briefly, on being interrogated; "he was too old a man to bear the fatigue of that long watching. If he had had a son it would never have been allowed. I wonder that his wife did not use her influence. A poor exchange, to nurse Job Simmons back to life and take him instead. We could get along without Job, I suppose, but real solid honest men like Solomon Smith are scarce."

"If he only hadn't gone to take care of Job Simmons!"

This Laura said to Mrs. Smith one morning when we were waiting to take a message from her to the doctor.

I was very sorry that she said it. There is nothing to make a sharper thrust in a burdened heart than that dreary "if you hadn't done thus and so." But Mrs. Smith did not seem to take it in that way. She went on quietly folding the paper on which she had been writing, while she made answer:

"Well, you know, child, we haven't got that to think about; and it is a mercy we haven't just now, when there is so much to tend to. There wasn't anything else to do; you see, the duty stared us right straight in the face, and there wa'n't nothing to decide about it. He was sick, and had to be took care of, and there was nobody to do it; and if 'whatsoever ye would that men should do to you, do ye even so to them,' didn't mean Job Simmons and Solomon, why, then Solomon said he was sure he didn't know what it did mean; and so you know that settled it."

X

CHAPTER XXVII

"DELIVERANCE."

THERE came a summer afternoon which we, who spent it in the little brown house in the Hollow, never forgot.

For in the large, pleasant room opening from the pleasant kitchen, a wonderful scene transpired; a wonderful guest held audience, taking with him when he went away one of the number, and taking us, who stayed behind, even to the gate of the city.

The room was in perfect order and neatness. No little thing had been forgotten. The white curtains were looped back enough to let in the glory of the western sky as the sun was setting. The white cloth on the little table by the bedside had the folding creases still in it, showing that thoughtful hands had made it fresh that day. The spread on the bed was as white and as carefully arranged as usual. A fresh glass of full-blown roses stood on the table by the east window and sent ever and anon a breath of perfume through the room.

Solomon Smith's large chair, in a fresh tidy of purest white, was drawn up beside the bed, as if its owner were expected to rise pretty soon and rest in it again. But one look at the worn face, from which the white hair was brushed carefully back, would have told those wise in translating such expressions, that earthly resting-places were not for him any more.

Solomon Smith was tired out; so tired that nothing on this side could rest him, and he had been sent for to go home. Beside him, sitting erect and quiet, her face illumined by a tender smile, her tender eyes fixed on his face, her warm hand clasping his, which was growing cold, sat Mrs. Solomon Smith. We had come in, Laura and I, all unprepared for the scene.

" About the same as usual," had been the message which we had received from the house in the Hollow, even that very morning ; and none knew at that early hour that that day was to be the day of days in which one of the redeemed should be presented for the first time, in all the glory of his new attire, at the palace of the King! So unprepared are we for great events, when they are right at our door.

"Let us go and see how he is this afternoon," I had said to Laura as we rose from the dinner-table. " I will take him a little of this lemon jelly, it is so cold. A taste of it may refresh him."

I had no idea what refreshment they were making ready for him in his Father's house.

" Seems to me he lingers in the same condition a long time. If I were Mrs. Smith I should want to try a change of physicians. The weather is cooler now; he ought to be gaining strength a little."

This Mr. Leonard said, and I resolved, as I made ready for the walk, to give a hint to that effect to the wife, if opportunity offered. Just so unprepared as that were we.

It was the doctor who opened the door to us, and

who said : "You may step inside the room. She saw you coming up the walk, and she wishes to have you."

"Mamma," Laura said, "he must be better. You go in ; I will wait here."

But the doctor held open the door and motioned her on, and then in another moment we saw that face, with its strange seal of immortality.

I recognised it at once, as those do who have watched it before, but Laura stopped, startled and frightened ; and Mrs. Solomon Smith glanced toward her for an instant, with a reassuring smile.

"Maria"—it was her husband's voice, low, feeble, yet in the stillness of the room distinct to us all—" I wouldn't have gone and left you if I could have helped it. If I'd had the planning of it, it would have seemed selfish ; but I couldn't help it, Maria, so it must be right, you know."

There was a wistful pleading in the tone, almost like that of one asking forgiveness for a possible wrong.

Her answer was prompt, steady, reassuring :

" Yes, Solomon, it is all right. You and I know that. We can trust Him. You was never selfish in your life, husband. You have thought of me from first to last ; and if you had your way you would bear it all now ; but the Lord sees that His way is the best ; you and the children will be looking out for me."

Then he smiled—a loving, grateful smile. "You're going to the very gate with the old man, and going to cheer him up to the last. I'll tell the children all about it."

This was her answer. Silence fell upon them for a little. The old man closed his eyes, and seemed to be resting, and the warm hand that held his cold one began to make little soothing passes down the wrinkled palm; then she laid her other hand on his forehead, and wiped tenderly the drops gathering there; and the room was still.

The door opened very softly, and the shadow of Job Simmons slipped in. I had heard how he had fairly haunted the house, longing to do, and trying to do beyond his strength; so eager to show his gratitude for one who had almost given his life for him. Laura had said, one day, that if Mr. Smith should die, she shouldn't think his wife could endure to look at Job Simmons ever again. I thought of it now, for she glanced up a moment when the shadow slipped in, and once more she smiled, and nodded her head in assent of his coming.

"You won't disturb him, I think," the doctor said in a low tone; whereupon the eyes of the sick man unclosed and rested on Job, on whose poor, sunken face there was a look as of mortal pain, and his hollow eyes were dim with unshed tears. He had not seen Solomon Smith for days, and the thought that he was actually going, I learned afterwards, had come to him almost as suddenly as it had to us. But Solomon Smith, looking at him, with the death-film gathering on his eyes, still recognised the face over which he had watched so long and well, and spoke:

"Ah, Job, I've got ahead of you somehow. I didn't think it, but He's sent for me first. Be faithful, and follow on."

Poor Job!

"I'd give my life for you this minute,' he murmured. "I'm worth nothing to nobody, and you are needed."

And then there came over the face on the bed that rare bright smile.

"He gave his life for me long ago; and he'll take care of all I'm leaving; won't he, Maria?"

Quick and firm came the answer:

Yes, Solomon, we can trust Him, you and me."

Silence again, and closed eyes.

The doctor moved nearer, spoke to me in a low whisper:

"He will not speak again, I think. Will you go around near to his wife?"

But even as he spoke those eyes unclosed again, and there had come over them a marvellous change. The languor of disease and weariness was gone out of them; they seemed to glow. There was a flush on his face, as if there might be the coming of health and youth; and his voice rang out and filled that room; not a note of weakness in it.

"Maria!"

"Yes, Solomon, I'm right here."

"Maria, mine eyes have seen the King in His beauty!"

Steady and true was the answer:

"Aye, and they shall behold the land that is very far off."

It was in time, I am sure, for the quickened hearing to catch the sound of the triumphant promise, and close upon it came the fulfilment, for even as

the sound of the last word died away, the doctor
said:

"He is gone."

"Yes," said Mrs. Smith, "and I am here."

It would be impossible for me to tell you of the
depth of controlled pain revealed in those few steadily
spoken words. There was even a note of astonishment in them; as if for a moment she could hardly
believe that he had actually gone to that land "very
far off" and left her behind! When had he ever
been known to leave her behind? She had gone on
journeys, errands of comfort or duty, several times;
but never before, since their lives had been made
one, more than forty years ago, had he gone to another
town, or city, even for a night, and left her!

Those who looked to see Mrs. Solomon Smith cry
out, or faint, did not understand her. She sat for a
moment as one dazed. She reeled for a moment on
rising, as one who was giddy; then she drew her
usually straight form erect, and looked about her.

"You are all good friends," she said, "and you
will do what is right, and you will let me go upstairs
and be all alone. If I am bereft of my husband, I
am bereft. And yet I am not alone. My heart
trusted in Him, and I am helped."

Then she turned and walked slowly and steadily
from the door.

"Mamma!" said Laura to me hours after that.

Everything had been done that we could do in the
little brown house, and after vainly urging its bereft
mistress to come home with us, we had come away,
leaving Job Simmons and his wife in charge. It
was the way she would have it. In her earliest

loneliness she remembered that poor man's broken-
hearted, almost remorseful grief, and his longing
desire to do something.

Laura had at first given way to such a passionate
outburst of grief as seemed utterly unnatural to
those who did not know her as her mother did;
but it told me plainly that all the unrest of the past,
which had been sealed over by a film of ice for a few
weeks, had broken forth again and had her in possession.

As I say, it was hours afterwards that she made
this confession.

"Mamma, to be able to endure trial as auntie
Smith did to-day would be worth giving up everything for; but I never could do it; I never could."

It was no time in which to ask her what that "it"
covered; so I said simply this:

"Don't you remember her words: 'My heart
trusted in Him, and I am helped.' Do you think
she bore it alone ? You have never tried his strength,
Laura."

What a strangely mingled thing our life is ! And
how surely and steadily and swiftly the Lord is working when we do not see his hand nor hear his step !
I wept much over my daughter that night. I saw
only too plainly that she realised that her earthly
vows actually held her away from making surrender
to the Lord. She understood that the sort of Christian
she must be, Norman Eastlake neither was, nor would
enjoy in her; and that their lives would be discord-
ant. Yet she could not resolve to settle the great
personal question first, and leave the second until
she could ask Him, as her guide, to point out the

way he would have her take. Did I think he would
leave her stumbling in that mire until her feet were
over the precipice? My faith seemed to be no
stronger than that. Yet he was making the way
plain even then.

It was the very next day but one, the afternoon on
which we laid Solomon Smith's tired-out body to
rest under the green and flowery sod, that Laura came
to me with an open letter, saying simply this:

"Mamma, read that."

Then she vanished up the stairs.

It was in Norman's handwriting, and began as was
usual with him: "My dear Laura!" It was the only
sentence that was as usual, and yet it sounded commonplace enough; the miserable formula that has
been used by dishonourable men ever since sin and
sorrow began. A series of platitudes about feeling
deeply, painfully, that their tastes and aims were not
in common, that he was not calculated to make her
happy; that they had both been very young, and
that, in short, he realised that with both of them it
had been a mistake, and like an honourable man he
hastened to release her from an engagement which
he felt sure was becoming distasteful to her, and a
great deal more in the same strain.

I did not wait to read it all. I let it drop from
my hands while I clasped them, and the first words
I said were, "Thank God for deliverance!" And yet
I fear I almost hated the source through which it
came. Too well I realised that it might be months,
possibly years, before my Laura could see deliverance
in it. I remember I thought confusedly of the
words:

"It must needs be that offences come, but woe unto him by whom the offence cometh!"

It was several days thereafter that I went alone to visit my stricken friend. I had not seen her since she laid her dead away. I had shrunk from the first call almost as much as Laura had. Indeed, I was inclined to think with the child, that the sort of exaltation in which she had borne the parting, when it passed, would leave her in the depths. It was the only condition in which Laura could conceive of her, knowing with what rare devotion she had loved her husband for almost half a century.

I remember just how pleasant the familiar room looked as I stepped into it that summer afternoon. Everything was exactly as usual. The square stand on which the Bible always rested stood in its place by Solomon's vacant chair; a fresh tidy was fastened to the chair; the mat on which his feet had always rested when he sat there was spread before it; the Bible was open, and his spectacles lay on the page.

"It is just as Solomon left it," she said quietly, following my glance, and pausing in the seam she was sewing to turn a tender look on it; "that last day he sat up, he read, and left the Bible open, and I didn't use that one. I wanted to leave it somehow, and it was open—where do you think? Why, at a verse for me: 'They looked steadfastly towards heaven as he went up.' Now, you see, I know as well as though I heard him say it, that Solomon wants me to keep my thoughts away from the grave, and keep them steadfastly toward heaven. That's where he is, and if I can keep my eyes looking there, I shall

see him soon, coming in the clouds with Jesus. It
don't do to look at graves."

I had gone to try and comfort, but the Master had
been there before me, and, instead of trying to bind
up a broken old heart, I sat and told her of a young
one that human folly and selfishness had brought
very low. I could not get away from the thought
that the Lord had given this old saint of his some
work to do for my child. She heard me through
without many interruptions, save to ask now and
then a keen question, which showed me that she saw
beyond the surface.

"Will you let the child come and stay a day or
two with me?" she asked at last. "Tell her I'm
lonesome, and her sweet young face will hearten me
up. I would like to have her come. I love the
child."

"I will go," said Laura suddenly, when I gave her
the invitation.

She had been going around the house with a white,
quiet face for a week or more. She had shut herself
within herself, refusing to let even her mother enter
into her bitterness. "Please don't mention him
again, mamma," was all the answer I received when
I tried once to speak to her of Norman Eastlake. I
knew she shrank terribly from coming into contact
with Mrs. Smith's keen eyes, and was going there
because it was a cross that she meant to try to bear.

Partly by accident and partly by design I let the
days pass until nearly two weeks were gone before
seeing Laura again, other than as I met her riding
or walking with Mrs. Smith. Company came to us
in the meantime, and Laura sent to me a coaxing

little note, begging that she might be excused from seeing them, and saying that she believed she was a comfort to auntie Smith ; and, anyway, the blessed old saint was a comfort to her, such as she should thank God for for ever. I took heart at this, and thanked him on my knees that night, that he had one disciple among us who was " looking steadfastly toward heaven" all the time.

There was a sweet quiet in Laura's face and voice when at last she returned to me ; and she came into the parlour of her own will to entertain the callers with which our house was full all the afternoon. It was quite dusk before we had opportunity for a word alone together. Then she came to me, and, kneeling beside me, put her lips to my cheek as she gave her sweet message :

" Mamma, He did not reject me. I have given myself to him for time and for eternity. And oh, mamma, he has showed me joy already in his service. I am not going to be a broken-hearted little idiot. I am a servant of Christ."

" I tell you," said Mrs. Solomon, with a strong light on her grave face, " there's two kinds of idols. One kind is made of clay, and all the Lord has to do when he wants to free a child from that, is to let it crumble to pieces before her eyes ; and there's some that are made of solid gold ; and when he has to take them away, he makes a place for them in his temple above."

THE END

LONDON :

WHITING AND CO., 30 & 32, SARDINIA STREET, LINCOLN'S INN-FIELDS.

www.ingramcontent.com/pod-product-compliance
Lightning Source LLC
Chambersburg PA
CBHW020322140726
47905CB00013B/2150